FAIR AND JUST

A PENELOPE PHAIR MYSTERY

ALEX P. BERG

CHAPTER ONE

Porcelain plates clattered off the counter, oil sizzled and spat on a hot stove, and above the constant roar of the kitchen, I heard the sous-chef's cry. "Order up!"

I turned myself sideways and thought skinny thoughts as Annabel came toward me with a tray of draft beers. She pivoted and lifted the tray, and we orbited each other between the food service racks with an ease that belied the many broken pint glasses who'd sacrificed themselves for us to get there. The grace with which she balanced the tray and darted down the hall made me think once again that she might make a great jammer for my roller derby team, but her scrawny arms and general lack of size would work against her no matter how serpentine she might be. Of course, asking her to join the Monster Maids would mean admitting to her I played roller derby in the first place, and despite having worked at Gil's Diner for the past five months, I still wasn't sure I was ready for anyone there to learn what I did in my free time. For some reason, having strangers watch me elbow chicks while wearing a pink polka-dot skirt and a matching tank top felt different than having friends do it.

The sous-chef cried out again, reminding me why I'd ducked into the kitchen in the first place. I danced to the counter and picked my order slip from the ticket holder, tucking it into my apron pocket as I loaded table sixteen's meatloaf and club sandwich onto a tray. With the earthy scent of Gil's signature smoked loaf thick in my nostrils, I swirled back down the aisle and through the swinging door, trading the clatter of the kitchen for the din of the dining room. The lunch rush was always hectic at Gil's, but not a single chair was empty today, nor a single mouth closed judging by the volume.

I wove my way between the booths, ducking to the side as a man sprung up from a padded bench to my right. I might not be as lithe as Annabel, but I was quick on my feet, a skill I'd honed long before I ever thought about strapping on a pair of skates and elbow pads. Waitressing may not have been a contact sport, but knowing how to move sure didn't hurt.

I slid between two chairs as I made my way to table sixteen by the windows. A pair of white collar types sat there, one a goblin with light green skin, wide set eyes, and pointy ears, the other an ogre or troll half-breed, almost as wide as he was tall, wearing a cheap suit, a too-tight necktie, and with a nose shaped like a butternut squash. The goblin stockbroker leered at me as I approached the table, but I flashed a forced smile anyway.

"Here you go, gentlemen," I said as I eased the plates off my tray. "One meatloaf for you, sir. And for you, a roast beef club, hold the tomatoes. Can I get you anything else?"

The overweight half-breed blinked at the sandwich in front of him. He jabbed a chubby hand at it accusingly. "What the hell is this?"

"It's... a roast beef club, without tomatoes."

Gourd Nose turned his fat finger toward me. "Don't get

fresh with me, young lady. I can see it's a sandwich, but it's not what I ordered."

"It isn't?" I cocked my head, though not on purpose. It's just my natural reaction when I'm confused.

Gourdy noticed my tilted head and jammed his finger further under my nose. "You're darned right it isn't. I told you I wanted a turkey club, *without* mayo, and I said I didn't want the bread toasted."

I may not have the most acute nostrils in the universe, but I know what a load of bull smells like. "Are you sure about that?" I started to slide the order slip from my pocket. "I could've sworn I wrote down—"

"Well, whatever you wrote, you got it wrong." Gourdy flashed me a set of crooked teeth. "Now get your tight little behind back in that kitchen and get me what I ordered."

My jaw tightened at the mention of my backside, but I knew the job, and I knew this was a fight I wasn't going to win. "Right. Sorry about that. I'll just get this out of your way..."

Gourdy slapped my hand as I reached for his plate. "You kidding me? I'm a busy man, and I've only got fifteen minutes to eat. If I want any lunch at all, I'm gonna have to choke down this slop. Just get me the turkey club to go. Come on. Skip to it!"

Between the two-crown suit and the rolls of fat that threatened to spill out of it, it wasn't too hard to figure out what Gourdy's gambit was. Gil's wasn't in the habit of handing out free meals, but it sure seemed like the ogre had figured out how to game the system.

"You bet," I said between clenched teeth. "I'll get right on that."

Gourdy shouted at me as I turned, his voice carrying over

the clamor. "And get us some refills on these waters while you're at it, Toots!"

I missed a step at the sleazebag's call. I could deal with the fact that he and his leering goblin friend hadn't ordered anything to drink that would fatten my tip, but him tossing sexually charged slang my way really burned my biscuits. Nonetheless, I gave him a sideways nod and said, "You got it."

With my tray clenched between steel fingers, I waltzed back through the kitchen's swinging double doors to the order counter. I leaned across the polished steel and hollered so I'd be heard over the hiss and sizzle of the stove. "Hey Tony! Had an order mixup. Need a turkey club on the double, eighty-six the mayo! Put it in a doggy bag, and don't toast the bread unless you want me back here in a hot minute."

Tony was in mid-twenties, same as me, with a strip of pale fuzz across his upper lip that made him look even younger than he was. He looked up from the grill, sweat pouring from under his white cap. "Gods almighty, Nell, can't you keep an order straight? I'm deep in the weeds here, and table twelve didn't order hockey pucks." He flipped a couple of the patties on the grill for emphasis.

"Give me a break, Tony," I said. "It's not my fault. The guy at sixteen's acting like a real George Eddy."

Tony waved his spatula at me. "Alright, alright. Gimme a minute!"

I grabbed a pitcher of ice water and headed back out. Table six needed their glasses refilled, twelve asked for the check, and the guy at twenty-one gave me the old lifted finger. He ordered another round of cheese fries for his table and got his glasses refilled too, so by the time I got back to sixteen it had been a couple minutes and my pitcher was feeling a little light.

Gourd Nose scowled as I picked up his sweaty glass and refilled it. "Hmph. Took you long enough."

Once again I kept my composure, even as his lunch mate Leery McStevens kept undressing me with his eyes. "We're slammed. Trying to do the best we can."

"Well, try a little harder, will you? And where the heck is my sandwich?"

I glanced at Gourdy's plate, which was picked clean except for the lettuce we'd served it on. *Slop, my ass...*

I sloshed the icy dregs into Creepy's glass. "I'll check on that. Just a moment."

Another table tried to flag me down as I retreated to the kitchen, but I put my blinders on and acted like I hadn't noticed. The swinging door slammed against the backstop as I pushed through and bore down on the order counter.

"Tell me something good, Tony," I called.

Tony stood before the prep table, arms blurring cartoonishly as he stacked and assembled. "Keep your shirt on, Nell. Just gimme a sec."

"Oh, come off it. You'd love it if I took my shirt off."

He snorted and slid the paper bag across the counter toward me. "Don't you dare. If the health department catches you, my wallet's gonna get real slim real quick."

I scooped up the bag and flashed him a thankful smile. "Thanks, Tony. Owe you one."

The cook was too busy to crack a retort, already having scuttled back to the grill. I plunged back through the swinging doors and made a beeline for sixteen, once again ignoring the pleading eyes and wagging finger of the guy at seven.

Gourdy gave me the stink eye as I approached, yet still I smiled. I scooped up his clean plate and slid the to-go bag into its place. "Here you go, sir. Turkey club, hold the mayo, plain bread. Anything else I can get for you today?"

Gourdy snapped open the bag. His eyes bugged out and he snarled, not with faked righteous indignation as he had the first time but with actual rage. *"You've gotta be friggin' kidding me! What the hell are you trying to pull, Doll?"*

If Tony pulled a prank on me, I'd not only refuse to give him a peek at what was under my shirt, I'd pry his toenails off one by one with a hot poker. As it was though, since I didn't know what was in the bag, I kept my teeth pressed into a smile and pretended to give a damn. "Is there a problem?"

"You're damned right there's a problem!" Gourd Nose dumped the sandwich on the table. Tony had wrapped it in waxed paper, but the turkey and other fillings showed through where he'd sliced it in half. Gourdy jammed his finger into the middle, pointing at a juicy slice of red vegetable. "You want to tell me what that is?"

My patience tank was running on empty, and I'd already figured I was getting stiffed on my tip. I didn't have many darns left to give. "It's a tomato. They grow on vines. Good for digestion. Lots of people like them on sandwiches."

Gourdy's scowl deepened. "Don't get smart with me. I know what it is. I want to know what the hell it's doing on my sandwich!"

I sighed. "It comes on a club. If you didn't want it, you should've told me to hold it like you did with the mayo."

"I *did* tell you to hold it!" bellowed the guy. "You got wax in your ears or something?"

"You asked me to hold it on your *first* club," I said. "Remember it? The roast beef one you *didn't* order and *didn't* want but treated like a bowl of chocolate ice cream?"

Gourdy pushed himself to his feet. His arm darted out, and his chubby fingers wrapped around my arm. "Now listen here, you hash-slinger. It's bad enough you got my order wrong, but I'm not about to get smart-mouthed by some dumb broad."

My muscles tightened, not just the ones in my arm but all over. I unclenched my jaw enough to speak. "Let go of me."

Gourdy sneered. "Or what?"

In retrospect, I don't think I hit him that hard, but I've always been a poor judge of my own strength. I'm no delicate flower, no matter how many men I've met over the years might've wanted me to be. I could dish it out even better than I could take it, which was one of the reasons I liked roller derby so much. Even beyond my temperament, I had some size. Word was my grandfather on my dad's side was a half-troll, though I'd never met the man, and many of the humans and elves and dark elves who'd sown their seeds into my family tree were on the taller end of the bell curve.

No, I don't think it was the force of my blow that did it but rather the fact that I hit Gourdy square in the neck. The big guy choked and sputtered. Both of his hands shot to his throat, as if he might be able to pry the force of my blow from his windpipe by force. He stumbled and tripped on air. His wide rear hit the table first, but the rest of him wasn't far behind. Leery's glass of ice water leapt toward the ceiling, followed by the remains of his meatloaf, the silverware, the salt and pepper shakers, the bottle of katsup, and Gourdy's uneaten turkey club of course, which unwrapped itself as it flew, spreading slices of turkey, lettuce, and tomato over everyone within a three table radius.

At least there wasn't any mayo on the bread.

Gourdy hit the tile like a sledgehammer, but it was the rain of lunchmeat that quieted the cacophony in the dining room to a disgruntled murmur. I felt about fifty sets of eyes turn on me, and over the newly subdued grumble I heard the sharp crack of my manager's voice. "Miss Phair! A word."

He stood by the bar, his lips twisted in anger, one eye narrowed. On the best of days, my shift manager's disposition was about as warm and sunny as a January snowstorm, but the look on his face told me my conversation with Gourdy was about to become only the *second* worst one of my day.

CHAPTER TWO

The door to my apartment creaked as I pushed on it. Mid-afternoon sun streamed through the living room windows, but the beams couldn't cheer me any more than they could during my walk home. I slammed the door shut and kicked my shoes off, tossing them in the general direction of the boot tray.

I stomped past the moth-eaten floral print couch toward the kitchen. A pastel green Frigidator stood in the middle, its enameled paint as glossy as the day Mick got it for me, though the stainless steel handle no longer gleamed. Mick claimed he'd bought it as my birthday present, and in his defense, it had been my birthday when he showed me the magazine ad, but in every other respect the purchase had been a cop out. Mick knew I hated to cook—Tony at Gil's joked I could burn water, and he wasn't far off—but beyond that, the first generation Sherman Electric we'd replaced with the Frigidator could barely keep a bottle of milk cool in February. Mick claimed the Sherman's last gasps were coincidental with when I'd happened to be born, but lo and behold, two days after the new Frigidator got installed, I'd found two cases of his favorite beer lounging inside the chilly molded interior.

I could've used a beer as I tugged on the Frigidator's handle, but not a single bottle greeted me from within, of beer, milk, or anything else. The fridge was as barren as a buffet ravaged by a full scrummage team. The only things in it were a sack of carrots who'd all sprouted roots and a casserole that had turned into the home of a brave and resilient group of neon orange fungal spores—brave and resilient because they'd grown over the pale green fungus that had died upon tasting the casserole the first time around.

I sighed as I closed the fridge. If my manager had even half a heart, he would've poured me a drink before canning me, but apparently he thought being dressed down in front of a packed house was a stiff enough libation for a young woman of my 'limited social graces'—his words, not mine.

Luckily, not every beverage in Mick's and my apartment needed to be kept at crisp, winter temperatures. I stooped down, rummaging in the cabinet underneath the toaster for the liquor. Most of the bottles were on their last legs, but a fifth of gin still had a full belly. Not exactly the best spirit to drink on its own, but as pirates of yore used to say, any port in a storm, and today had caught me in a derecho.

I dug some ice cubes out of the tray in the freezer, tossed them into a glass, and filled it with a few fingers of gin. The cubes clinked against the sides as I swirled it all together. Before it had even cooled, I lifted the glass and took a long drag. The liquor burned my throat, but once the contents hit my bloodstream, I'd feel better... *wouldn't I?*

I set the glass down with a sigh. Mick wouldn't be happy I'd lost my job, even if he brought home more than I did. He covered our apartment's rent in its entirety, but he always told me I had to pay my fair share. He brought it up when he'd purchased the Frigidator not-a-present, reminding me not so subtly it was my responsibility to keep it stocked. Now I wouldn't be able to do even that, though on the bright side, it meant I'd probably burn fewer meals.

Not that I wouldn't be able to find a new waitressing job. It wasn't like film or radio or any number of old boys clubs. I wouldn't get blackballed from every diner in New Welwic because I'd punched some fat-fingered jerk in the neck after he put his hands on me. There were never enough young women willing to smile and nod patiently while jackasses ogled them and decided how much they should earn for the next thirty minutes. I could land another waitressing gig.

I just really, *really* didn't want one.

It wasn't just that the pay stunk or that waiting hand and foot on insufferable jerks was demeaning. It was that the only reason for me to be doing the job at all was the threat of starvation. I wasn't so naive as to think anyone had a fierce enthusiasm for waitressing, but most of the folks who did it had bigger dreams. They waited tables while working on their passions on the side. Almost every waiter and waitress I'd ever met was an aspiring something-or-other. Aspiring actor. Aspiring writer. Aspiring musician or dancer or artist. I had aspirations too, but the difference was that successful actors and musicians and painters, while few and far between, could theoretically make a living off their artistic endeavors. If I was being honest with myself, I had to admit the same couldn't be said of my roller derby efforts. The best paid girls on the team only made enough to pay for a nice meal out every other week. By all accounts, even the team's owner Arturo had refinanced his home to keep the team liquid. I think the only person making money off the Monster Maids was the guy who owned the rink on which we played. Similarly, none of the other athletic endeavors I'd tried growing up were money-makers, not unless you counted semi-nude oil wrestling as a sport. So what the hell was I doing wasting my time waitressing?

I took another pull from the gin, but the second swig didn't go down easier than the first. I set the glass down roughly, and over its angry clink, I heard something. A rustling, as well as what I thought was a shush.

I swept my eyes across the living room. It was empty, but to the side of the kitchen, the door to Mick's and my bedroom was closed. Strange. We usually left it open except for when we slept.

I approached the door and turned the handle. As I pushed it open, I found Mick hunched over, fixing the sheets on the bed. His hair was rumpled, and he wore nothing more than a pair of red and white checkered boxer shorts. He looked up as I entered, his eyes wide with surprise.

"Nell! Hey! What are you doing back so early?"

"I could ask you the same thing," I said. "Were you sleeping?"

He planted a hand on his hips and flashed me his teeth in a way that was more grimace than smile. "Yeah. I, ah... wasn't feeling well. Had a bad headache. Thought I'd come home. Close the blinds. Get everything nice and dark and try to sleep it off."

I nodded to the blinds, through which the mid-afternoon sun streamed. "The blind are open."

Mick nodded. "Yes, well, I'm feeling better now, thankfully.

I opened them when I heard you come in. Speaking of, what are *you* doing back so early?"

I sighed as I crossed to the bed. "It's a long story. Actually, that's not true. It's cut and dried. I got fired."

Mick rounded the edge of the bed toward me. *"What? Why? What happened?"*

"I punched a guy in the throat."

Mick had been reaching out to console me, but he froze. "Are you serious?"

I nodded. "Yeah."

"Like... *a customer?*"

"Yes, Mick, a customer, and he deserved it for what it's worth. He was saying rude things to my face, and he put his hands on me. He grabbed me by the arm. I told him to let go."

"And, what? You just *laid him out?*"

Mick wasn't small, but I'm a tall girl. We see eye to eye, and what I saw in his eyes at the moment was shock and disbelief. Not a whole lot of concern, though. "I'm not hurt by the way. Thanks for asking."

I turned toward the closet, figuring I might burn my uniform after I changed into something more comfortable, but I was stopped by a forceful yank.

"Wait!" said Mick.

I turned and stared at Mick's hand. He grabbed me around the arm just as Gourdy had done at the diner. Same arm, same spot.

Mick saw the look on my face and dropped my arm like a hot coal. "Sorry. I didn't mean to do that. It's just... Look, the fact that you got fired for clocking a guy surprised me, but that's no excuse for reacting the way I did. I'm sorry that happened at work, Nell, and it's not your fault. You didn't deserve it, and you shouldn't have gotten fired."

The ice I'd felt at the steel touch of his fingers melted slightly. "Thanks, Mick. I appreciate that, but in this case, I think my manager was justified in showing me the door."

Mick coughed nervously. He waved his hands as if trying to fan away the awkwardness in the air. "Whatever. You never liked working there anyway. You'll find another job. In fact, we should go celebrate. Get some drinks."

I couldn't believe Mick was taking my firing so well. I was sure he'd berate me over the loss of income. Maybe he'd finally realized money wasn't everything and there were more important things to worry about in a relationship. "You really want to celebrate the fact that I got *fired?*"

"Why not?" said Mick, an easy smile crossing his lips. "I already told everyone at the office I was taking the rest of the day off. Might as well make the most of it." He rushed to his side of the bed and started throwing his clothes back on, which he'd dumped unceremoniously on the floor.

I smiled, his infectious charm getting the best of me. "Alright. Let me slip into something a little more festive."

Mick lunged toward me, stumbling with his pants around his ankles. "No! You're fine the way you are. You don't need to change."

I ignored him as I opened the closet. "Mick, if you think I'm going out in my Gil's uniform then you've lost your—"

My voice trailed off as I caught sight of the five-foot nothing gnome hybrid nestled amongst my dresses, clutching what I had to assume were her clothes to the front of her mostly nude frame. She smiled and shrunk further into my wardrobe, muttering a squeaky "Hi..." as she did so.

My jaw tightened as I turned. I stared at Mick with daggers in my eyes.

Mick finished pulling his pants to his waist. He held a hand up. "Now hold on there, Nell. I can explain."

My first instinct was to ask what was going on, but I'm no idiot. Mick's state of undress. The rustling and shushing I'd heard. The half-naked woman in the closet. The fact that Mick had never had a migraine in his life. I knew exactly what was going on.

I took a slow breath. "Mick, I've had a really bad day."

"It's not what it looks like," said Mick. "She's from work. She, ah... spilled a drink on herself at lunch. She needed a change of clothes, but she lives forty-five minutes out. She came back with me to borrow something of yours."

My cheeks burned, from anger as much as embarrassment. I couldn't believe I hadn't suspected anything sooner. "She's half my size, Mick. Gods, *shut up.* You're such an ass."

I turned and stormed toward the exit. Mick stumbled after me, catching me once again by the arm as I passed through the bedroom door.

"Stop it, Nell," he said. "I'm trying to talk to you."

My teeth ground against each other as I stared at his fingers coiled around the muscle of my arm. *"LET... GO."*

Mick pulled me close. "Damn it, Penelope, listen to me for a second. I—"

I'm better with a running start on wheels, but I've never shied away from close quarters encounters. My elbow took Mick in the nose, and I heard a sharp crack.

Mick let go of me. He stumbled into the door frame, blood streaming from his nostrils. *"Son of a...!* What the hell, Nell?"

He tested his lips with a couple fingers, both of which came back red. "I think you broke my nose."

"You should be happy that's *all* I broke," I snarled.

Mick pushed himself off the wall and came at me with a raised finger, his cheeks flushed. "Now listen here, woman—"

Maybe it was the way he said the word that broke the griffon's back, or maybe I'd already committed to my course of action when I saw the color in Mick's cheeks and the way he stomped toward me. Either way, I wasn't about to become a statistic. I grabbed Mick by the arm, swept a leg underneath him, twisted, and threw. Mick flew across the living room, slamming into the coffee table spine first. The wood splintered and cracked as it collapsed under his weight.

Mick groaned and pushed himself to his feet. "Why you... *you bitch.*"

That did it. Until now, I could've claimed to have been protecting myself, but no more. As Mick straightened, I rushed forward and slammed a knee into his groin. He wheezed and doubled over, groaning as he tried to gather himself, but I didn't give him the chance. I threw a solid right hook that took him in the chin. He crumpled, bouncing off the loveseat on his way to the floor.

"Call me a bitch one more time, Mick!" I shouted, my cheeks burning with anger. "I dare you."

Despite everything, Mick reached for my ankle. *"Bitch."*

I kicked away Mick's outstretched hand, then followed that with a heavy foot to Mick's midsection. He grunted and wheezed, but the blow shut him up.

I stood there, breathing hard and wondering if the final kick had been necessary, when I heard the floorboards creak. I turned to see the petite half-breed, now dressed, sneaking through the bedroom door.

She smiled demurely as she crept toward the exit. "I'm just going to let myself out, if that's okay."

Somehow, words made it through my clenched teeth. "You might want to try running."

Believe it or not, she took my advice.

CHAPTER THREE

R umor has it prison is far worse than jail, but if true, I don't want to find out.

My jail cell at the Williams Street precinct was cold, clammy, and stunk as much of despair as it did of urine. I shared it with seven other women. Two of them, an overly skinny elf and a human woman who must've been pushing three hundred pounds, were likely prostitutes based on their excessive quantities of eyeshadow and their short imitation leather skirts. A dark elf sat against the cinderblock wall, shivering uncontrollably and rocking back and forth, though probably not from cold. Her dilated pupils and the recurring twitch in her eye made me think she was high as a kite and possibly already on the way down. A pair of dwarven women, one fresh-faced and the other with a shock of gray hair, had taken ownership of one of the cell's corners. The younger one had a black eye and the older a haunted look upon her face, suggesting they'd been through some trauma, though being the victim of it didn't explain why they'd been locked up. The last two women I couldn't quite place, a human with a buzz cut and a giant breed based on her height. They had a few bruises on their arms, and the giant woman was missing two of her front teeth, but they hadn't said a word between them since I'd been escorted into the pen. Strangely enough, despite the latter's surly demeanor, *I* was the one everyone refused to approach. Not a single one of them had come within five feet of me since I'd taken my seat along the bench.

Then again, I was the one with cuts and scrapes on my knuckles without a bruise upon me to show for it.

Regardless of the reason, I wouldn't look the gift horse of privacy in the mouth. Even though I'd shown twice in one day that I was capable of defending myself, I didn't think getting into a third bare-knuckle brawl would help my case come my judicial hearing.

While Gourdy had stormed off from Gil's while my manager tongue-lashed me, Mick hadn't been so forgiving. After his mistress took off, I'd called the police myself, figuring a neighbor must've heard the clamor and might beat me to the punch if I didn't. After giving the operator an account of what happened, I'd descended to the apartment's front steps and waited for the authorities to arrive. Maybe I just wanted to get in front of any charges and show I was trying to be helpful, but I also couldn't stand the thought of spending another second in Mick's apartment. I hadn't even changed out of my uniform before heading to the sidewalk.

I'd only been waiting for a couple minutes when the officers arrived. One of them stayed with me while the other went to check on Mick. At first, the officer who lingered with me spoke softly as he inquired about what happened, but as he heard my side of the story about how I'd beaten Mick senseless, the empathy he reserved for victims of domestic abuse disappeared and was replaced with mirth. Apparently, women being beaten by their boyfriends was a tragedy, but the opposite was worthy of a chuckle.

Mick didn't think it was funny. Once he'd been roused and given his account of things, he demanded to press charges. Since I didn't dispute his version of the events, the officers had no choice but to cuff me and push me into the back of their squad car.

So it was I found myself in the cell, wondering how my life had fallen to pieces. A day ago I'd been in a stable position, if not necessarily happy. It's not as if Gourdy's insults and his friend's leering bug eyes made me realize I hated waiting tables. I'd known that for a long time, and if I was being honest, my relationship with Mick had started to crumble long before I found a half-nude chest-height gnome in my closet. Now that I'd beaten the snot out of him, all the horrible ways he'd treated me seemed painfully obvious. The constant verbal abuse about our finances. The way he expected me to do all the cooking and cleaning and shopping. His occasional grabbiness. The way he'd ignore my problems and focus only on how they affected him. I didn't know how long Mick had been cheating on me, but the relationship was as done as Gil's infamous char-broiled steaks. It had just taken some bloodied knuckles for me to realize it.

Of course, even though I might be better off in the long run without Mick, I most certainly wasn't now. The apartment was in his name. Everything I owned was in it, or had been when I'd been unceremoniously pressed into the back of an NWPD squad car. Given the look on Mick's face as I'd driven off, I wouldn't be surprised if my clothes and personal effects currently littered the sidewalk underneath his window, being picked through by guttersnipes and lookie-loos.

Even that wasn't the worst of it. Though I technically had an account with my local bank, it was about as empty as the Frigidator at Mick's. I didn't have two silver eagles to rub together. There was no way I could put a month's rent down on a new apartment, not even a dump in the Erming across the river, and without a place to stay, how was I supposed to land another job? I didn't even have a decent outfit to interview in. Maybe someone I knew would take pity on me. Not my parents. I'd burned that bridge long ago, but Annabel perhaps, or if she didn't want to associate with me after the show I put on at Gil's, maybe one of the Monster Maids. Cyreth or Mary.

Of course, losing my home wasn't my most pressing problem. Being in jail was. In my mind, my attacks on Mick had been in self-defense, but would a jury see them that way? If Mick took me to trial, jurors would probably be lenient because of my gender and the nature of our dispute, but that was a long way down the line. What happened now? Did I need a lawyer? How would I get out of jail, and how would my homelessness affect matters?

My chest ached. The weight of the world pressed down on me as I thought about all the ways in which I was totally, fully, and completely screwed. I wanted nothing more than to curl into a tight ball and cry, but I refused to let myself do so. The fact that I looked like a hard-ass was the only thing keeping the other women in the cell from bothering me. Nonetheless, emotions don't care much for intimidation tactics, and within a few minutes of me sitting there, stewing in my misery and dark thoughts, I felt a touch of wetness tickle the corners of my eyes.

I squeezed them shut, willing the tears away. As I did so, I heard a heavy clank and the grate of steel on steel.

A gruff voice called out. "Penelope Phair?"

I looked up, wiping my cheeks surreptitiously as I took stock of the officer at the cell door. "Yes?"

He nodded to the exit. "Time to go. You've made bail."

I stood, blinking. "What?"

"You hard of hearing? Someone bailed you out. Let's go."

I approached the cell's metal door. "I didn't call anyone."

The officer's look suggest he didn't care. "You want to stay in here or not?"

Once again I had to remind myself not to look the gift stallion in the mouth. I stepped into the hallway as the officer slammed the door shut behind me. "Follow me," he said.

The uniformed officer led me through the double doors at the end of the hall, along the edge of a floor filled with desks bustling with beat cops and people being booked. As we walked, I wondered who'd coughed up the bail money. Tony, after hearing the account of what transpired this afternoon from Annabel? Some of the roller derby girls? Or gods forbid, *Mick*. If I found him standing there, telling me he'd thought it over and was willing to drop the charges if we got back together, I'd find myself right back in the pen after planting a boot in his tenders.

I didn't have to wonder long, though. As we reached the lobby, I spotted an old woman seated against the wall, her pointed ears sticking through her long white hair. She smiled as she caught sight of me. "There you are, Nelly."

I blinked, and suddenly my chest didn't feel quite so empty. "Nana Daggers."

CHAPTER FOUR

Technically, Shay Daggers wasn't my grandmother. She was my great-grandmother, but she'd always introduced herself as Nana when I was little, and the name stuck. Despite the cane she used to help her walk, she moved with a certain grace. White hair cascaded down her shoulders and a legion of wrinkles creased her brow, but neither could hide the fact that she'd been a lovely woman in her youth.

Looking at her slender form and elfin features made me wish my ancestry was a little more to order and less of a potluck. It wasn't that I thought I was ugly, I just often felt mismatched. I had enough dark-elf and troll blood in me to give my tan skin a bit of an olive undertone, and my technically brunette but basically black hair fluctuated between curly and wavy based on the humidity. My nose was a little wider than I wanted it to be, and my shoulders were *way* wider than I wanted *them* to be—sometimes, anyway. They were nice for sports, less so for fitting into dresses and blouses. At least I had a nice ass, but I don't think any of my ancestors could take credit for that. That was from all the roller skating.

The officer disappeared as I met my great-grandmother by her chair. "Nana, what are you doing here?"

She stood and pulled me into a gentle embrace. While there, she leaned in and whispered in my ear. "I'm busting you out of here, young lady. What does it look like I'm doing? I'm not as spry as I used to be, though. I can probably only whack two or three of these officers on the head with my cane. How many can you handle?"

I snorted as I pulled back, smiling despite my predicament. "Ask a silly question, get a silly answer. I guess I brought that on myself. What I should've asked is how you knew I was here."

Nana steadied herself on her cane as she let go of me. "About that. Do you remember when you ran away from home when you were fourteen?"

It wasn't an experience I'd ever forget. I'd roamed the streets and slept on park benches for seventy-two hours, getting progressively hungrier and more miserable until the police picked me up for loitering. "You sprang me that time, too."

Nana shrugged. "When they found you, they hadn't been able to contact either of your parents. My name was listed as a secondary contact as a result of the guardianship agreement following the divorce, which is how I arrived and rescued you that rainy day a decade ago."

I sighed. "Let me guess. Once again my father couldn't be reached." Chances were he was too drunk to pick up the phone, same as always.

Nana Daggers shook her head. "Believe it or not, the police don't worry about contacting the next of kin for people who've been arrested. That's reserved for rebellious minors. But I still have some connections in the department after all these years. When your name crossed the sergeant's desk, he recognized it from the runaway incident ten years back and gave me a call."

I didn't know all the details, but I remembered enough stories to know Nana had been a member of the force a lifetime ago. I knew she'd been a detective, but I couldn't remember how high she'd risen. Captain, I thought. Regardless, I shouldn't have been surprised she'd tracked me down.

I hung my head. "So you know what happened then."

Despite her age, Nana Daggers was fairly tall, too, so her fingers didn't have to rise far to tilt my chin back up. "Sweetheart, all I know is you needed my help. You know I'll always be there for you."

I felt the tears coming back, but I blinked them away. "Thanks, Nana."

She snuck her arm through mine and gestured at the front doors with her cane. "Come. Let's get going. Baul is waiting outside. We'll need him to fetch the car."

With Nana Daggers hanging onto me, I headed out of the precinct onto the stone stairs leading to the street. Pedestrians clogged the sidewalk at the base of the steps, but at the top not ten feet from the door stood Nana's enormous bodyguard slash chauffeur slash butler Baul. He was a full-blooded ogre, closer to seven feet tall than six, with dark skin and a jutting lower lip. He wore a black suit and a matching rimmed cap, which I suppose helped him look less threatening, but I'd never thought of him as anything but an enormous teddy bear. After all, he'd been at Nana's side as long as I could remember.

He smiled as he saw me. "Miss Phair. Good to see you." He turned his eyes to Nana. "Should I get the Lancerette?"

Nana nodded. "Please, Baul."

The big man pushed himself off the railing and headed

down the stairs. I moved with Nana to the side, out of the way of people coming and going from the station. The sun was on its way toward the horizon, sending late summer rays through the gaps between buildings. A slight breeze blew, wicking away the perspiration that dotted my brow.

"You know," said Nana, "this probably should've been the first thing I asked, but... are you well, dear?"

I tore my eyes from the fading sunlight to focus on my great-grandmother. How much did she really want to know, and how much did I want to burden her with? "I'm fine."

Nana snorted and shook her head. "I know the norms have changed since I was young, but it used to be that girls who got thrown in jail for assault didn't qualify as *fine*."

I frowned. "I thought you said the sergeant didn't tell you anything."

Nana Shay lifted an eyebrow. "Your knuckles are scraped and raw, and you have a nice lump sprouting from your elbow. There are also a couple droplets of blood on your uniform, though not yours unless I'm mistaken. Once a detective, always a detective, my dear."

I sighed. "I don't want to talk about it."

Nana nodded respectfully. "Of course. I understand."

I made it about twenty seconds before giving in to Nana's unrelenting wall of silence. "Okay, fine. Maybe I got angry at work when some fat jerk tried to stiff me on a tip and grabbed my arm and told me I was a hussy. Maybe I clocked him and maybe when I got home I found Mick in bed with another woman and maybe I got angry again. Maybe I smacked him around a little, too. Maybe he needs a new coffee table because he broke his with his back, and maybe I need a new place to stay because I have no boyfriend and no job and no apartment and nothing but this stupid Gil's Diner uniform which I want to strip off and burn at a thousand degrees!"

Nana pulled me into another embrace. I didn't even realize I was crying until I saw the wet spots my cheeks left upon her shoulder.

"There, there, dear," she said. "It's going to be okay."

I wanted to be angry and yell and stomp, but I also wanted to be held, and it was entirely possible the only person in the world who truly loved me was standing in front of me with her arms already around me.

I held on weakly, shaking my head as more tears fell. "How is it going to be okay, Nana? I'm a screwup. I've always been a screwup, and this time I've really loused it up. Worse than ever before."

Nana pushed me back, but she held onto my shoulders. "Oh, I don't know if I'd say that. Remember the time you sent that one boy to the hospital when you *accidentally* knocked him down the escarpment into the canalized portion of the Earl River? Or when you crashed your father's car after sneaking out without his permission? Or when you set fire to your mother's boyfriend's home?"

My cheeks warmed as I wiped away the last of my tears. "Are you trying to make me feel better? Because you're only confirming I'm the world's biggest bungler."

Nana's face twisted from melancholy. "No, Nelly. Not at all. What I was getting at is that you've always made mistakes, but the mistakes don't lessen who you are. You're a smart woman, strong and strong-willed—very much so. Those are wonderful qualities, but they can get you into trouble, too, especially when you *react* to others instead of *acting* on your own behalf. I know you have a big heart, but sometimes it's better to listen to your head instead."

"So, what?" I said defensively. "I'm too emotional? Is that it?"

"Sometimes, yes, but that's not a bad thing. You just have to learn to control your emotions, and learn when to listen to reason rather than your gut." Nana smiled and her eyes twinkled. "You know, there's someone else who had the exact same problems you do, someone you've always reminded me a lot of."

I snorted. "Is there, now? So this is the portion of our talk where you tell me you were just like me when you were young?"

"Oh, I wasn't talking about me. I was referring to your great-grandfather Jake."

I only had vague recollections of the man. He'd died when I was a toddler. He'd been older than Nana Daggers, and he didn't have any of her long-lived elf blood in his veins, either. I knew he'd worked as a detective alongside Nana, but if I'd learned more about him over the years, I'd forgotten it. "Was he a royal screwup, too?"

"The worst," said Nana. "You wouldn't believe how many problems he had when I met him. He was an alcoholic. He was divorced and had a son he barely knew. He was cocky, brash, and sexist. To be honest, he was something of an asshole."

"Nana! Language!"

She shrugged. "Well, he was. I'm not going to sugarcoat it."

I lifted an eyebrow. "So you're telling me you fell for an alcoholic, sexist jerk?"

"No, I fell for the sweet, gentle, compassionate, intelligent man who was hiding within him. It didn't happen right away, either. He chased me for a while, and in that period he transformed himself. Gave up booze. Got into shape. Challenged himself mentally and emotionally to overcome the bad habits he'd acquired, but it wasn't until he came to grips with the fact that he had to change for himself and not for me that he really grew into the man I'd always known he could be."

"Great," I said. "So all I have to do is find Mr. Right and go on a transformational journey to keep my life from falling apart. I'll get right on that."

Nana snorted. "For the record, Jake had a flair for sarcasm, too. My point is, you have the tools you need to overcome the obstacles in front of you, same as he did. You're smart, strong, resilient, and most importantly, despite the fights and mistakes and screwups, your heart has *always* been in the right place, just like Jake's was."

I swallowed a lump in my throat as Baul pulled up in the navy blue Lancerette. It felt nice to have someone tell me I was worth something, that I wasn't a waste of space and time and someone else's love, but I wasn't totally sure I believed her. Nana was family. She was supposed to believe in me and support me, no matter what—not that being family had ever stopped my parents from not giving a damn.

I sighed as I inspected my shoes. "Did Papa Jake ever struggle with his self-confidence?"

Nana Daggers snuck her hand through my arm. "The fact that he was so outwardly cocky gives you your answer. Come. Let's not keep Baul waiting."

As I helped Nana down the stairs, my eyes on the sparkling blue car in front of me, I couldn't help but think about my predicament. Each step took me further from Nana's love and closer to reality.

Tears threatened to break free from the corners of my eyes

again, and my throat felt tight. "Nana... I don't have anywhere to go."

Baul exited the car and held the back door open for us. Nana patted my arm as we reached it. "Nonsense, dear. As long as I'm alive, you'll always have a place to rest your head. You're coming to stay with me for a while, like it or not."

CHAPTER FIVE

I t seemed like ages since I'd been to my Nana's house, but it all came back to me as Baul pulled onto her street. Twenty foot saucer magnolias lined the road, thick with teardrop-shaped leaves and mostly free of the pink and white flowers that bloomed in spring, though an odd tree or two still held a few confused blossoms. The houses along the road were all old world New Welwic, with brick facades and slate roofs, though most of them had been remodeled over the years to add subterranean garages and extra stories on top. Nonetheless, the remodeling efforts had been done with an eye to uniformity, probably at the behest of a historical building commission or a persnickety neighborhood association.

Baul pulled the car into Nana's driveway, stopping across from a keypad on a post. He rolled down the window and punched a few numbers into it. In response, the garage door rumbled and began to pull itself up.

I blinked. "Whoa. Is that new?"

Nana smiled. "We had it installed a year ago. No sense in

having Baul go out in the rain and snow when technology can do the job for him."

Baul pulled the Lancerette forward into the spot and killed the engine. He opened the back door and helped me and Nana from the car. For a big guy, he was surprisingly spry, beating us to the door to hold it open as I escorted Nana inside.

"Thank you, Baul." Nana handed him her shawl as we stepped into the foyer. "If you could get some water started in the kettle. And check with Marcel to see how dinner is coming along?"

Baul bobbed his head. "Of course, Mrs. Daggers."

With Nana's arm still hooked around mine, we headed toward her sitting room. Though the house didn't look enormous from the street, you nonetheless could've fit three copies of Mick's and my apartment into the first floor alone. A chandelier hung in the entryway, the light from dozens of candle bulbs reflecting through the crystals dangling underneath. Though the home's furnishings felt outdated to my eye, there was no question they were expensive, from the hand-carved legs on the card table to the plush floor rug with palmette patterning to the velvet upholstery on the sofa pushed against the back of the sitting room—an entirely superfluous space whose very existence said something about Nana's wealth, even if the presence of Baul and her private chef and the immaculate Lancerette hadn't made it abundantly clear.

Hints of vanilla and patchouli tickled my nose as I helped my great-grandmother onto the sofa. "Remind me, Nana, what positions did you and Papa Jake hold in the NWPD?"

Nana sighed as the couch took the pressure off her feet. "Well, Jake started as a patrol officer, though he spent most of his years as a detective. That's where I began, but I ultimately worked my way to captain. It was an interim position the first go around, but I got the job for good later on. Ordering others around was intimidating, but the stability and structure the position provided was more appealing to me once I had kids. Jake just liked solving mysteries, though. He refused several promotions over the years. Why do you ask?"

I looked around the sitting room, perhaps with my eyebrows higher on my forehead than they normally were. "I never realized police work paid that well."

Nana laughed. "It doesn't. Don't get me wrong, we would've made it work on our salaries alone, but most of what you see around you is thanks to Jake. He made a big bet on Sherman Electric when it was being formed, and it paid off *very* handsomely over the years."

I whistled. "Talk about striking while the iron is hot. Way to go, Papa."

Nana rolled her eyes. "Don't give him too much credit. He was the furthest thing from an investor. Back then, Sherman was a budding electric and lighting company. They hadn't branched into telephones and radios and stoves and fridges, and Jake had no reason to think they ever would. Well... no sensible reason, anyway."

I paused by the windows overlooking the front garden, which was bright and green and buzzing with insects. "What's that supposed to mean?"

Nana sighed. "The only reason your great-grandfather bought stock in Sherman Electric was because he claimed a time-traveler from the future told him the investment would pay off."

My mouth fell open. It was still open when I faced Nana. "So Papa Jake was a lunatic? *He's* who I remind you of?"

Nana gave me a reproachful glance. "Now, now. I'm not saying I totally believed him on *that* one, but we ran across a lot of strange things in our years on the force. Wild beasts of all shapes and sizes, mysteries we could never explain, not to mention all sorts of dangerous and potent magics."

Now it was my turn to roll my eyes. "Come on, Nana, not with the magic stuff again."

Daggers' grandmotherly glance took on a steely edge I'd seen few times before. "Just because you don't see it every day doesn't mean it's disappeared. There was a time before electricity and technology infected every aspect of our existence that magic was alive and well. I'll admit it was also something of an oddity when I was young, but it still exists. It hasn't gone anywhere, there are simply fewer practitioners now who know how to harness it."

I didn't want to get in a fight, certainly not with Nana, but there were some things I wasn't willing to believe in. Thankfully, Baul kept me from saying anything that might get me in trouble. He stepped into the sitting room, his bald head now freed from underneath his chauffeur's cap. He gave a short bow. "Mrs. Daggers. Miss Phair. Dinner is served."

Baul crossed to the couch to help Nana up, and suddenly I felt self-conscious again. Nana had said that as long as she was around, I'd always have a roof over my head, but we hadn't talked specifics on the ride over from the station. I didn't want to upend her life. "You're sure there's enough dinner to go around?"

Nana waved me to come along with her. "You may not believe this, darling, but when I got the call from the sergeant, I had a sneaking suspicion you might be joining me for supper. I told Marcel to add an extra portion to the meal before I left.

Even if I hadn't, there probably would've been plenty. He always makes enough to last through the following day. Baul is very good at polishing off leftovers."

The big ogre smiled. "That I am, Mrs. Daggers, although perhaps you should tell Marcel to cook a little less. My pants are more snug around the waist than they used to be."

Baul led us to the dining room. There, Nana's chef Marcel served us a delectable three-course meal. First came a salad of mixed greens, three different colors of tomatoes, and slices of grilled peach, followed by a tangy green soup that Marcel said contained cucumbers, yogurt, and lemon. Finally came the entree, a roasted chicken leg and thigh that smelled like heaven, complete with a side of herbed potatoes and green beans. Nana picked at her meals, never eating more than half of anything, but I couldn't help myself. Not counting the swigs of gin I'd tipped back at Mick's, I hadn't put anything in my stomach since before my shift at Gil's started, and I'd never been the kind of girl who stopped getting hungry when she's stressed. I cleaned all three of my plates, and if not for the threat of reproachful glances from my great-grandmother, I would've picked up the chicken with my bare hands and torn every last strip of meat from the bones instead of using my knife and fork like a civilized girl. Marcel poured us wine throughout, and by the end of it, with a full belly and a warm sensation coursing through me thanks to the Saldea Valley blanc, I was starting to feel as if the world wasn't ending anymore.

Throughout the meal, Nana regaled me with tales of ages past: some of Papa Jake, some of my grandmother, and even some of me as a young girl, though thankfully none about my father. As Marcel cleared the last of the dishes, Nana swirled the remaining two fingers of wine in her glass. She chuckled as she stared into the past. "I still can't understand how you got away from all of us in the first place. You barely knew how to walk and yet somehow you managed to make it to the stairs without any of us being the wiser. Lucky for you your grandmother's stairs were carpeted. My goodness, what a terror you were when you were little."

Honestly, I preferred the stories about Papa Jake and Granny Abigail to the ones about me. The latter all seemed to reinforce the idea that I'd been getting into trouble since the day I was born. "I'm not sure I ever *stopped* being a terror."

"Well, once you get older people phrase it differently. They say you're *difficult* or *impulsive,* or even *impetuous* if you've really twisted their knickers."

I sighed. "Doesn't really matter what anyone calls it. It's all the same thing. I've been on this earth nearly twenty-five years, and I haven't changed over any of them."

Nana's brow furrowed. She stared at me intently as she set her glass on the table. "What have you been doing outside of waitressing, Nelly? Still playing... what was it called? That game with the sticks?"

The line of questioning caught me off guard. "Lacrosse? No. It's roller derby now. Has been for a couple years."

"What do you get out of it?"

I frowned. "I don't get paid much, if that's what you're asking."

"I more or less assumed that," said Nana. "So if not for the money, why do you do it?"

"Uh, because it's fun. Obviously."

Nana lifted her eyebrow into an expertly crafted arch. "Humor me for a minute, Nelly. What is it that draws you to the sport?"

"Well, I like that's it's physical."

Nana didn't say anything. After a moment, I realized she wasn't satisfied with my response, so I brought out my shovel and kept digging. "I guess... I like that the other girls don't look down their noses at me. That once we step onto the rink, we're equals, same as it was playing lacrosse. I like that people who watch see me as someone who's in control instead of a screwup who can't hold down a waitressing job. I like the way it makes me feel. Strong. Powerful. Confident." I sighed. "I wish I could feel that way all the time."

Nana nodded as she ran a finger along the rim of her wine glass. "Strength. Power. Confidence. These are qualities you desire, and I daresay you already have them. The more important question is what do you *need?*"

I blinked, confused. "Pardon?"

"You've always known what you've wanted, Nell, but I don't think you've ever stopped to think about what you need. They're different things. Have you ever stopped to think that the qualities you most desire are the same ones that keep getting you into trouble? What you *need* is something that allows you to be the person you want to be while keeping you grounded and safe and stable. What you need is a sense of purpose. A reason for existing."

I lifted an eyebrow. "Don't tell me some nice man in a suit showed up at your door and convinced you to join their church, Nana."

My great-grandmother smiled. "Some people find purpose in religion, it's true, but that wasn't what I was referring to. People can't flit through life like a leaf on the wind. They need to know they've made a difference. Some people strive for big changes—businessmen, scientists, even politicians, for better or worse—but most people find purpose in smaller efforts. They make their communities a better place, they garden, they bake bread. They do things to put smiles on their friend's faces. Some people find all the purpose they need in a family."

I snorted. "Yeah, I don't think I'm going to be starting a family anytime soon."

"Based on how you got thrown in jail, I figured as much," said Nana. "But there are any number of ways to make your impact upon the world. What I'm saying is you need to find something, be it an activity or a career, that lets you be the person you want to be while fulfilling you at a deeper level. As much as your sports escapades might make you feel powerful, I'm not sure they're doing the latter."

The part of me that liked roller derby and lacrosse wanted to huff and moan and throw something, to stamp my feet and tell Nana that she didn't know what the heck she was talking about. My problems were clearly external: my lack of a job, losing my home, my boyfriend cheating on me, not the fact that I needed to find inner peace or some similar pile of bull. Then again, my Nana was over a hundred. I had to admit it was at least *possible* she'd learned some valuable life lessons on her journey through the cosmos.

I sighed. "What did it for you?"

"What gave me purpose?" said Nana. "It wasn't any one thing. Your great-grandfather Jake had something to do with it, as did our children and grandchildren and now even you. But if I'm being honest, my job helped me put the world into perspective. I put a lot of bad actors behind bars, and together with the rest of the department, I have to think I helped a lot of people. Not all of them, but many, and that's all I ever could've hoped for."

I shook my head. "Must be easy to make a difference when you're a cop."

"Who ever said anything about it being *easy?*" Nana's eyes twinkled as she pushed herself from her seat and gathered her cane. "It's time for me to retire. These old bones need more rest than they used to, but feel free to stay up as late as you like. Baul will have fixed up one of the guest rooms on the second floor for you when you decide to rest your head."

I gave her a hug as she hobbled to my chair. "Thank you, Nana. I don't know what I'd do without you. Can I help you to your room?"

She brushed me off. "If I don't use my legs, pretty soon they won't work at all. I'll be fine. And remember, dearest. There's no problem so great it can't be fixed." She gave me a kiss on the forehead. "Goodnight."

"Goodnight, Nana."

Once she retired to her room, the house grew so quiet that I wondered if she and Baul had transformed into mice. I cleared the last of the dishes into the kitchen, all except for my wine glass. That I kept with me as I shifted to the solarium overlooking the garden behind the home. There, I nursed the last of the Saldea Valley blanc late into the night, but I didn't drink much of it.

Mostly, I stared into the rustling trees behind the home and thought about what Nana Daggers had said to me.

CHAPTER SIX

Sunlight trickled through the drapes as I cracked my eyes. I rolled away from it and snuggled deeper into my pillow, but my bladder poked me and complained. I tried to ignore the thing, but it insisted, so I rose and crossed to the attached bath. I yawned as I returned, a sense of relief spreading through my lower abdomen, and paused by the thick purple drapes. The sunlight was bright white against the window frame. As I pulled one edge of the drapes back, light flooded in like teenage girls rushing into a concert. I shielded my eyes from the glare, and when they'd adapted, I turned to the clock on my nightstand. The hour hand had crept past eleven and was already on its journey toward noon.

I blinked. Apparently Nana's beds were more comfortable than mine.

I pulled the drapes all the way back and secured them, but I didn't stand by the window. Even though the guest room faced the garden behind the home, the view wasn't totally obscured from the surrounding homes, and lacking any nightgowns, I'd slept in my undergarments.

I crossed to the wardrobe and threw open the doors. Despite being a guest room, there were a few of Nana's clothes hanging upon the rack inside. The dresses looked like they hadn't been worn in fifty years, but style wasn't my main concern. Finding something that fit was. I was tall enough that all of them would expose my knees, but my shoulders would be the bigger problem. Luckily, there was a sleeveless yellow sundress hiding in the corner. The fabric was stretchy, so I could probably fit into it, even if it wouldn't leave much to the imagination. Not that it mattered. Baul was too much of a gentleman to stare.

I squeezed into the dress, fixed it as best I could in the mirror, tamed my hair to a gentle frizz, and opened the door. There I paused to see if I could hear signs of life from downstairs, and good thing, too. If I hadn't I would've tripped over the green leather suitcase sitting in front of my door. I figured it was Nana's, but there was a card sitting on the top near the handle.

I picked it up. The writing inside was in Nana's hand.

NELL,

INSIDE YOU SHOULD FIND SOME OF YOUR PERSONAL EFFECTS. I instructed Baul to make a visit to your former residence this morning. As it turns out, he can be quite persuasive at convincing others to return property. If you're missing anything, let me know and Baul can make another trip in the afternoon.

I also had Baul stop at Marshall May's on his way home. He talked to a sales associate there who put together a care package fit for a young lady who had been displaced from her home. You *should find everything from toothpaste to makeup to undergarments alongside your clothes from Mick's.*

Marcel won't be back until mid-afternoon, but Baul made waffles. Help yourself if we're not around when you wake.

Love,
Nana

I SMILED AS I CLOSED THE NOTE. APPARENTLY NANA meant it when she said I'd be taken care of. I hefted the suitcase into the guest room, though I didn't immediately change. I'd need a shower first, and for now, the promise of waffles was a greater priority. I headed down the stairs, through the foyer, and into the kitchen. The only sound in the home was the creak of the occasional floorboard under my feet and the hum of the refrigerator, so I assumed Nana and Baul were out. True to Nana's note, however, I found a stack of waffles on a platter in the middle of the eat-in table next to a carafe of maple syrup.

Sadly, the waffles' buttery, yeasty aroma no longer hung in the air. Sure enough, the fluffy rectangles were stone cold to the touch, but I couldn't blame Nana for that. She probably hadn't expected I'd wake at the crack of noon.

I snagged a couple of the waffles, stuck them in the toaster, and depressed the lever. The thing hummed as it came to life. As it warmed, the buttery scent I'd yearned for started to permeate the kitchen. My stomach caught wind of it as soon as my nose did. A growl rumbled from my mid-section, so I helped myself to a cold waffle while I searched the cabinets for a plate. I found stacks of them almost immediately, but they all seemed too fancy for breakfast, with fine filigrees inlaid into the ceramic or with landscapes embossed onto the bottom. Didn't Nana have any cheap Festiveware?

I gave up my search when I heard the toaster's bell. I singed my fingers as I plucked the waffles from the slots and dumped them onto a plate that looked fit for a dinner party. I poured some syrup alongside them before I cast my gaze around the kitchen, wondering where the silverware was hiding.

My stomach grumbled again, and I gave up that search, too. Instead of sitting at the round table, I headed down the hall, dipping a waffle into the puddle of syrup as I made for the solarium. The windows in Mick's apartment provided a splendid view of the faded red bricks of the apartment complex across the alley, so I tended to take any opportunity that provided itself to stare at something green. I caught sight of Nana's vibrant hydrangeas and their rose colored petals as I reached the solarium, but something from inside the house also drew my eye. A door down the hall standing half open, the chamber within dark. Nana's bedroom was at the end of the hall, but I couldn't remember what lay between.

Curiosity got the best of me as I pushed into the room, hitting the light switch by the door with my elbow. The bulb overhead flared to life, bathing the space in a warm yellow glow. It was a study, small but efficiently packed, with built-in shelves across three of the walls and a solid maple desk pushed against the other. Two portraits hung on the free wall, each at least fifty years old based on the ages of those portrayed. One was of Nana Daggers, dressed in a captain's uniform, her collar crisp, her tie perfectly knotted. Even in a broad-shouldered jacket that didn't flatter her she looked gorgeous, with lustrous brown hair and bright blue eyes. The other painting I could only assume was of Papa Jake. Instead of a uniform, he posed in a black leather jacket that had been well-loved, for lack of a better term. He wasn't quite the looker Nana had been, but he wasn't ugly either, with a weathered face and a strong jaw. His posture and the tilt of his head made it look as if he was challenging me to an arm wrestling contest, and the glint in his eyes made it seem as if he didn't care one whit what the world thought of him. Nana said I always reminded her of him. Was that how I faced the world?

I turned from the paintings to the bookshelves as I continued to eat my waffles. One of them was packed with books: a good deal of them law texts, but also books on history, engineering, botany, economics, and a series of what appeared to be mystery novels about a guy named Rex Winters. The other two shelves also had books scattered amongst them, but the shelves were built taller to accommodate framed photographs and curios and display cases. One shadow box had Nana's name engraved at the bottom. It contained her assorted medals and commendations, some simple multicolored ribbons, others bronze stars with faces of old guys or eagles spreading their wings on the front. One medal hung in its own box, an iron cross that hung from a purple ribbon. The words 'Distinguished Service' were engraved around the edge with the number forty at the bottom. Was that the number of years Nana spent on the force? There were also a pair of matching framed letters on aged, yellow paper, one addressed to Papa Jake and another to Nana, though her last name had been Steele back then. They were signed by the mayor and police commissioner of the time, thanking them for their service in defense of the city. They weren't form letters, either. They contained heartfelt personal thanks for saving their lives and those of their families. I'd have to ask Nana about what happened.

By far the most common thing on the shelves was photographs. I'm not entirely sure when photography became mainstream, but Nana looked to be about forty or so in the oldest of the photos. There were lots of photographs of her and Papa, but others were featured, too. There was a photo of Papa Jake with some ancient guy in a wheelchair with a jar-shaped head and sagging jowls. The old guy looked about as happy as a cat being thrown out in the rain, but Papa Jake was smiling. I found multiple photos of Papa and Nana with a pair of other couples, one a regular human duo, the guy with light hair and easy good looks and his partner cute as a button, the other a ragtag pair of a bucktoothed guy who was the same size and shape as a wardrobe and a moon-eyed woman with jet black hair that fell to her waist. Everyone but the cute woman seemed to be officers based on their attire.

It was some of the more recent photos that struck me though, the ones that weren't staged like the older ones. There was one of Nana shaking hands with gleeful crowd in front of a park and another of her hugging a woman in front of a dull brick tenement. The woman was crying, but there was a look of relief in her eyes, too.

A slim book with a black leather cover poked over the edge of a shelf. I slid my empty plate onto the desk, wiped my fingers on my dress, and picked it up. A photo slipped out as I opened it, but I caught it before it floated to the floor. In this picture, Nana stood at the front of a huge crowd in a banquet hall, Papa Jake at her side. Everyone was smiling, and the words "Happy Retirement!" were plastered across a banner in the back. As I slipped the photo back into the book, I caught

sight of a few handwritten messages of thanks and appreciation on the first page. I flipped through the book, and each
page held more and more notes. The entire book was filled
with them, a hundred pages worth. I had no idea Nana made
such a difference in so many people's lives. And to think I'd
entertained the idea that I might know more than her about
life or finding meaning or *anything*—well, maybe roller
skating.

I heard a creak and the thumps of feet, followed by Baul and
Nana's voices. I slipped the book back into place, gathered my
plate, and headed for the kitchen. I slid my dish onto the eat-in
as I rounded the corner into the foyer, where Nana stood as
Baul brought bags in from the garage.

"Morning, Nana!" I crossed over to give her a kiss.

Nana's eyes darted to the grandfather clock against the wall.
"That it is, for a few more minutes anyway. Did you just wake?"

I shrugged sheepishly. "Guess I was tired. Fighting takes it
out of a girl, you know."

"Indeed it does." Nana flicked a couple fingers toward my
dress. "Didn't you find the suitcase Baul left you?"

"I did, thank you. And thank you, too, Baul."

The big ogre came in with another two bags of groceries.
"You're welcome, Miss," he said before heading back out again.

"—but I didn't find it until after I'd snagged this dress from
your wardrobe. I'll put it back after I change." I eyed a stain
suspiciously close to where I'd wiped my syrupy hands on the
cloth. "After I wash it, of course."

Nana gave me a sly grin, as if she knew something I didn't.
"The Daggers blood is strong in you, in more ways than one.
Keep the dress. I haven't worn it in ages, and you fill it out far
better than I ever did."

I frowned. "To be honest, I'm not sure it's supposed to be filled out *quite* this much..."

"Nonsense," said Nana. "You have a nice figure. Show it off. Now, why don't you help me outside? The air is cool, and we can enjoy the garden while Baul prepares lunch."

I nodded, helping Nana out the back door and into the wicker chairs in front of the brick fire pit. Bees buzzed over the flowers and dragonflies over them, looking for a mid-day snack, and a sweet smell hung in the air, perhaps from the bee balm. As I got Nana situated, I couldn't help but think about the photos and medals I'd seen in her study, as well as the book filled with messages of thanks. I'd always seen my Nana as just that—my great-grandmother, old, smart as a tack, clever, mischievous, loving, and doting, but I'd never put much thought into who she'd been before I came into the picture. There was so much I didn't know about her.

More importantly, there was so much she could teach me— if I'd be willing to listen.

I settled into a chair across from her, ideas coalescing in my head, clearer than they'd been as I'd mulled them over the night before. "Nana, what was your job like when you were in the force? I mean the day to day, nitty-gritty kind of stuff."

Nana blinked as if I'd caught her off guard. "I guess it depends on what portion of my career you're talking about. Things were quite different after I made captain than when I was a detective. Why?"

I shrugged. "I was in your study. I saw the pictures and medals. I guess I had some idea of how many people you helped throughout your career, but I didn't realize *how* you did it. You saved the lives of the mayor and the commissioner?"

Nana gazed into the distant reaches of the garden. "Jake and

I did, yes. My, that was an adventure. We battled fires and a hurricane. I got kidnapped, and Jake and I both risked our lives, not to mention we battled strange forces that, well... I'm not sure you'd believe in them if I told you."

"Was that normal, though?" I asked. "Did your cases often involve action and adventure and mystery?"

"Not always, but more often than not. Being a detective was exciting work. It made me feel *powerful* and *confident*." Nana's eyes twinkled. "Why do you ask?"

If not for that twinkle, I might not have suspected I'd been played, but I'd already come to the decision on my own, even before Nana put on the hard sell. "Just curious. So... what does it take to join the police, anyway?"

CHAPTER SEVEN

I headed up the subway steps to street level, coming out at the corner of 12th and Grand. I knew my address, so I cast about, searching for the building numbers over the heads of other pedestrians. Eventually, I found them, affixed to the front of the world's plainest building, a towering hunk of grey concrete and steel. A suspicious individual might suspect the building hid something nefarious behind its bland exterior, like a money laundering operation or a religious cult, but the reality was more mundane. The building was a government testing facility.

I checked my wristwatch and found I had thirty minutes to spare. In the past, I hadn't bothered wearing one, but the past three months of police academy had beaten that habit right out of me. *An officer of the law should always be aware of the time so as to accurately report the timing of criminal activity when witnessed.* That was from chapter two of the police academy training manual, the one that covered uniforms. While the sergeants at the academy generally hadn't expected us to memorize specific passages from the manual, they'd taken a stand on proper dress, knocking that lesson into our heads early—sometimes literally.

Most of my time at training academy hadn't been spent getting rapped on the knuckles with rulers, however. Every day, the other recruits and I sat through lessons on law and criminal investigation, though most of it we'd been expected to learn on our own from reading assigned texts. We'd also been taught elementary first-aid and been given de-escalation training, but by far, most of our time at the academy was spent on three things: self-defense, firearms training, and driving. I couldn't say I was particularly upset about getting to spend so much time on those activities. All the drills were exciting to participate in, and it didn't hurt that I happened to be pretty darn good at two out of the three.

The self-defense training had by far been the easiest to learn. I'd always known how to move thanks to my background in athletics, and I picked up the moves the instructor taught us quickly. At first, the instructor matched participants by gender, but after it became apparent the other females in my class weren't up to the task of taking me down, the sergeant began assigning me male sparring partners. As he put it, all the women would have to work their way up to male partners eventually since we wouldn't have the luxury of picking our opponents when we made it to the streets. I just got a head start. Some of my male colleagues thought it was funny to be matched with me, others went easy on me, and others still used the exercises as an opportunity to play grab ass, but all of them figured out pretty quickly that they had to put in effort if they didn't want to end up with their noses in the dirt. Still, enough partners took me seriously that I was able to learn a great deal: from how to properly execute a throw to how to protect myself if someone wrapped an arm around my neck from behind to how to throw a punch that would knock a jerk like Mick out for hours instead of merely daze him.

Even though I'd never held a pistol prior to entering the academy, I turned out to be a pretty crack shot with one. Once I adopted the standard two-handed technique with its boxing stance and slightly bent elbows, the paper targets at the end of the range went from looking like slices of improperly fermented cheese to looking like a ping-pong ball flew through their centers. For some reason, the men in my class took greater offense at me being able to outshoot them than when I'd pin their arms behind their backs and tackle them to the ground, as if the ability to hold a gun straight was in any way dependent on what failed to dangle between my legs. If all we'd done with our revolvers was target practice, I might've been ostracized, but there were so many exercises and lessons regarding firearms that it was hard to get bent out of shape over any one. Besides stationary marksmanship, we practiced shooting under pressure, shooting around obstacles, and traversing a simulated live fire environment, not to mention holstering and unholstering, revolver maintenance, and sundry tests of trigger discipline.

I probably wouldn't have made a single friend at the academy if my driving had been as good as my shooting, but I proved myself mortal as soon as I got behind the wheel. To be fair, I'd never been a great driver. There was a reason I'd wrecked my dad's car when I was sixteen, and I hadn't improved much in the years since. It wasn't that I was terrified of operating a motor vehicle, as some of the recruits had been of the revolvers at first, but based on the number of orange cones I crushed under my tires during my first route of the test course, perhaps a bit of apprehension would've paid dividends. Still, like with any other exercise practice paid off, and by the end of the academy I could not only parallel park but do it without hitting the cars in front or behind me.

Although I'd passed my courses at the academy, the final written exam still awaited me. I'd have to pass that too before the NWPD could hire me. There wasn't a guarantee they would, of course, but I figured if I scored highly enough, the department would have to give me a shot, despite the thornier parts of my permanent record. Nana said she'd put in a good word for me, but I told her that as much as I appreciated her putting a roof over my head and loaning me the funds to pay for the academy, I wanted to earn my spot on the force fair and square, same as she had. Nana had mumbled something about white lies never hurting on an application, but I think she respected my choice, as she didn't bring it up again.

Butterflies fluttered in my stomach as I looked at the nondescript building on the corner. I'd never put much effort into any of my studies, but I did my best to commit the training manual to memory, spending upwards of an hour each night reading and rereading sections. Still, there remained a voice in the back of my mind saying I could've done more. I could've spent more time reading supplemental texts, picking my instructors' brains, and learning from Nana. I wasn't sure how much faith I put in the voice, but its very presence was a novelty. I tried to think of it as a positive. The fact that I'd put in so much effort and was now nervous meant I actually wanted to reach the finish line I'd set before me.

I swallowed back the lump in my throat and headed into the building. I took the elevator to the fourth floor and followed the signs to room four fifty-six. Upon arriving, however, I found the door locked and the lights inside turned off. Had I written the room number down wrong, or even worse, mistaken the address on the building itself? I couldn't have, not with the bland exterior and the city seal embossed on the tiles in the lobby. No, I simply must've arrived at the wrong room. If I found someone downstairs, I could ask them and—

A gruff voice interrupted my panic. "Here for the cadet's exam?"

I turned to find a goblin half as tall as me, green of skin and with her hair held in a tight beehive, peering at me from over her spectacles.

I sighed. "Yes. I thought this was the room, but clearly I made a mistake. If you could point me—"

"You're in the right place. Not often anyone beats me here. Only the overachievers." The woman slipped around me, pulled a key from her pocket, and unlocked the door.

Me? *An overachiever?* I scoffed as I followed her inside. "There's less than half an hour until the exam starts."

The goblin scoffed back. "Most people don't even arrive on time." She clambered into the chair at the front of the room, dumped her bag on the desk, and began to rifle through her things. After forty-five seconds of that, she looked up at me. "Well? Have a seat."

I did as I was told, picking a desk near the middle. I rapped my fingers on the worn desktop as I checked my watch again. Twenty-four minutes until test time. Suddenly another thought struck me.

I put my hand in the air, silly as it felt.

The goblin glanced at me over her glasses. "Yes?"

"Was I supposed to bring my own pencil?"

The goblin's eyes widened. *"You forgot your pencil?"* She clicked her tongue. "And I had such high hopes for you."

I sighed, feeling like the same old screwup I'd always been. "Great. Do you think they sell any in the lobby? I should have time to get one, right?"

The woman at the front rolled her eyes. "Relax. I'm pulling one of your freakishly long legs. I'll provide the pencils."

"Oh." I blinked, feeling like a fool.

The woman stuffed her head in a book. "You'll be fine by the way. Your kind have nothing to worry about."

My brow furrowed. *"My kind?"*

The woman glanced at me over the pages. "Yeah. Early birds?"

"Right." I thought the goblin might've meant something else, but I dropped the subject as another cadet showed up. Slowly, more and more prospective officers arrived, and despite the room being only half full, the proctor stood and distributed the exams as the clock struck two.

As it turned out, I needn't have worried. The goblin was right. I knew I aced the test before I handed it in. If anything, I was disappointed in the breadth of knowledge the exam tested. It was almost as if the police department didn't expect that much out of new recruits, but as I handed my exam in, I was sure that being over-prepared would only help me further down the line.

At least, that's what I hoped.

CHAPTER EIGHT

I paused outside the front doors of the Williams Street precinct under the giant seal of a soaring eagle with a pair of scales clutched in its razor sharp claws. I'd been inside the building before, first when I'd been arrested for beating Mick to a pulp and more recently for my interviews, but I'd never before stepped inside the precinct *as a police officer*. As soon as I took one more step, I'd stop being a civilian and start being a public servant. My life would never be the same. I'd be fully committed to upholding the oath of honor I'd taken at my commencement ceremony, even when I wasn't wearing my uniform. I'd have to put other people's wellbeing before my own, and I'd be obligated to treat everyone I encountered in the line of duty fairly, justly, and without bias.

It was a lot of responsibility, but I was ready for it. For the first time in my life, I had a purpose, and it felt good! Apparently, Nana had been right about that, too. At some point, I'd have to buy her a gift to show her my appreciation—once I'd settled into my new life and paid back her loan to cover the academy, of course.

With a deep breath, I pushed on the doors and stepped inside.

There, I paused again. I exhaled, searching for the new sensation that was surely inside me now that I was officially a cop. A tingle in my fingertips, a twitch in my toes. I couldn't sense anything off the bat, but perhaps—

I grunted and stumbled as someone slammed into me from behind. I tipped forward, narrowly catching myself before I fell. I turned to find a large, gruff-looking officer holding onto a hand-cuffed crankhead by the arm behind me. He glared at me as he adjusted his belt. "What the heck are doing standing there? Clear the doors."

I bobbed my head. "Right. Sorry."

The officer pushed past with his charge, and whatever tingly feeling I'd thought I'd feel vanished along with him. Shaking my head to clear the cobwebs, I pushed into the precinct, heading down the hall on my right to the ladies' room. There I found my locker, though my name hadn't been slid into the removable nameplate yet. The room contained a bare twenty lockers, but only half had names affixed to the front. For all the progress Nana claimed the NWPD had made in the years since she served, it appeared it still had a long way to go.

With my shirt buttoned tight, my tie straightened, my frizzy hair fixed in a bun at the back of my head, and my hostler secured on my belt, I pushed out of the locker room—and almost into my second collision of the afternoon. I pushed myself against the wall as an officer with his eyes glued to a clipboard almost took me out. I tried to say sorry, but it came out as a startled squawk, which caused the officer to veer at the last second.

"Oops. Sorry... Oh. Hey, Nell."

The officer in question was none other than Cliff Bradley.

He was tall, about two inches taller than me, with brown eyes and medium brown hair that he kept cropped close on the sides but grew to a rebellious inch and a half under his cap. When I'd first met him at the academy, his cheeks had been shaven clean, but as he realized the instructors didn't expect him to look as if he'd stepped out of a barber's shop at roll call, he'd let his beard grow to a mild scruff. Only a small percentage of men could successfully pull off the look, but Cliff was one of the lucky ones. His stubble gave him a rugged appearance, like a lumberjack or a longshoreman. Maybe it was his strong jaw that did it.

I brightened. "Hey Cliff. How's your first day been?"

"You mean once I woke up?" He smiled. "Not too bad. Patrolled my beat. Handed out a few tickets. Only got chewed out twice. Now I get to file some paperwork." He lifted the clipboard.

Cliff had been assigned the first shift to start, from six in the morning to two in the afternoon, whereas I'd gotten the second shift from two to ten. I'd blame my Nana for me drawing the best slot to start, but I knew it was chance. The academy assured us we'd get rotated through all the shifts, frequently in some cases, and as a rookie, I fully expected to get stuck with more than my fair share of nights.

"So how's your TO?" I asked.

TO meant training officer. All officers patrolled in pairs, but for the first year of a rookie's career, they were assigned a senior officer to oversee their development and teach them the ropes. A rookie might have a few different TOs to account for shift assignments, but by and large, whoever you got your first day was who you were stuck with for your next journey around the sun.

"Quiet, but reasonable as far as I can tell." Cliff lifted his clipboard. "Though he might be less so if I don't get these forms filed. See you later?"

I nodded. "Yeah. See you."

He flashed me a warm smile and headed down the hall, while I worked my way to the stairwell, up to the second floor, and into the briefing room. There, I sat in one of the available chairs and pulled a notepad and a pencil from my pocket. I wasn't the first to arrive, and the room filled quickly after me. A heavyset guy with a jutting lower lip collapsed into the seat at my right. I said hi, and he grunted in response and sipped on his coffee.

At a minute until two, a gnome, four feet tall, wearing thin wire-framed glasses and with a crop of ginger hair, strode purposefully into the room and closed the door behind him. As he spun, I took note of the three white chevrons upon each of his shoulders, and I caught the name Zaxby engraved into his badge. There was a podium at the front of the room that was taller than he was, but apparently a step stool was hidden in its lee because the gnome disappeared behind it only to pop up a second later. He gripped the podium's sides and fixed his eyes on the clock.

At the precise moment the clock's minute hand struck zero, he spoke. "Good afternoon, officers. Roll call. Aynsley?"

A voice called from the back of the room. "Here."

"Coldwell?"

"Here."

Sergeant Zaxby read out the dozen plus names of the assembled officers, and I responded when called. At the response of Officer Wormwood, the sergeant looked up from his podium. "Very good. Now, before we get started, let's address the baby elephant in the room. We have a new recruit in our midst. Officer Phair?"

I didn't know what I was supposed to do, so I stood. A few of the officers, all men, craned their necks to look at me, but no one clapped or said a word.

The gnome fixed his green eyes on me. "In case you hadn't figured it out, I'm Sergeant Zaxby, the watch supervisor. If you have an administrative issue, come to me. If you don't understand your assignment, come to me. If your tie's not on straight, fix it before coming to me, and if for some reason you file your reports incorrectly, well... don't bother coming to me. You may as well save both of us the time and head home. Do I make myself clear?"

I belted out a clear, "Yes, sir."

"This isn't training academy anymore. An inside voice will do. I'm sure everyone will give Officer Phair a warm welcome, and we look forward to your contributions on the squad."

Zaxby waved me down, and I sat.

The gnome continued. "To our first order of business. Twelfth Street is closed between Grant and Gondolyn Parkway due to a cement truck that lost control of its brakes and careened into the shops on the east side of the road early this morning. Cleanup crews are on the scene, but we're going to need additional patrol officers directing traffic at the cross streets. Also, there's a concert tonight at The Leaning Lorry on Fifteenth. The band is some anti-establish punk group, and their fans have been known to riot after shows. We're not expecting it to impact this shift, but depending on how cheap the booze is and when these yahoos get started, you never know, so we'll be placing additional officers in the area starting at seven.

"We've also got a BOLO for a couple suspects who are wanted in connection with the robbery of a hardware store on Marquette. The first is a human, male, five foot five to five foot eight, short black hair, thick black beard, last seen wearing a dark short-sleeved shirt and tan cargo pants, the other a dwarf, about four eight to four ten, braided hair, last seen in a green dress. Presumed female. Fled the scene in a blue Grandoise Town and Field, no license plate recorded. Also we still have a BOLO for the nimrod who relieved himself on Officer Miramoira's car yesterday."

Zaxby paused and took off his glasses. His demeanor shifted as he swept his eyes across the room. "I also don't have to remind you we're still looking for the Tarot Card Killer. The city has its best and brightest working the case, but as of now, we don't have a lot to go on, at least nothing the chain of command has decided to make public. That means I don't have specifics to give you to lookout for, but if you see any suspicious activity, any young women being trailed or stalked, intervene immediately. And for Pete's sake, assume whoever you're approaching is armed and dangerous. We can deal with aggrieved boyfriends who think they've been unjustly detained, but if we lose a cop to this psycho, there'll be hell to pay. Are we clear?"

I'd been training to be a police officer for the last three and a half months, but I could've been living under a rock and still heard about the Tarot Card Killer. The first murder occurred six weeks ago. The woman had been found in a parking lot outside a bowling alley, her head twisted around nearly a hundred and eighty degrees. Supposedly there hadn't been any bruising to the soft flesh of her neck, and she'd been found with a single tarot card sewn into the hem of her dress. Those two pieces of information were all that leaked to the media, but it was enough to spawn a flurry of conspiracy theories. Those had only grown more fervent when another young woman had been pulled from the wreckage of a car only for police to discover she too had a tarot card sewn into her clothing. To the best of my knowledge, the details of the crash hadn't made it to the newspapers, but the way the department had been tight lipped about her death made it obvious to everyone she hadn't died in a simple car crash.

Everyone in the room nodded solemnly at the mention of the Tarot Card Killer. Even the overweight officer beside me pulled his eyes out of his coffee long enough to nod in response.

"Good," said Zaxby as he returned the glasses to his nose. "Now. Assignments. Phair. You'll be assigned to Officer Stonefist. The two of you are on patrol from Sixteenth to Twenty-Eighth. Coldwell? That means you're with Wormwood now. The two of you are on the cement mess at Grant and Gondolyn Parkway."

Zaxby nodded toward the exit, and I figured that was my cue. I stood and headed out as he read more assignments. Of the three officers who'd stood and made for the door, I wasn't sure which was Stonefist, but I figured it out quick as a guy who was a good six inches shorter than me approached.

"So." He hooked his thumbs in his belt. "You're Phair."

Stonefist didn't have the traditional clean-cut look most of the other officers did. His long reddish-brown hair snaked down his back in a thick braid, and his coarse beard of the same color expanded across much of his chest. His skin was swarthy and weathered, and even though he didn't even come up to the tip of my nose, he was nonetheless far too tall to be a pure-bred dwarf. Maybe he had some troll or ogre in him. He was broad in the shoulders, that was for sure.

I nodded. "That's right. Penelope Phair, though most people

call me Nell."

The man lifted a brow. "Yeah? Well, at the bar the guys call me Razi, but we're not at a damn soiree are we? We're at work, and as long as we're wearing the uniform, you'll address me as sir, Officer Stonefist, or if you want to get fancy, Training Officer Stonefist. Are we clear?"

Clearly, Stonefist wasn't the chummy type. "Yes, sir."

"Good." Stonefist gave me a once over. "You just graduate from the academy?"

"The ceremony was the Saturday before last."

Razi sucked on his teeth. "Well, relax a bit. You're in good hands. I've trained a half-dozen rookies, though never a woman. You're not going to embarrass me, are you?"

I blinked, confused. "How so?"

"You know. Woman shit. Being irrational. Emotional. Not mixing it up when the need arises. Letting your feelings get in the way of the job."

I bristled and stood straighter. Though I tried to keep my voice even, it came out cooler than I'd intended. "I'll try my best to be professional, *sir*."

Razi put his hands up. "Alright, put the claws away. I'm just trying to see who I've got on my hands. Fact of the matter is, I don't care if you're big, small, male, female, brown, cream-colored, or see-through. All I care about is results. If you do your job, follow the rules, and have my back, we'll get along fine. Sound good?"

I relaxed a little. Maybe what I'd interpreted as sexism was Razi's version of a meritocracy. "Sounds good, Officer Stonefist."

"Great." He clapped me on the shoulder. "Now lets stop by the armory for a few items and hit the road."

CHAPTER NINE

We drove along a commercial stretch of 25th Street, Razi behind the wheel of the patrol car and me in the passenger's seat. I figured Stonefist would make me drive—forcing work upon rookies was a time-honored tradition in pretty much any field, not just policing—but either he'd heard something from the sergeants at the academy or he considered driving to be a privilege rather than a punishment. Either way, being relegated to being a passenger left me without a lot to do other than keep my eyes on the street and listen to the crackle of the police radio.

"So," I said, breaking the silence. "Any idea what we'll be up to today?"

Stonefist shifted in his seat. "Zaxby put us on patrol, which means we don't have a specific assignment. Unless we happen to come across an assault or a robbery in progress, that means we're stuck with the boring stuff. We'll drive around, keep an eye out for anything suspicious, probably hand out some traffic tickets, and hope dispatch radios in with something interesting."

I frowned. "Is that it?"

Stonefist snorted as he stopped at a red light. "I know you just got out of the academy, but contrary to what the instructors might've told you, actual police work isn't all gunfights and car chases. It's pretty dull most of the time, which is a good thing. Boring means safe, and keeping law-abiding folks safe is the name of the game. So yeah. That's it."

I stared out the window, wondering if Nana had sold me a bill of goods. "There's got to be something else we can do."

"You rookies and your unbridled optimism. Keeps me young." Stonefist smirked at me before pulling the car forward as the light turned green. "Well, go on. Entertain me. What other naive illusions do you have about the job?"

I sank into my cushions. "You're really suggesting there's nothing for us to do but drive around and keep our eyes open?"

"Oh, I didn't say that," said Razi. "There's always something we *could* be doing. We could stake out a stop sign and bust anyone who rolls through without bringing their vehicle to a complete stop. Or if you're really feeling ambitious, we could rustle up some fugitives with outstanding warrants."

I sat up straighter. "Now, that sounds more interesting."

Razi scoffed as he took a turn. "Settle down there, hotshot. It's mostly an exercise in checking addresses we have on file and asking people if they've seen whoever it is we're after. Plus, we need to stay in our patrol area, which limits who we can go after."

"Fair enough," I said. "Do you know of anyone in this part of town who fits the bill?"

"Sure," said Stonefist. "There's a guy by the name of Mort who hangs around a pool bar on Eighteenth, for one. I could probably think of a few more if I wracked my brain."

"What's this Mort guy wanted for?"

Razi shot me a raised eyebrow. "Does it matter?"

"It matters if he's wanted for violent crime. We've got to be prepared so we can keep each other safe, right?"

Razi's eyebrow rose higher. "You *sure* that's why you care?"

"Why wouldn't it be?"

Razi peered at me for a second. As he turned his eyes back to the road, he slowed the car and pulled into an open spot at the side, next to a musical instruments shop.

The squad car clunked as he put it in park, and Razi turned to face me. "Alright, rookie. First day on the job, so no better time than now for your first test. Answer me something. What do you think the job is?"

I squinted at Stonefist. "Is this a trick question?"

Razi waved his hand toward the street. "Not a trick. Just answer. Why are we out here? What's our purpose as officers of the law?"

"To catch criminals? To help people?"

Razi lifted both eyebrows. "You asking or telling me? Come on. Try again. I know you can get this one. It's in our motto, after all."

"Right. To serve and protect." I'd known that, but Stonefist asking such a basic question threw me off guard.

"Exactly," said Razi. "*Serve* and *protect*. Now if you ask me, the first part of that is superfluous. Of course our job is to serve. We're public servants. It's in the word. But protect? That's the key. That's our job, and it's very different than what you first said."

"It is?"

"Of course. You said you thought our purpose was to help people."

Now I was confused again. "Protecting people is different than helping them?"

Razi's eyes widened. "Of course it is. They're entirely different concepts. When you help someone, you're guiding them through a task or offering your services to make things easier for them. That's *not* our role. We're here to *protect* people. To keep them safe from harm. We do that by separating the good folks from the bad and putting the bad ones behind bars."

I probably should've kept my mouth shut, but I couldn't help but think Razi was putting too much weight behind specific words. "Right. Catching criminals. That's what I said."

Razi's eyes narrowed, suggesting his surprise at my ignorance was turning into annoyance. "No. When you *catch* a criminal, you're bringing them in after the damage has been done. They commit a crime, you find them, and punish them. But you didn't protect anyone. They've already murdered and raped and stole. What I want to do is *stop* criminals."

I blinked. "What are you talking about? Are you suggesting you should arrest people *before* they commit a crime? Like using precognition?"

Razi smiled, but there wasn't any humor in it. "I can't tell if you're being smart with me or you're genuinely confused, so I'm going to give you a pass. I'm not talking about foresight, as great as that would be. I'm talking about identifying people who are *likely* to commit a crime and staying on their asses until they slip. Sometimes all it takes is a nudge for them to lose their shit, and then you've got 'em. Another criminal off the streets before they can do real damage. Now sometimes, you can't stop criminals the first time, no matter how hard you try. But once they reveal themselves, you don't have any excuse not to act. You were asking why there's a warrant out for Mort Withers? Parole violation, but my point is, it doesn't matter. We know he's a bad guy because we already locked him up once, and it's our job to put him back behind bars where he can't hurt anyone else. Serve and *protect*."

What Razi was talking about was criminal profiling—targeting people who were likely to commit crimes because they were poor, uneducated, desperate, or hungry—and it was decidedly *not* something I'd been taught in the academy. Nonetheless, that wasn't the part of his argument that rubbed me wrong the most. "I think the original offense matters. If this Mort guy is a serial rapist, then you're damned right we need to take him down, but if he got busted for jaywalking the first time—"

Razi extended a finger. "Nope. Don't give them an inch. Once a criminal, always a criminal. Trust me. This is how you protect folks. By believing people when they show you who they are, and by using that knowledge to identify the rest of the bad apples. Not only do we know Mort's a bad guy, but we can look at his associates, his friends, his family. They made him who he is. Chances are there's more rot in the wood that needs to be torn out."

I didn't want to get in an argument, not on my first day, and certainly not with my TO, so I nodded. "Right."

Razi put the squad car back into drive. "One more thing. The protection part of our motto isn't just about protecting civilians. The people we protect first and foremost are our own. Got it?"

I nodded.

Apparently, that wasn't good enough. Razi raised his voice. "I said, *got it,* Officer Phair?"

"Yes, sir," I said. "Loud and clear."

"Good." He gave the car some gas. "Now let's get to work."

CHAPTER TEN

I figured after Razi's lecture that we'd head straight out and try to find Mort, but we did nothing of the sort. Either as a punishment to me for questioning Mort's offenses or as a reminder that police work wasn't the glamorous profession I'd made it out to be, most of the afternoon was spent driving around and handing out tickets for minor traffic infractions. We did get a call from dispatch to deal with a hit and run, but no one had been injured in the accident. A woman's car had the side mirror knocked off by a speeding motorist, so we took the woman's statement and notes for our report but did little else. At about seven, we pulled next to a mobile food truck parked outside a warehouse that was being torn down and replaced with apartments. We ordered sandwiches that tasted like cardboard and ate them in the car, and it wasn't until eight, as the sun's last light faded from the sky, that Razi pulled the squad car onto Eighteenth, drove to Dartmoor, and parked in an open spot outside a bar by the name of Slick Ernie's. There were a few neon signs in the window, two of which spelled out the words

Beer and Music, but a third showed a crude depiction of a pool ball and cue.

I tried to keep my excitement under wraps, figuring Stonefist might turn the car around and keep driving until the end of our shift if I so much as smiled, despite all the stuff he'd said about making it a priority to nab criminals off the streets before they could strike.

I nodded toward the place. "This the place Mort frequents?"

Razi nodded as he unbuckled. "Sure is. I figure it's late enough he might be off work and have made his way here. Let's check it out."

I felt like a heel as I got out of the car and slammed shut the door behind me. Instead of assuming Stonefist was a hypocrite or a vindictive jerk, I should've assumed he knew what he was doing and wasn't wasting time for no good reason. "So what's the perp look like?"

Razi adjusted his belt as he closed his own door. "Skinny. About my height. Looks like he's flying high on three ounces of crank and hasn't washed in a week. You'll know him when you see him."

Stonefist pushed into the bar, and I followed. It was a typical pool joint, with a half-dozen tables on either side of the bar. Lamps with green glass fixtures hung over each table, their warm glow spreading across the green felt and worn wood. The neon signs in the front window buzzed like angry hornets, and it was only their colorful glow that kept the players from looking like dryads in a moonlit glade. Cigarette smoke hung in the air, as did a greasy scent that suggested the kitchen only served food cooked in a deep fryer. Most of the patrons were too engrossed in their games and drink to take notice of us, but those who did nodded and muttering to their friends as they did so.

Stonefist sauntered across the floor, eyeing the patrons as he made his way to the bar. A decent number of folks sat there for a Monday evening, but Razi didn't have to shoulder his way into a free seat. As soon as the folks in front caught sight of his uniform, they stood and left for the tables on either side.

Razi deposited himself into one of the stools at the bar, and I took a spot next to him. The bartender, a youngish guy with hair that swept across his face and hid one of his eyes, gave him a nod of acknowledgement as he tended to folks enjoying their beverages at the far end.

After extricating himself, the bartender gave us a nod. "Evening officers. Anything I can help you with?"

Razi laughed. "Come on, Orelius. Don't act the stranger. You know my usual."

The young man nodded, his one visible eye refusing to meet Stonefist's. He smiled a bit as he met mine, though. "Anything for you, Officer?"

I shook my head. "No, thank you."

As the bartender retreated to the taps, I leaned into my training officer's ear. "Isn't it against the rules to drink on duty?"

"I'm aware of the rules, Phair," he said. "This isn't about the beer. Watch and learn."

The bartender returned with a pint glass filled to the brim with an amber-colored brew. He put it on a coaster in front of Stonefist. "Anything else I can do for you?"

Stonefist smiled. "As a matter of fact, there is. We're looking for Mort Withers. Seen him lately?"

"Uhh... sorry, Officer," he said. "I'm not sure I know who you're talking about."

Razi pushed his beer to the side. "Come on, Ori. You know Mort. Skinny little punk, never pays his tab, looks like he inhaled a line of black ice anytime you say his name? He comes in here all the time."

Orelius looked around, clearly wishing he was anywhere else. "I guess he sounds familiar. What about him?"

Razi leaned in. "I already told you. When was the last time you saw him?"

Ori shrugged. "I'm not sure. I think he dropped by a few nights back."

"How many is a few? Two? Three?"

"I don't know. Three, I think."

Razi scoffed. "You think?"

"I don't remember. He didn't even get anything from the bar. Made his girlfriend order."

"*Girlfriend?*" said Razi. "Now we're getting somewhere. What did she look like?"

Ori sighed. "Blonde. Thin. Sunken eyes. I wasn't paying much attention." Someone hollered from the other side of the bar, and he acknowledged them with a wave. "Excuse me. I've got a job to do."

Razi shouted after him. "Don't go far. I might need more." He shook his head and snorted. "That kid. I'll break him yet."

"*Break him?*" I said. "Is he a suspect?"

Razi tilted his head and peered at me over his nose. "Use your noggin, Phair. He has nothing to do with Mort, and as far as I know the only law he's broken is for not reporting his owner for serving watered down liquor. I'm talking about making him compliant. You think I made him serve me this beer for kicks?"

"Honestly, I thought you were going to drink it."

Stonefist's eyes twinkled. "Now, Officer Phair. That would be against the rules."

"So why have him pour it?"

Razi sighed. "You're missing the point. In our line of work, we don't ask. We tell. We set expectations, and folks meet them or suffer the consequences. Ori here? I've almost made him realize it. A few more house beers, and I think the message'll sink through."

I glanced at the brew. "You're not going to pay for it?"

"And ruin the hard work I've put in? Gods, what do they teach you in the academy these days?" Razi shook his head as he stood. "I need to use the phone. See if anyone in the filing office at Williams Street has an address for Mort's girl. Go wait in the car."

Razi hitched up his pants and headed toward the payphone on the far side. I shot another glance at the beer and one at Ori, but he was busy taking orders from other patrons. A knot had started to form in the pit of my stomach, and I was pretty sure I knew why. Other than refusing to pay for his drink, Stonefist hadn't done anything wrong, not by the letter of the law, but the manner in which he'd approached the bartender rubbed me wrong. By Razi's own admission, Ori hadn't done anything illegal, yet Razi treated him with nothing but contempt. A mark to be broken. Why? Wouldn't the man give up what he knew if we'd just asked? Razi insinuated such a path was laughable.

I shook my head and headed for the door, ignoring the looks I got from patrons on the way out. I settled into my seat and stewed in my thoughts, listening to the static on the radio and sniffing the fumes of passing cars on Eighteenth. After a few minutes, Razi emerged and settled into the driver's seat.

I cleared my throat. "Get anything?"

Razi buckled in. "Better believe it. An apartment complex a few blocks north on Twenty-Third. Let's check it out."

Razi pulled the car out and hooked onto the nearest cross-street. I tried to put the events that had transpired behind me and instead look forward to catching a wanted felon, but I couldn't seem to get too excited about it. Stonefist said Mort was wanted for a parole violation, which told me nothing about why he'd been arrested in the first place. Razi's description made it sound like the guy might've been picked up on drug charges, but who knew? Not that it mattered. Our job was to follow the letter of the law and let the judges and attorneys sort the rest. Maybe that was my problem. I was overthinking things on my first day. I'd settle into a groove soon enough, and I was certain my Nana would tell me the same if I confided in her.

Razi slowed the car as we reached the sixty-seven hundred block of west Twenty-Third. He nodded toward my side of the street. "Keep your eyes peeled. This place should be around here somewhere."

I asked for the address and Razi gave it. As I looked past the streetlights toward the sooty faces of the buildings beyond, the radio crackled. "Calling all units. We have reports of shots fired at New Age Alchemical on the corner of Twenty-Ninth and Hoover. Please respond."

My heart leapt into my throat as I looked at Stonefist. "That's only a couple minutes from here."

Razi's teeth flashed from within the expanse of his ruddy beard. "Screw Mort. Call it in."

The squad car's tires squealed as Stonefist hit the gas, and I picked up the handset. My voice was raspy as it pushed past my lips, and I could hear blood pumping through my ears. "This is unit eighty-seven responding. We're en route."

CHAPTER ELEVEN

O ur siren wailed as we careened up Hoover. My heart pounded in my chest as I went over every training exercise I'd undertaken in the academy. *Stay calm,* I told myself. *Move quickly, act decisively. Stay in cover, don't expose yourself, and trust your instincts.* That's what the instructors told us. All of it made sense, except for trusting your instincts, which seemed like it was dependent upon the individual, not the situation. What if your instincts were terrible? What if your instincts told you to run and hide, or to careen into danger pell-mell? Presumably the instructors assumed anyone with instincts unsuited for police work would be weeded out during the program, but it still seemed like a bad piece of advice.

Luckily, I didn't have much time to second guess myself. Within a minute and a half of us taking off outside the apartments, we rocketed into the intersection of Twenty-Ninth and Hoover, narrowly avoiding a couple cars that had swung to the side to get out of our way. In the six blocks we'd traversed, we'd transitioned from a low-income residential district to one that was decidedly more commercial.

Razi hit the brakes and pulled the car onto a free patch of pavement at the side of the road. The car shuddered as the tires bumped onto the sidewalk, and my head jerked forward as we came to a stop.

Razi growled. "Where is it? You see the place?"

"New Age Chemical, right? None of these buildings look like factories." I spotted a fabric store that had closed shop for the evening, and the building to our side had a sign in the window advertising tax preparation services.

"Damn it!" Razi picked up the radio receiver. "Dispatch, this is eighty-seven. We need an address on that chemical facility."

The radio crackled as Razi released his thumb from the button. That's when I spotted it. "There. Across the street. Brown and white sign."

Razi depressed the button on the radio again. "Never mind. We've got it." He tossed the receiver to the console and unbuttoned his holster. "Let's go!"

He popped out of the squad car and raced across the street, his reddish-brown braid dancing on his back as he ran. A pedestrian carrying a bag of groceries on the far side saw us coming and reversed course, lickety-split.

Razi rushed to the building's front doors, his revolver gripped tight between both hands. He took position behind a concrete support beam as he peered through the glass. "This can't be the place. It isn't a chemical plant."

I took position on the other side of the doors, slipping my own revolver into my hands. "The sign says New Age Alchemical. Maybe it's a store."

"Looks like an office." Razi leaned closer to the windows. The lights were off inside, making it hard to see. "Is it even open?"

"Lights on upstairs." I nodded toward the glows coming from the third and fifth floor windows.

As the words left my lips, a sharp crack ripped through the air. I ducked instinctively, as did Razi. My partner flattened himself against the concrete and pulled his head back. "Where did that come from? You got eyes on the shooter?"

I heard a low rumble from the alley at my back, and a thought struck me with the force of a bat. "That wasn't a gunshot. That was an engine backfiring!"

Razi blinked in confusion. As he stood there, I took off into the alley, following the sounds of the motor. I raced past stinking garbage bins and stacked pallets, the gloom deepening the further I ran from from the street. The rumble of the engine intensified as I approached a yawning black maw where the alley intersected a larger one that ran parallel to Hoover. I slowed as I reached it, and the decision might've saved my life.

A car roared past, heading north. I ducked, flattening myself against the New Age Alchemical building as a whoosh of air caught me. My hair fluttered and my heart skipped a beat, but a tiny voice inside my brain screamed at me to not waste the opportunity. I pushed myself off the wall and ran into the alley, focusing on the car as it sped away. Sparks sprayed into the air as the vehicle scraped against the side of a dumpster. Its tires screeched as it pulled onto Thirtieth, and it was only as it pulled free from the alley's gloom that I got a decent glimpse of it. Glossy black paint. A flat top with a rounded end and fender skirts over the back tires. I only caught the first two letters of the license plate before the car disappeared around the corner. A and F, I was pretty sure.

I turned back into the narrow cross alley to see Razi jogging up behind me. *"What the hell are you doing?* You can't go running off like that."

I pointed toward Thirtieth. "A car sped past. I got a good look at it. Could be the shooter. We need to get to our patrol car!"

Razi held up a hand. "Hold your guffalopes, Phair. You have no idea who just took off. Could've been the shooter, could've been any random guy who heard a gunshot or our siren. In the meantime, you ran off alone during a possible active shooter situation! What the hell were you thinking?"

My body tingled from adrenaline, but I felt something else underneath it. A realization of guilt. "I heard the car. I thought it could be the perp."

Razi's brow furrowed, and even in the darkness I could see red in his cheeks. "You ran off without saying a thing. Even *if* you'd been justified in taking off after the noise, you needed to tell me. You don't leave your partner behind, *ever.* Got it?"

I swallowed back the lump in my throat. "Yes, Officer Stonefist. I'm sorry. I—"

"Save it," he said. "We still might have a shooter inside the building, and we're wasting time. Stay behind me, and do as I do. Can you handle that?"

I nodded. "Yes, Officer."

He took off back down the alley toward Hoover, and I followed. Razi worked his way to the front doors. He moved his pistol to his right hand and tested them with his left. One was locked, but the other wasn't. He crept inside the lobby of the building, scanning the darkness with the muzzle of his pistol as he crept forward.

Stonefist motioned toward the end of a hall. "We'll take the stairs. Stay close and keep your eyes peeled."

We pushed into the concrete stairwell and headed up. Razi paused at the second floor landing and poked his head into the hall, but the lights were dark as they'd appeared from street level, so we kept going to the third. Again, Razi poked his head into the hall, but this time the lights were on. He motioned me forward, staying quiet as he did so. We both moved up, but Razi held out a hand. He pointed to a pair of open doors on our left, away from the windows. The first was cracked, but the furthest was wide open, with light spilling into the hall.

He whispered. "I'll sweep the first room while you keep your gun trained toward the second. If it's all clear, we'll keep moving."

I nodded, and we crept along. Despite the fact that he looked built for power rather than dexterity, Razi didn't make a sound. I walked as carefully as I could behind him, hoping the soles on my shoes wouldn't betray me.

Razi stopped a foot shy of the cracked door. He nodded to me and tapped his ear. I listened, and I heard a sound. Not crying. More like a soft moan.

Razi's voice lowered so I could barely hear him. "On three. *One. Two.*"

My partner barreled into the room, pistol held before him. He voice punched the air like a heavyweight's jab. "Get on the ground! Now!"

I moved to the doorframe, my gun trained down the hall, but I spared a glance inside. A diminutive older woman, maybe with some gnome blood in her, cowered against the far wall, telephone in hand as she tried to hide behind a desk. She dropped the phone as Razi barged in, scrambling to the tile. "Please! I called shots. They told me to stay on phone!"

Razi growled. "Who got shot? Where?"

The woman's arm shook as she pointed. "Down hall. In lab. Mr. Tovar. I not know if he... if he..." Her voice trailed off.

Stonefist kept his revolver trained on the woman as he nodded to me. "Go. I'm right behind you."

I hurried down the rest of the hall, pausing outside the open door. I kept my body protected as I poked my head around the corner, scanning the contents. I saw polished stainless steel tables, Bunsen burners and tongs, wire-frame racks packed with beakers and vials and jars of chemicals, and coat stands with pristine white garments hanging from their jutting hooks.

The tile underneath was anything but pristine, though. It was covered in blood.

CHAPTER TWELVE

I padded into the laboratory, trying to ignore the body on the floor as I checked for signs of movement. A slight chemical tang hung in the air as Razi crept to the far side of the room and swept through it, same as I did. As I cleared the wire racks, I knelt to get a look under the lab tables. I couldn't see through them to the other side as they all had modesty panels to hide where the gas and electrical wiring snaked up. Some had drawers built in underneath, and one of them hid a heavy gray safe whose door stood open, but I saw no signs of anyone other than the body on the tile.

I rose to my feet. Razi tipped his head toward me. "Clear?"

I nodded. "Clear."

My partner put his gun away. I did the same. Once I'd secured it in place, I returned to the body I'd sidled past on my way through the lab.

I'd seen dead people before but never outside a funeral home, and certainly no one who'd just been murdered. For obvious reasons, that wasn't the sort of experience the academy could recreate. Nonetheless, as I stood there eyeing the man on the ground, his blood glistening as it spread behind him on the white tile in an oblong pool, I found myself feeling strangely calm. There was a nervous tingle in my fingertips, but I'd felt that since the call from dispatch came through. If anything, the sensations of fear and excitement that initially coursed through me had faded. My heart rate had fallen, my breathing returned to normal, and I had full sensation in my extremities. Shouldn't I feel something at the sight of a man on the ground, shot dead at my feet?

His death wasn't particularly visceral. He'd been shot three times in the chest based on the bloody holes in the front of his lab coat. Maybe if he'd been savaged, stabbed, or beaten, his body would've produced in me a stronger response, but as it was, I couldn't bring myself to feel more for him than the distant relatives whose funerals I'd attended as a child. Perhaps my emotions were dulled because I didn't know the man, but I didn't think that was it. I'd always been more spiritual than religious, but it seemed to me the soul of a person had nothing to do with the flesh. As soon as the spark of intelligence left someone in death, all that was left was an empty vessel. The life lost might be worth mourning, but not the body that lingered behind.

"Don't touch anything," said Razi from the other side of the room.

"Relax," I said. "That's one of the first things they teach us at the academy."

I leaned over to get a better look at the dead guy. His mouth hung open. Combined with eyes that had rolled back, it gave him a look of surprise. His jaw was smooth shaven, but the hair on top of his head was more disheveled: black, four or five inches long, wavy, and with the odd gray hair that suggested he was at least in his forties. Broken glass surrounded him, and a slightly sour aroma wafted from the chemicals that had spilled onto the floor. The man's left arm extended over his head. The watch he wore on it was exposed, and the face had cracked, likely after a high speed greeting with the floor. I could hear it ticking, despite the impact, so I doubted it would tell us the man's time of death. The way the arm sprawled across the floor made it look as if he were pointing. From his hand trailed a few stainless steel links and pins, as if from a watch band that had been ripped to shreds, though the man's own band seemed no worse for wear. Further along the direction of the arm was the safe I'd spotted earlier. From this vantage, I could see inside it, and the interior was clean as a bone.

"Hey. *Detective Phair*. You going to hang out and gawk or should we get some work done?"

I straightened. "I'm just observing everything for my report. Speaking of which..." I checked my wristwatch. Five minutes until nine. It had taken us a few minutes to get up the stairs and clear the room. I should be able to back out the exact time we reached the scene.

Razi struck his thumbs in his belt as he took a step forward. "Just so we're clear, *your* job is to stay out of the way so the detectives can do *their* jobs when they arrive. Which they won't do until you call in the murder." He nodded toward the door.

That was a fair point. "I'll be right back."

"Stop by the other room on your way back," said Razi. "Get a statement from that woman on the phone."

It seemed to me that was something Razi could do while I went to the car, but perhaps there was a reason he was asking me to do it. Razi scared the woman pretty badly when he barged in. She might be more comfortable answering questions that came from my mouth than his, or perhaps Razi felt the need to protect the crime scene.

Then again, maybe he was just lazy.

I shook my head as I took the stairs down two at a time. I'd been on patrol with Stonefist for less than a shift, so it was natural that I didn't have a complete grasp of his motivations, but it frustrated me that I couldn't pigeonhole him. Half the time he seemed indifferent to the plights of those around us, displaying a clear aversion to anything resembling police work, and the other half of the time he exhibited real passion, albeit for what I considered a perversion of justice. I mean, protecting people by proactively weeding out those who might cause problems? It might lower crime, but doing so came at the expense of liberty and the concept of being innocent until proven guilty. The question was, was his worldview a product of who he was or what he'd seen on the job?

Once I reached the street, I jogged to the squad car. I called the murder in via the radio, then headed across the street and back into the building, noting the distant wail of another approaching police siren.

When I got to the third floor, I found the woman Razi had scared half to death still hunched against the wall, head between her knees. She'd replaced the phone's handset on the base, but she was still making the same pained moan I first heard as we crept up the hall. A bucket with a mop in it stood in the corner, and based on the woman's faded coveralls, I suspected they were hers.

I pulled a notepad and pencil from my pocket as I took a careful step into the room. "Excuse me. Ma'am? I need to ask you some questions about what happened here."

The woman lifted her head. Tears didn't stain her cheeks,

but her eyes were wide and her knees wobbled despite the fact that she was sitting. She was clearly terrified, either of what she'd seen or of Razi and me. Maybe both.

She nodded gingerly. "Um. Yes. I try." Her voice had an accent to it that I hadn't taken note of at first, but she was easy enough to understand despite it.

The room was an office with a half-dozen desks in it, but only a couple appeared to be in use. I pulled a chair from one and helped myself to it as I eyed another. "Can I get you a seat?"

The woman didn't meet my eye, but she shook her head.

Seeing the look on the woman's face convinced me Razi had been right to have me take the statement, regardless of his intentions. "Can I get your name?"

"Katrina. Katrina Naimpar. I work cleaning."

That was going to be my next question. "You're the one who found the man in the other room? The one who's been shot?"

She nodded her head, eyes still averted.

"You knew him?"

She finally turned her head my way, and there was a twinkle of something wet in her eyes. "Mr. Tovar. He call by Gus. He hire me."

Gus Tovar. I wrote that down. "What was Mr. Tovar's role here?"

The woman squinted, unsure. "Sorry?"

"What did Mr. Tovar do? Was he the owner? A scientist? Technician?"

Katrina nodded, holding up a finger. "Science. That one."

I wrote down scientist. "Can you tell me what happened tonight? From the first thing you heard or saw, please."

"I up on floor..." She hesitated and held up five fingers. "I clean. I hear bang. Loud. Then more, *bang bang, bang bang*. I scare, so I wait. But I come. I find him. In lab. I very scare, so I call. That all."

I wrote as she spoke, filling appropriate grammar in where necessary. "So you heard five shots?" I held up a hand's worth of fingers for emphasis.

She nodded. "Yes. Five." She held the fingers up too, seeming thankful for a reminder of the word.

"When did you hear the first shots? The time?" I tapped my watch.

She looked glum. "Sorry. I not know."

"And when you came down from the fifth floor, did you see anyone? The shooter? The person with the gun?" I mimed the act of shooting with my fingers in case I'd lost her.

She shook her head. "No. I no see."

"No one at all?" I asked. "As far as you know, it was just Mr. Tovar in the building?"

The cleaning woman frowned, and I could tell she was trying to figure out how to phrase what she wanted to say. "I see man. Here. Before."

"So you noticed someone else in the building before the shooting?"

The woman smiled and nodded. "Yes."

"Do you know who it was?"

Another shake of her head.

"Can you describe him?"

The woman's eyebrows furrowed. "He have long hair. Color..." She looked around and tapped a portion of the speckled tiles.

I focused on the tip of her finger. "Brown?"

She shook her head and tried again.

"Grey?"

She nodded. "He also have hair on face. Here, not here." She mimed hair on her cheeks and lips but not her chin.

That seemed distinct. It would help us narrow suspects down for sure. "Thank you. That's very helpful, Ms. Naimpar. Do you by chance know if this man with the long hair was still in the building when you heard the shooting?"

"No. I sorry. I on five." She pointed up again.

"Was anyone else working here tonight while you were cleaning?"

The woman shrugged. "I not know. I sorry."

Something told me I was lucky to have gotten all I did out of her. I coerced a home address out of her one number at a time, thanked her once more, and asked her to stay until the detectives arrived. As I finished my interview, I heard the siren reach a crescendo outside before being turned off. I tucked my notepad into my pocket as I returned to the laboratory. There I found Razi lounging in a seat on the far side, paying Gus Tovar's body as much attention as he would a raindrop in a thunderstorm.

"I got the statement," I said, sparing the dead man another glance. "Now what?"

Razi smirked as he looked up. "Now you get to do the same thing I've been doing for the last eight minutes. You wait until someone else shows up to take over. Might as well get comfortable. Who knows how long it'll be."

CHAPTER THIRTEEN

I tried to sit and wait, but apparently I didn't have the same gluteal fortitude Stonefist did. First another pair of patrol officers arrived, the ones I'd heard parking as I'd finished my interview with Ms. Naimpar. They helped secure the building and search the premises while Razi and I did the hard work of making sure no one snuck in and made off with the body. Eventually, another one-two punch hit us. First a photographer arrived. He started snapping pictures as soon as he crossed into the lab. Two minutes later a pair of techs with the crime scene unit showed up. They got busy dusting for prints and swabbing surfaces without so much as a hello.

There was only so much of Stonefist's apathy I could take, so after a few minutes of watching other people engage with the scene, I got up. Razi reminded me not to touch anything, but I told him I just needed to stretch my legs. I don't think he believed me, but I didn't care. I was starting to have my fill of the guy's attitude. As if being the first to arrive on the scene of a murder wasn't something to get enthused about. And on my first day on patrol no less! Obviously, I hadn't wanted anyone to die, but in terms of calls to get from dispatch, this was about as good as it got.

I paced the laboratory, careful to stay out of the way of the photographer and the techs. Part of me wanted to rifle through Tovar's pockets and sift through the files in the cabinets, to unearth clues that might provide insight into the events that transpired before we arrived, but not only would I get in trouble, I knew it wasn't my job. I was a patrol officer, not a detective like Nana had been. Beyond that, solving mysteries wasn't why I'd joined the force. I'd become an officer to help people. To perform the same services Nana told me had made an impact on her and given her a sense of purpose.

But that didn't mean I wasn't curious about what happened.

One of the techs had started marking points of interest with placards. I followed her at a reasonable distance, watching as she marked a couple bullet holes in the wall. The cleaning woman said she'd heard five shots. I'd counted three that hit Tovar, but there was no telling how many were stuck inside his corpse and how many had passed through. While the tech moved to mark broken beakers and vials near the body, I eyeballed the holes. The first was dark and indistinct, but the second bullet must've hit a support beam instead of passing through the plaster, as I noticed a metallic gleam not far inside the puncture. The strange part was it looked golden in color rather than dull gray.

"Having fun?"

I stood at the sound of Stonefist's voice. He sported a frown, but I didn't let his sour demeanor get me down. "I'm not touching anything."

"You realize the detectives are only going to ask for our report and the witness statement, not your insight, right?"

I took a slow breath. "Aren't you at all curious about what happened here? Have you witnessed so many murders that you're completely jaded by them?"

"It's not my job to be curious. It's my job to stop this shit from happening, and we failed. That pisses me off." Razi sighed. "You wouldn't understand. You're still wet behind the ears, so I'll give you a pass. Just know you've only got thirty more minutes to enjoy this."

"Why?" I said. "What happens in thirty minutes?"

Razi tapped his wristwatch. "Our shift is up, that's what. Get it together, Phair."

As Stonefist shook his head, I heard voices in the hall. I shifted my attention toward the door just in time to see someone walk through. He was a tall drink of water, a good three or four inches taller than me, with broad shoulders and sharp features. His skin was dark, more grayish in tone than brown, though there was a bit of a warm undertone to it. Pointed ears stood tall and proud at the sides of his head, which combined with his off-white hair, shorn short and parted at the side, gave away his dark elf bloodlines as clear as any birth certificate could've. A sports coat caressed his frame—not a cheap, off the rack coat from a department store but a tailored one with shoulders that fit the flesh and blood ones underneath and sleeves that ended shy of his wrists, letting the bright white cuffs of his shirt peek from underneath.

He stopped inside the door to the lab, scanning the room with ice blue eyes. As he did so, Razi turned and caught sight of him. My partner's eyes widened. "Holy shit. They sent Alton Dean?"

Throughout the day, I'd seen Stonefist miffed, disappointed, even piqued, but this was the first time I'd seen him surprised. I kept my eyes on the handsome new arrival while I spoke softly. "Am I supposed to know who that is?"

Razi shrugged. "Maybe not yet, but you will. He's the NWPD's hotshot detective *du jour*. He gets all the weird, tough cases."

"Weird and tough how?"

Razi gave me a look. "You didn't hear it from me, but he's the one tracking the Tarot Card Killer."

My eyes widened a little themselves as some of what hit Razi smacked me in the gob. "Oh. What's he doing here?"

"Beats me," said Stonefist. "Maybe all the other gumshoes were busy brewing coffee."

Another couple followed Dean into the room, chatting as they did so, and a more mismatched pair I couldn't imagine. The first was a woman, though she was gorgeous enough that she might've been part fairy. She was five and a quarter feet tall if that, petite with long dirty blonde hair and bright amber eyes. She had ruby red lips perfect for pouting, and her nose was thin and had a concave curve to it, the kind of nose most girls wished for, all except for those who realized breathing was more important than looks. Her hands were stuffed into the pockets of a shiny leather jacket that hung open in the front, revealing a frilly yellow blouse and a rack that wasn't as petite as the rest of her.

The guy who followed was over a foot taller than her and, if I had to guess, somewhere between three and four times her weight. He was a full blood ogre like Nana's butler Baul, with dark brown skin, a head the size of a watermelon, and a nose and mouth to match. He chuckled at something the diminutive woman said, flashing a mouth full of surprisingly pearly white teeth. Not only did he have quite the smile, but he was impeccably dressed. While Dean had opted for a blazer, this guy wore a three piece suit, black with pinstripes matched with a flat black vest with glossy buttons that might've been real horn rather than plastic.

The new pair let their conversation fade as they took stock of the situation. I nudged Stonefist. "And those?"

He shrugged. "I don't know. They work with Dean. Moss and Justice, I think."

I followed the flick of his finger as he listed them off. "That big guy's name is *Justice?*"

Razi lifted a brow. "You want to bring it up with him, be my guest."

Dean, who'd stood there staring at the body and the carnage surrounding him, turned his attention to the photographer. "Glen, have you snapped shots of the supply cabinets yet? There might be records of what's in here, and we'll need something to compare them against. This could've been a robbery, and we can't presume to know what the shooter was after. Speaking of, snap a shot of the combination dial on that safe. Forensics? Be careful, okay? We've got puddles on the ground from these broken beakers. Who knows what chemicals were in them. The smell in here isn't too pungent, but better safe than sorry."

Dean turned to the two detectives who'd followed him in. "You seeing this the same way I am?"

The petite woman stepped forward, stopping a few feet from the guy on the floor. Her voice was small, just like her, but warm rather than high-pitched and squeaky. "Not a ton of good angles in here due to these shelves. I'd say the shooter had to be close. Probably around here. Any further back and the bullets would've cut through some of the glassware closer to the door." She pointed at the glass shards on the floor past Tovar, then toward the bullet holes in the far wall that had been marked by the techs. "At least two shots gone awry, from this close no less. Looks like three hit. I wouldn't say the shooter was much of a marksman, but they could've been rattled."

Dean jutted his chin toward the massive ogre. "Ogden?"

The big guy stepped to the side of the much smaller woman. When he spoke, his voice was deep but buttery smooth, like a singer in a jazz club doing the two AM set. "There's a broken watch band on the floor. Maybe got grabbed and ripped, which further suggests a short range scuffle. Also, I see a wet glimmer inside the safe. If it was open when this guy was shot, that gives us a series of events. Shooter demands the contents of the safe, the guy on the floor complies, hands it over, maybe fights back a little, then *blammo*."

Dean nodded. "Could be. Any shots fired that close will have left tons of evidence on our perp, that's for sure. If they're dumb enough not to do their laundry right away, could make this an open and shut case."

Dean's eyes had scanned me and Razi upon entering, giving us the same quiet, analytical treatment everything else in the room had gotten, but now the tall dark elf focused on me. He waved with a couple fingers. "Officers?"

I perked up and headed over, going around the far side of the tables to stay out of the way. Dean and his fellow detectives met us by the door.

I didn't salute, but I did stand at attention. "Officer Penelope Phair, at your service, Detective."

"At ease, Officer. I'm Dean. These are Detectives Moss and Justice." His forehead adopted a single crease. "You new?"

Behind me, I heard Razi snort. I let my shoulders drop to their normal position. "Yes, sir. Is it that obvious?"

He didn't smile, though the edge of his lip curled up ever so slightly. "Only a little. Mostly I haven't seen you before." He glanced at Razi's badge. "You and Officer Stonefist were first on the scene?"

Razi pushed his way even with me. "That's right, Detective. We got the call from dispatch while on Twenty-Third. We arrived within two minutes, though we didn't get up here until five minutes after that." He punctuated his displeasure with a glare in my direction.

Dean turned back toward me. "What happened?"

Even though he'd asked me, Razi answered. "Officer Training Wheels here heard an engine start up behind the building. Took off into the nearby alley before telling me what she was doing. We had a chat before heading up."

Dean lifted an eyebrow, but I couldn't tell if the action was one of disappointment or surprise. "Did you see anything?"

"A car sped past on the cross alley as I reached the intersection," I said. "It was flying. I don't want to assume it was fleeing the scene, but it was moving fast, sir."

Dean's eyebrow drew back down, and he focused on me. It was an intense gaze. "What kind of car was it?"

I'd revisited the encounter in my head several times while waiting, thinking I might be asked such a question. "Something with a rounded back and fender skirts. Maybe a Pearl Motors Townsman. Black, I think, but everything was so dark it was hard to tell. Should be able to confirm, though. The car scraped against a dumpster before turning onto Thirtieth. Might've left a paint chip or two behind."

Dean's eyebrow crept back up, and this time I was certain it was out of surprise. "Indeed it might've. License plate?"

"Started with AF. That's all I caught."

"And the driver?"

"Didn't get a look at him. Sorry."

Dean turned to his fellow detectives. "That's more than we usually get. We'll take it. What happened after that?"

Razi pushed forward, sneering in a way that made me think no amount of Dean's thanks would get me off his shit list for leaving him behind. "We hurried back around and came up here. Found some janitor cowering in the room down the hall. Apparently she was the one who called in the shooting. Found the stiff here afterwards. Been here since."

"You take the cleaning staff's statement?" said Moss.

"I did," I said. "She said the man on the ground is Gus Tovar. Said he's a scientist, though he might've been part owner of the company, too. The cleaning woman said he hired her, so maybe it's a small operation. Anyway, she said she didn't see the shooter, that she heard five shots while cleaning the fifth floor and by the time she got down here the room was as we now see it. She did say there was another man here earlier. Long grey hair, mutton chops and a mustache but no goatee. She's not sure if he was still here at the time of the shooting. I've got everything written down in my notepad if you want to see it."

Justice and Moss shared a look, and Dean held up a hand. "That won't be necessary. Just file the statement in your report. We appreciate your help, officers."

I almost clicked my heels. "Anything else we can do?"

"As a matter of fact, yes," said Dean. "You said the car you spotted turned onto Thirtieth. I'm going to need you to head up there and canvass the businesses for a few blocks. See if anyone saw more of that plate or caught a glimpse of the driver."

Razi cleared his throat. "We'll get right on that, Detective." He jabbed me in the arm and nodded toward the hall. He looked none too pleased.

CHAPTER FOURTEEN

Razi's face turned red as we descended the stairs. "What the hell were you thinking, Phair? Asking if they needed our help? Did you forget our shift is almost up?"

I sighed. I might've been new to policing, but I wasn't a stranger to human decency. "What was I supposed to say? *Well, that's all I've got Detective Dean, good luck with the dead guy, see you later.*"

"You're supposed to shut your mouth," said Stonefist. "You're supposed to know better than to ask for more work to be shoveled onto your plate. Now I'm going to have to radio for another squad to swing by and wait for them to arrive before we can vamoose."

I paused as we reached the lobby, which was now brightly lit. "But... Detective Dean gave us an assignment."

"Yeah, he told us to ask around to see if anyone got a better look at the car you failed to get a full plate on. Like that's going to pan out. In case you hadn't noticed, there's not much of a bustling restaurant and bar scene here. You'll be lucky to find a single store open at this hour, much less anyone who paid heed to a car going by an hour ago. But that's neither here nor there. The point is, it's somebody else's problem now."

I stood my ground by the door. "Detective Dean gave us an order. It was implicit."

Razi set his jaw. "He gave *an* order. He didn't give *you* an order. You think he gives a damn who ends up walking up and down Thirtieth asking questions? Please. As if you're somehow more apt at this job than literally any other cop who's got more than a day's experience."

My back stiffened. I forced my hands to my sides, because if I didn't, who knew what kind of trouble they might get me into? "You know what, Officer Stonefist? I do think I'm the right officer for this assignment. For one, I'm the one who actually got a look at the getaway car, and for another, I want to do the work, which is probably more than you can say for whoever comes to replace us. Maybe Detective Dean doesn't give a damn who does it, but I do. I wouldn't have stuck around the academy for three months if I didn't care. So yeah, I'm going to canvass the businesses, and then I'm going to report back to Dean before I punch out."

Razi snorted, and his lips curled upward in a smile. He didn't look happy though. More like a tiger sizing up his prey. "To think I thought you'd be an easy one when I introduced myself. Guess we all make mistakes." He threw his thumb over his shoulder. "I'm going to call dispatch and see who they're sending over. I'll wait for them, but I'm not going to wait for you, if you catch my drift."

I wasn't sure what to say to that, and Razi didn't give me a chance to figure it out. He turned and crossed Hoover, heading toward the squad car.

I sighed, and my shoulders slumped. Perhaps standing up to Stonefist wasn't the smartest thing I'd ever done—I'd never been very good at picking my battles—but what was I supposed to do? Ignore an order from a superior? Detective Dean had every right to tell me what to do, and I intended to do right by him, even if it meant working past the end of my shift. That said, I was pretty sure I'd come to regret my decision sooner or later, even if I was following orders.

I hoofed it up Hoover and turned east on Thirtieth. I took note of a couple tire marks on the sidewalk as I passed the alley, but I didn't investigate the dumpster. If any paint was left on the side, it would be up to the crime scene unit to find it, not me. All I had at my disposal was a flashlight, and for as much confidence as I had in myself, there was only so much I could do without tweezers, brushes, and appropriate forensic knowhow.

As I walked past darkened storefront after darkened store-front, I had to admit Razi might've been right. Perhaps if this stretch of Thirtieth were packed with nightclubs and twenty-four hour diners, I'd have a chance of getting something useful regarding the car I'd seen speed off from New Age Alchemical, but after a block and a half of walking, the closest thing I found to a witness was the mannequin standing in the front of a fabric retailer by the name of Fleece by the Foot. Nonetheless, I didn't give up, and as I neared the intersection with Terrace Avenue, I spotted the lights of a convenience store spilling into the street.

A door-mounted bell rang as I pushed my way in. The shop was on the small side, and the copious amounts of junk inside made it feel even smaller. A sleepy looking guy with a mustache that was more fuzz than hair stood behind the counter, his face framed by a lottery-ticket dispenser on one side and a rotating spit of hot dogs on the other. He rested his chin on one of his hands, and he looked in danger of slipping and smashing his face on the counter.

I sighed as I envisioned my slim hopes for a lead fleeing faster than the black Townsman had. "Excuse me?"

Just as I'd predicted, the cashier's face slipped off his hand, though he caught himself as his nose scraped across his forearm. He lifted his head, blinking a few times as he focused on me. "Uh... can I help you?"

I tapped my badge as I approached the counter. "I'm Officer Phair. Trying to track a suspect. Any chance you saw a black Townsman tear through here around nine o'clock?"

The guy scratched his head. "We get people of all races stopping by. Not sure how many are out-of-towners, though."

"A black *Townsman*. It's a car."

"Oh. No, then. No cars in here. They don't fit through the door."

Normally, I might've responded to words that choice with a quick moving open hand, but this young man looked dumb enough to be serious. He was working the night-shift at a convenience store, after all. "Don't suppose you saw an older guy come through? Long grey hair, mutton chops?"

The kid blinked. *"Mutton?* Like... lamb?"

That answered my question about how smart he was, at least. "I'll take that as a no. Thanks anyway."

I pushed back outside. This stretch of Thirtieth wasn't totally deserted. The occasional car passed by, although there wasn't any foot traffic to speak of. I'd travelled three blocks from the corner of Hoover, and Dean hadn't specified how far I should go. I spotted several more stores with lights on further up the road, but I didn't think grilling the folks inside would get me anywhere. With each street that passed, the chances of the getaway car still being on Thirtieth went down by a factor of three. Even if I did come across an eagle-eyed pedestrian who'd been standing at the street corner an hour ago, there wasn't much of a chance they'd had anyone to spy on.

I checked my watch. Quarter after ten. Technically after the end of my shift, but depending on the department's response, Razi might still be waiting for me. Heck, he almost certainly was. Chances were he'd threatened to leave me behind as a motivational tactic. He'd probably be a real treat to ride back to Williams Street with.

I turned west and returned to Hoover at a trot, fully expecting to see Razi hanging out his window and sneering at me as I took the corner. Instead, I found an empty spot across the street and another squad car parked a few spots in front of it.

My breath wheezed out of me like air bleeding out of a balloon, and my heart sunk. "Well, crap."

CHAPTER FIFTEEN

The New Age Alchemical laboratory wasn't as crowded as when I'd left it. The two CSU techs were still there, as were Detectives Moss and Justice, but despite the presence of the squad car outside, there wasn't any trace of the new patrol officers. In addition, the photographer had left, as had Detective Dean. Shame, that. From the moment he'd walked into the room, he'd radiated a focused energy that suggested his status as the department's golden boy wasn't unfounded. I'd figured I might be able to learn a thing or two from him, even if it was only how to accept assignments without getting my TO mad at me. Plus, he'd been easy on the eyes.

As I walked in, Detective Justice stood by the filing cabinets. He'd pulled some of the binders from within and set them on the nearest lab table. While he flipped through the contents, Detective Moss spoke with one of the forensic techs. "Yeah, let's grab prints off the handles on the stairwell and the front door. Might as well dust the elevator, too, to be safe. Thanks."

The tech nodded and headed my way. I squeezed against the wall as she pushed into the hall, and Detective Moss returned her focus to the body of Gus Tovar. She held a clip-board in her hands, and as she surveyed the man's still form, she made a note. She knelt, took a closer look at the gunshot wounds, scribbled another note, and stood before tucking the tip of the pencil between her lips.

Though her mind was occupied, the only person she was engaged with was dead. I didn't figure I'd get a better opportunity. "Excuse me. Detective Moss?"

She looked over her shoulder and nodded. "Officer Phair. What can I do for you?"

"I finished canvassing the businesses on Thirtieth up to Terrace. Is Detective Dean still here?"

"He had to step out," said Moss. "Get anything useful?"

"Unfortunately, no." I stepped up beside her, taking another look at the body. "The only place I found still open was a convenience store, and let's just say the help there proved true a whole lot of stereotypes."

Moss shrugged. "Don't sweat it. Sometimes you get something, sometimes you don't. The fact that you were able to catch a glimpse of the car at all could be a major help in finding who did this. If you hadn't been so quick on your feet, we'd be even further behind the eight ball."

I shook my head. "I don't know. Officer Stonefist made it seem like I made a huge mistake taking off the way I did. I never should've left him."

Moss pursed her lips. "Your only mistake was not telling him what you were doing. You made the right choice taking off after the car. You've got good instincts."

"Thanks." I kept my eyes on the deceased. The blood was in the process of draining from the man when I'd arrived. In the hour since I'd first laid eyes on him, the color in his cheeks had faded, making the dark red blob of cloth stuck against his chest all the more jarring. He didn't seem to have any injuries apart from the gunshot wounds: no welts or cuts on his face, no bruised knuckles, no torn clothing. Between that and the fact that the only broken glassware was in the line of fire, I guessed he hadn't fought back against his attacker. That meant he'd known him, right? At the very least it suggested he didn't expect to be shot.

Moss's voice broke the silence. "First homicide?"

I nodded. "Yeah. *Thankfully*."

Moss's eyebrows furrowed. "What do you mean by that?"

"Well, it's my first day. If this weren't my first homicide, I'd be reconsidering if this city was safe enough to live in."

Moss's eyes widened. "This is your first *day?*" She whistled. "That explains some things. When you told Dean you were new, I thought you meant it in a general sense, not that you were on your first shift."

I shrugged. "I'd always hoped the job would be exciting. Beginner's luck, I guess."

"If you can call it that." Moss glanced toward the door. "So how are you handling everything?"

I looked at Tovar's cold, dead eyes. "Honestly? Surprisingly well. Maybe it's because there's not much gore, but seeing death so close isn't affecting me as much as I thought it would."

Moss tapped her clipboard with her pencil. "I wasn't talking about being exposed to death. I meant getting ditched by your TO."

I blinked. "How did you know I got ditched?"

Moss smiled. "Come on, Officer. I'm a detective. I pick up on clues. I heard the rumble of your squad car as your partner left and figured out the rest."

Detective Justice's mellow bass filled the room. "Don't believe her. The officers taking over for you came up and explained what was going on." He smirked at Moss from his vantage by the filing cabinets.

There was a twinkle in Moss's eye as she responded. "Stuff a sock in it, Og. You're just jealous I'm a more natural detective than you are."

Detective Justice lifted an eyebrow. "Sure, Ginger. I guess that's why while you've been working your jaw muscles, I've been over here actually making progress on the case." He pulled a piece of paper from one of the binders and flapped it seductively.

Detective Moss snorted. "If you wanted me to come over, all you had to do was ask."

Moss sauntered to Justice's side—and I do mean *sauntered*. Romantically speaking, I'd never thought about switching sides, but I could appreciate a good strut, and Moss had one. She'd probably broken it out a few hundred times too many, though, as Justice seemed completely numb to it. He stood there, oblivious as she undulated to his side.

Moss plucked the page from the ogre's mitts and slapped it against her clipboard. "What do we have here, exactly?"

"Nothing much," said Justice. "Just a threatening missive from some religious nut."

Moss scanned the page and started reading. "Dear Mr. Tovar. I am sorry to hear you do not share our organization's concerns over the investigation of alchemical methods. It is bad enough you insist on prying into the divine methods by which our Lord and Savior created the earth beneath our feet, but to attempt to unlock the secrets of the most holy Philosopher's Stone is an affront to the Creator himself. These powers do not belong in mortal hands, and to recreate the Stone's power is to risk not only a cataclysmic economic collapse but also divine retribution at the hands of the Almighty. I warn you. Cease and desist your heretical scientific endeavors before you unleash a power that no mortal is fit to wield. Most sincerely, Brother Roncalli."

Moss blinked and looked up into Justice's dark eyes. "What the heck is this?"

"Well," said Justice. "It's this thing called a *letter*. People write them to each other to communicate information. Sometimes—"

Moss planted a fist into Justice's arm. "Oh, shut up. You think this Roncalli zealot shot our scientist?"

"He doesn't sound pleased, that's for damned sure," said Justice. "Letter's dated last Tuesday. Seems like a reasonable time frame for things to escalate."

"You find any more of these?" Moss waved the letter.

"Not yet," said Justice. "I think that one got misfiled. Most of these binders are full of formulas and experimental notes."

Moss slapped the page against Justice's broad chest. "Well, bag this one, and we can track Roncalli down tomorrow."

"Yes, ma'am." Justice gave a mock salute. "You want that in a clear baggie, or maybe something with a little color to it? Pink might make the threats pop."

Moss shook her head as she returned to me. "Sorry about that. Justice can be *a real smart ass when he wants to be.*" Her voice got noticeably louder as she said that last part.

"I'm always smart," said Justice. "I *choose* when to be an ass."

Moss smiled, suggesting she wouldn't have it any other way.

"Anyway, where were we? Your TO ditched you while you were canvassing Thirtieth?"

I nodded. "Yeah. Said he would, too. I didn't take his word for it. Guess that shows how smart *I* am."

Moss gave me a sidelong glance. "It shows something, but I'm not sure it's an indictment of your intelligence. Your training officer, on the other hand..."

Moss seemed nice enough, but I'd only just met her and there were still Justice and the other tech in the lab, to boot. I didn't want to get into trouble, so I didn't say anything.

I think Moss read me, nonetheless. "Tell you what. The coroner should be over any minute. Once they arrive and I get them squared away, I'll give you a ride back to your precinct. Williams Street?"

I nodded. "Yeah. Thanks."

"Hey? What about me?" said Detective Justice. "I'm supposed to walk back to Fifth?"

"Don't be dense," said Moss, shooting the big guy a bright smile. "There's a subway station a few blocks from here."

Justice threw up his hands, and Moss shot me a wink. I figured there was more to it, but it wasn't my place to get involved, so I gave Moss my thanks again and went into the hall to wait.

CHAPTER SIXTEEN

Moss's car rumbled as we rolled down Hoover. It was a half-hour until midnight, and most of the traffic lights had been switched to a constant blinking yellow. I sat in the passenger seat, same as I had in Razi's car, drumming my fingers on my knee. Strips of yellow light flickered across the dash, bright then dark, bright then dark.

"Thanks again for the ride," I said, speaking over the crackle of the radio. "Though you didn't have to. I could've made my way back."

Moss waved me off. "Please. Taking the subway after getting abandoned by your training officer is like the walk of shame after a one-night stand, except in this case you're the only one who knows what happened. It's the least I could do."

I tipped my head. "I'm not sure about that. There are probably a lot of cops who'd figure I earned every second of that subway ride."

"A lot of *male* cops, you mean." Moss glanced at me over her shoulder, one hand steady on the wheel. "Trust me, I've been in your shoes. It wasn't even that long ago. There are good TOs and bad TOs. Everyone gets hazed to a certain degree, but women get the worst of it. Even guys who don't think they're part of the problem have sexist tendencies. It's ingrown in the system. Institutional. Wasn't much I could do about it as a patrol officer, and there's still not a whole lot I can do as a detective, but a ride back to your station? That's within my power."

I gazed across a sea of brightly lit signs hanging over the shops at the side of the street. Neon catchphrases adrift in an ocean of night. "I don't know if Officer Stonefist's actions were due to my gender. I get the feeling he'd treat me almost as miserably if I was a guy. Who knows? I could be wrong. I guess I figured things had changed since my great-grandmother's time."

Moss batted an eye. "Your great-grandmother was a cop? How long ago was that?"

"I don't know. Seventy years? All I know is it was *really* rare to have women in the force back then. She ended up becoming the first female captain of her precinct."

Moss's eyes narrowed. "Which precinct?"

"Fifth Street."

Moss whistled. "No shit. You're Captain Daggers' great-granddaughter?"

Now it was my turn to look surprised. "You know her?"

"Never met her, but I see her picture on the wall every day. She as no-nonsense as she looks in her official painting?"

I laughed. "I'm not sure I'm the best judge of that. She's always pampered me, to be honest."

"Well, give her my regards the next time you see her," said Moss. "It's always easier following in someone's footsteps than blazing the trail yourself. She didn't break the glass ceiling, but she cracked it, that's for sure."

Moss might've been my superior, but her conversational tone was chipping away at the wall of formality between us. I figured she wouldn't mind if I chiseled away a little more. "Can I ask you something about Detective Justice?"

Moss's eyes twinkled again. "He's a handsome one, isn't he? If the question is if he's taken, I'm pretty sure the answer's no, but I've been down that road before. He never takes the bait. He's too professional to get involved with anyone at work."

Justice wasn't the one I thought was handsome, but I wasn't about to get into that with Moss. "Actually, I was going to ask if Justice was really his last name."

Moss laughed. "It is now. He made it official with the courts a few years back. But you're right, it wasn't his given name. He didn't have one."

"He didn't have a name?"

"Not a last one," said Moss. "It's an ogre thing. Name was just Og, not even Ogden. He changed that, too. Wanted to be seen as more professional. Always with the professionalism, that one."

"But *Justice?*" I said.

Moss shrugged. "It fits him. He plays by the book, but underneath that thick exterior, there's a lot of passion. All he wants is for people to get what's coming to them, good as well as bad. I respect the hell out of him for that."

Moss slowed as the Williams Street precinct rose out of the gloom. She turned into the tight lot at the station's side, pulling the cruiser into one of the open spots. The engine growled as she put the car into park.

I gave her a nod as I eyed the station's battered bricks. "Well, thanks again, Detective. I appreciate the ride. Good luck with the investigation."

Moss's voice cut across the car as I reached for the handle. "Can I offer you a bit of advice, Officer Phair?"

I paused, arm outstretched. "Sure."

Ginger gave me a look as long as her lashes. "As much as I appreciate you sticking around to do the work Dean asked of you, it probably wasn't the smartest decision. I get it. You were stuck between a rock and a hard place, and you made a choice. However, in the future, you'll make life a lot easier on yourself if you do what your TO tells you."

"Even if he's being an asshole and tells me to do something stupid or against the rules?" I regretted calling Razi an asshole as soon as the words left my lips. He was my superior, even if I didn't much like him.

Moss wasn't taken aback by my choice of language, though. "You should absolutely do what he says, *especially* if he's being an asshole. Trust me, you're not the only one who's dealt with a Stonefist. We've all encountered his ilk before. Guys like him get off on punishing people, and that includes you. The more you struggle and the more obvious it is he's getting your goat, the worse he'll make things for you. On the other hand, if you embrace the suck, he'll stop getting a kick out of it and give up."

I felt a hot resentment creeping up my throat. I wanted to reply that it was stupid and unfair that the best way to stop a bully was to give into his poor behavior, but I knew Moss was trying to help. I let my breath out slowly and bobbed my head. "Nod and smile. Right. I used to be a waitress, so I'm familiar with that charade."

"That said," continued Moss, "tomorrow is going to suck for you, *bad*, no matter how you slice it. Your TO isn't going to let the fact that you disobeyed him go without a serious dressing down. Then again... maybe I can help. At least for a day."

I half expected to see another twinkle in Moss's eye, but there was nothing there but concern. I guess she didn't have an elaborate prank planned. "I'm all ears."

"To put it simply, Detective Dean has a lot on his plate. I'm not entirely sure why we got assigned the New Age Alchemical case, but suffice it to say, most of the work is going to fall on Justice's and my shoulders."

"Because of the Tarot Card Killer?"

Moss lifted a brow. "Didn't figure you knew about that, but I suppose having a former police captain for a great-grandmother gives you a better handle on internal affairs than most."

I shrugged. "Actually, Stonefist told me."

Moss rolled her eyes. "Of course he did. Probably felt like a big man letting that piece of gossip slip. Whatever. The point is, Dean's been hyper-focused tracking that psycho down, as he should be. That means a lot of work we normally share has been getting pushed onto Justice's and my desks. I might need an extra set of hands tomorrow."

I blinked. "I'm a patrol officer."

"So? Everybody in the department works together. Detectives, photographers, forensic techs, coroners, sketch artists, patrol officers, even management sometimes, though don't tell my captain I said that. If his head swells any bigger, it might burst. The point is, there's all kinds of stuff I'll need help with regarding this case, some of which might be suited to you. So if your TO is riding your ass and it gets to be too much, just call into dispatch, give them your name, and tell them you've got a message for me. I'll know what that means, and I'll see what I can do to lighten the suck, if you get my drift."

I didn't entirely, but an invitation to having my life suck less wasn't something I'd ever dismiss out of hand. "I appreciate that, Detective. I'll keep it in mind."

"Please," she said. "Call me Moss."

CHAPTER SEVENTEEN

The door to my apartment creaked as I let myself in. The floor lamp in the living room was on, keeping the demons at bay with its gentle glow. The apartment wasn't big. Just a standard one bedroom with a half wall that separated the kitchen and the living room. Floral wallpaper peeled back from the plaster at the ceiling, green in spots that stayed in shadow and yellow where the sun shone upon it for hours a day. The wood floors were worn smooth from use, and the fridge in the kitchen looked like it was the first one off the Sherman Industries assembly line. Nonetheless, for all its flaws it was infinitely better than the last place I'd lived, mostly because this one didn't have Mick in it.

I crossed into the kitchen and filled a glass from the tap. As my shift with Razi stretched into what seemed like a dozen, I'd been certain I'd find myself digging through the cabinets again, looking for a bottle to help take the edge off, but amazingly enough, Detective Moss had done a crack job of that herself. I knew she'd just been giving me a hand up after seeing me on the ground, but seeing as most of my interactions throughout the day had been characterized by indifference or outright hostility, having someone to talk to and confide in made all the difference. I'd have to remember to pay her kindness forward when I made detective someday.

I blinked and put my glass down half drained. *When I made detective someday.* I'd never had that thought before. In fact, I'd never given much thought to what I'd be doing more than a month or two in the future. *Ever.* When in high school, the guidance counselor expressed to me multiple times that I wasn't taking my studies seriously, and she'd been right. I'd paid far more attention to after-school sports and to the boys in my classes than to anything I was being taught. It wasn't that I was incapable of following along, I just found the subjects *boring.* I guess it hadn't come as a surprise to anyone that after graduation I'd bounced between retail and waitressing jobs as quickly as between boyfriend's apartments, the latter being the main reason my father disowned me. He might've been willing to look past many of my unladylike traits, but he couldn't forgive my approach to suitors. As if *he* didn't share the blame for my complicated relationships with men.

Regardless, though I'd often dreamed of futures in which I became a successful roller derby diva or found a winning lottery ticket on a street corner, I'd never made any real plans for my life, at least not until Nana put the worm into my head to join the academy. Even then, I'd had a discrete goal. Become an officer. Today, I'd achieved that. It hadn't turned out the way I'd hoped, but there was time for it to change. Still, it appeared my subconscious was already making plans for the *next* chapter of my career.

Me? A gumshoe? I shook my head as I drained the last of my water. If there was anything I'd proven myself to be good at throughout my life, it was getting ahead of myself. It only figured I'd keep the streak going, thinking I'd get to be a detective after bungling my way through my first day on the job and making an enemy of my partner.

I pushed the glass to the side and headed to the bedroom door. It was closed, so I cracked it open and stepped into the darkened room beyond. Quietly, I stripped off my clothes and stepped into the attached bath. I got the water going while I brushed my teeth and hair. Steam poured from the shower as I stepped into the tub, and though I hadn't logged the hardest of days from a physical perspective, the hot water felt like a tonic as it washed away the day's grime and drew the strain from my muscles. I could've stayed under the shower head for an hour if I'd let myself, but it was close to midnight and I needed my sleep, so I hopped out, dried off, and snuck back into the bedroom. There, by the light of the moon that trickled between the window shades, I wiggled into a nightgown, quiet as a mouse—or at least one that wore combat boots.

As I turned toward the bed, I smashed my foot into one of my nightstand's legs. The lamp on the stand rattled, as did the stand, but it was the cry that escaped my lips and the curse that followed that really shattered the silence.

A figure upon the bed stirred and turned. "Nell?"

I punched a balled up fist into the mattress a couple times as pain radiated into my foot. Nothing was broken, but it hurt like hell. "Hey, Cliff. Sorry."

"No, it's fine. You okay?"

"Yeah. Just hurts." I grimaced as I slid into bed beside him.

He turned onto his side to face me, and in the dim light, I could see the thin flash of his white smile. He hadn't shaved since I'd run into him at the precinct, but he didn't look any worse for it. If anything, he seemed more handsome than before, with his hair tousled from his pillow and his chest bare.

Cliff slid an arm around my midsection. His voice carried that bleariness of sleep as he spoke. "How was your first day?"

Cliff and I started dating about a month into police academy, though we hadn't let anyone know. Strictly, it wasn't against the rules to date a fellow cadet, but we both knew the instructors would frown upon it. We'd kept the relationship secret throughout graduation and while applying for positions. I hadn't even told Nana about Cliff, though she wasn't a fool. She knew my history, and the fact that I'd found a new place to stay before I started earning my paycheck certainly clued her into what was going on, even if she hadn't met the second half of the equation. Still, someone would discover our relationship sooner or later. I just hoped when it happened it wouldn't jeopardize our burgeoning careers. Not that it should. Neither one of us was in a position of power over the other. We weren't partners. There shouldn't be any conflicts of interest due to our relationship. Then again, if Cliff and I both believed that, why were we hiding the fact that we were together?

I nestled into my pillow, ignoring the possible consequences and focusing instead on the strong touch of Cliff's arm across my stomach. "My day was fine."

Cliff stirred again. "Fine isn't good."

I shook my head, staring at the ceiling. "I don't want to talk about it, and you need to be at work at six. Get back to sleep."

"Well, I'm awake now," he said, nestling closer into my shoulder. "What's wrong?"

"It's... complicated," I said. "My TO was a jerk, but I guess I wasn't a saint either. He caught me off guard with his views on policing, and at the end of the day, I had to choose between following his orders and those of a detective who arrived on the scene. I made the wrong choice. Maybe. I'm still not sure."

"You had a detective show up? What happened?"

Cliff really did need his sleep, and I didn't want to be responsible for him nodding off on his second day. "Nothing. I'll tell you later."

Cliff sighed, his warm breath rolling across my shoulder. "It sounds like you and your TO got off on the wrong foot. I'm sure everything will be fine tomorrow."

I didn't believe that for a second, but I kept my opinion to myself. I also knew I should stay quiet, I couldn't help myself. After all, I was still pretty awake myself. "Do you think your TO is a good person, Cliff?"

He shifted again. "Huh?"

"I don't mean is he a good cop. Did you get the impression his heart is in the right place?"

"I don't know," said Cliff, his voice still laden with sleep. "I think so. Why?"

I shrugged. "It's nothing. Goodnight."

Cliff moaned an affirmation. He snuggled closer, his muscular chest pressing against my side. His arm drifted across my midsection as his hand made its way to my chest. He cupped one of my breasts in his hand and gave it a gentle squeeze, his thumb and index finger lightly pinching my nipple.

I felt a simmer between my legs, and I suppressed a moan. "What are you doing, Cliff?"

"I told you, I'm awake now."

Much as I enjoyed his touch, I'd meant what I said. I slapped his hand away. "Tomorrow. Get some sleep."

He sighed, but his arm drifted away. "Fine. Goodnight."

"Goodnight."

Cliff stayed where he was, thought it didn't take more than a couple minutes before his light breathing turned into a gentle snore.

Unfortunately, it took me a lot longer than that to fall asleep.

CHAPTER EIGHTEEN

I was on my best behavior when I arrived at the Williams Street precinct for second shift the next day, but it didn't matter. Razi was full of piss and vinegar from the get-go. He didn't say a word as we left the sergeant's briefing, just growled and flicked a finger at me to follow. We didn't exit the precinct right away as we had the first day, but the presence of other officers around us didn't prevent Razi from unleashing the hounds. He slapped a bunch of paperwork related to our stop at New Age Alchemical into my hands and told me to get cracking, but it was the way he treated me while I filled it out that was demeaning. He stood over me at the desk we shared on the first floor, grunting and wheezing and making sniffs of displeasure with every one of my pen strokes. He'd interrupt and micromanage me and tell me to rewrite every aspect of the report, which couldn't have been fun for him, but being able to lord his seniority over me clearly was. He had me get him coffee and doughnuts from the break room. He gave me a uniform review halfway through my Form 1020B. He ordered me to the ladies room to retie my hair because according to him I looked like 'ten pounds of shit in a two pound bag.' I wanted to set him straight that nobody in their right mind would put excrement in a bag, never mind such a small one, but I reminded myself time and time again of Detective Moss's advice and simply nodded and did whatever Stonefist told me, no matter how insulting and demeaning it might be.

After a couple hours, Razi lost steam, just as Moss suggested he might. With a scowl, he told me to check out our gear from the armory and meet him at the squad car. As I stowed everything in the trunk, Razi growled at me from the driver's seat to hurry it up. I didn't figure there was anything we were late for, but nonetheless I kept up my obedient routine and did as I was told. As soon as I'd settled into my seat, Razi backed the car out and gunned the engine as he pulled onto Williams. I didn't ask where we were going because any question was an invitation for abuse, so I simply watched the horizon as we sped east.

We didn't go far. Within a minute, Razi pulled to the side, snagging an empty spot beside Miller's Creek Park. I'd become pretty familiar with the fifteen acre spread of trees and its burbling creek over the past few weeks. Cliff's and my apartment was on the opposite side of it, after all, and I walked through the park to get to the precinct. I didn't think Stonefist knew where I lived, so the fact that he'd stopped here couldn't have been anything personal, could it?

He slammed the car into park and barked at me as he unbuckled his seatbelt. "Well? What are you waiting for? We're on patrol."

I nodded and hopped out of the car. Given the wooded area's proximity to the station, Miller Creek Park wasn't exactly a hotbed of criminal activity, though I'd heard of the odd individual being mugged late at night. Still, if Razi wanted to spend part of our shift wandering under a canopy of leaves and breathing in what passed for fresh air in New Welwic, who was I to argue? It was better than getting tongue-lashed for improperly dotting my i's and crossing my t's, that was for sure.

I followed Stonefist as he barged onto the gravel path that crossed the park north to south. As it was the middle of the afternoon, there were a number of couples and elderly folks taking their daily strolls, but the main path was wide enough to accommodate everyone. Nonetheless, the folks who were paying attention noticed Stonefist's scowl from a mile away and moved to the side to avoid entering his sphere of influence. For his part, Stonefist didn't say a thing, but he did keep his eyes peeled as he headed toward the plaza at the center of the park.

The trees opened up as we arrived. A light breeze blew, bringing with it a scent of pollen from the tall pines around us. A fiddler with his violin case open for tips played a jaunty tune at the edge of the pavers, and sitting on the lip of a burbling fountain in the middle sat a young shaggy-haired teen holding a box of candy bars. He called out in a disinterested fashion, as if he'd been at it all day. "Mallows. Get your mallow bars. Two coppers apiece."

Stonefist stopped. He turned, and for the first time all day, he smiled.

A shiver ran down my spine. Something told me he wasn't planning on punishing me by making me eat so much candy I got sick.

Razi nudged me forward as he called out. "Hey! Kid!"

The youth at the fountain turned and caught sight of us. I still didn't know what was going on, but he seemed to. His eyes widened, and the color drained from his face. "Um... hello."

Stonefist stayed at my side as we approached him, making sure I didn't fall back. "What do you have there, son? Candy?"

The kid shrugged. "Just some mallow bars, Officer."

Razi nodded thoughtfully. "Sure. Trying to make a few coppers. I get it."

It was hard to notice, but the kid perked up a touch. "Yeah. That's all."

Razi shot me another smile, this one more subdued than the first. "Of course. I don't blame you. Everyone can use a little extra coin in their pockets. But... you have a permit to sell them, right?"

Whatever speck of hope the boy held onto fled. His eyes widened. "A *permit?*"

"That's right," said Stonefist, watching me as he spoke. "A street vendor permit. You need one to sell food on public property."

The kid blinked, brushing the hair out of his eyes. "But... I'm just selling candy bars."

"And while I admit the nutritional value of those things is piss poor, they still qualify as food," said Stonefist. "Do you have a permit or not?"

The kid's head drooped, and his voice weakened. "No, Officer."

Razi's smile widened as he faced me. "You heard him, Phair. Write him up."

I stood there, a lead brick on my chest. I gave the kid a quick glance. If his head got any lower, he might bounce it off the fountain's lip.

I lowered my voice, hoping only my partner would hear. "He's twelve. Maybe thirteen."

Razi responded in a similarly hushed voice. "And? If a

twelve year old shot his old man in the back, would you let him walk, scot-free? He admitted to a misdemeanor. Peddling without a license."

My collar pressed against my neck, and I felt my blood pressure rising. "You want me to give a citation to a kid for selling candy in a park, Stonefist?"

Razi leaned in. "You seem surprised, Phair. Almost like you thought I wasn't smart enough to figure out a way to make you miserable. Well, guess what? I've met every type there is over the years. You might think you know how to weather the storm, but trust me, I've got you figured out. The sooner you accept I'm in charge and that you should be doing everything I say, as I say it, when I say it, the easier this is going to go for you."

My heart felt like it was going to leap out of my throat. "This isn't right. If you want to make my life hell, go for it, but leave random kids out of it."

Razi sneered. "Are you having a hard time hearing me, Officer? I said *write him up.*"

My teeth ground against each other. My muscles coiled, and I wanted nothing so much as to throw a fist into Stonefist's smug face, but I pushed my rage down through sheer force of will. I'd been prepared to deal with a deluge of my partner's crap, but I hadn't expected him to go after innocents to get under my skin.

I took a deep breath as I patted the front pocket on my uniform. "I forgot my pad in the car."

Razi scowled. "Well, go get it and hurry on back. I'll stay with the kid."

Stonefist easily could've written the citation himself, but that wasn't the point. The point was for me to do it. For me to look the kid square in the face and have him stare back at me with hate and desperation in his eyes. And I was sure it would be followed with a lecture about how teaching the kid a lesson now would keep him from committing worse crimes later—that or it might lead to him doing it before his next birthday, thus allowing us to sweep him into a cell sooner than we otherwise might've. All positives in Razi's book.

I turned and headed down the gravel path at a trot. Stonefist would give me hell if he didn't see me hustling, but the fact of the matter was I just wanted to get away from him, even if only for a minute. The pad was a decent excuse—I'd actually forgotten to bring it with me as we'd left the car—but I'd have used my female organs as an excuse if it would've bought me time. Another second stuck with Razi's leering face and I might've done something to ensure I never set foot in the Williams Street precinct ever again.

When I got to the car, I threw open the door and settling into the passenger seat. I took a few deep breaths before opening the glove compartment. There, amid maps of the city, a collection of pencils, and a box of latex gloves were a couple of citation pads.

I grabbed one and closed the glove box, but I didn't leave the car. I sat there, staring at the two-way radio, wondering what I should do. I wanted to prove I could fight my own battles, but a voice in my head whispered that I still wasn't aware of how big of an asshole Razi might be.

Discretion won out over valor. I picked up the handset and called in. "Hello, dispatch? This is unit eighty-seven. I have a message for Detective Ginger Moss."

CHAPTER NINETEEN

Razi sat behind the wheel of the squad car, a smirk across his lips. Forcing his anger out on a boy who hadn't yet hit puberty had sweetened his disposition from that of a rampaging bull to a wet hen. He simmered and stewed, but he did so because he wanted to, not because he felt like he was still batting for the losing team. As a result, I hadn't dropped my guard. Stonefist's smile made me suspect he was still hard at work coming up with ways to make me feel weak, powerless, and dirty. His roving eyes probably searched for homeless folks to roust or jaywalkers to ticket, but it was the legal acts hidden deep at the bottom of the city's charter that he was likely most focused on, the ones I'd never see coming.

Suddenly, Razi perked. He slowed the car and took a purposeful turn onto Twenty-First, and I suspected he'd come up with a new way to torment me. Luckily, as he straightened the car out a call came through on the radio.

"Unit eighty-seven, this is dispatch. A detective needs backup at sixty-two forty Riverside. Can you respond?"

Razi frowned at the unit. "The sixty-two hundred block of Riverside? That's in the Delta district, by the river."

He turned his eyes on me. I shrugged. "I'm not that familiar with the area."

Razi picked up the handset. "Dispatch, this is eighty-seven. We're on Twenty-First and Schumacher. Don't you have any units closer to the area?"

The radio crackled as the woman responded. "Negative, eighty-seven. Can you respond?"

Razi sighed and rolled his eyes. "Copy that. We're on our way."

Razi replaced the handset and turned as we reached Twenty-Second. He eyed me once he'd gotten on the straight-away, looking as if he wanted to ask something, but after a moment of indecision, he kept his trap shut and focused on his driving.

It took us ten minutes get through the worst of the down-town traffic, but as we reached Riverside and headed north, the architecture slowly changed. The buildings got squatter, the walls thicker, the windows smaller, all due to the fact that the Delta was a historic district and the buildings hadn't been remodeled in ages. As I understood it, the place had once been the city's center of immigration with a huge processing facility on the river's edge. People streamed into New Welwic from far and wide, most of them traveling by boat, and though the city had been a sprawling metropolis for centuries, immigration really swelled during the industrial revolution. While I suppose that had been a boon for the tycoons of industry who ran the sweatshops and factories, landlords were probably the only other ones who benefitted. Over time, rents went up and jobs got filled, and immigrants found new places to settle. New

Welwic being what it was, there would always be an influx of starry-eyed yokels moving in from the country, but the giant processing facility had been shuttered long before I was born. Last I'd heard there were plans to renovate it into an arena, but since I'd given up roller derby upon beginning my training, I hadn't bothered to keep up.

I kept my eyes peeled once the addresses reached the six thousands, and it wasn't long until we reached our destination. A church, not too big and not too small with a pair of towers flanking a rose window in the depressed region between them, faced the river with the address given to us by dispatch carved into the stone at the base of the steps. Despite a thick construction that hinted at its age, I suspected the church didn't belong to one of the city's more popular religions. It butted up against a run-down bar on one side and an auto body shop on the other, and both of those businesses seemed to have more patrons than the church.

Detective Ginger Moss's black Howardson Hornet was parked in front of the building. Razi drove past it, pulled a u-turn, and parked behind it. As we exited the vehicle, Moss got out and met us on the sidewalk.

Moss, wearing a white button shirt and jeans but the same leather jacket I'd seen her in the night before, gave us a nod. "Officers Stonefist. Phair. Thanks for coming. Did dispatch appraise you of the situation?"

Razi blinked. I could tell he wanted to ask why we were there, but Moss's straightforward manner didn't give him an opening. "Ah... no. Just asked if we could respond."

Moss shot a thumb toward the church. "This is Saint Onassi of Reins, a church of the Divine Creation. Inside, to the best of my knowledge, is a man by the name of Giovanni Roncalli, a pastor. Yesterday, at the scene of Gus Tovar's murder, we uncovered a letter tying him to the deceased." Moss mentioned it as if I hadn't been there when it happened, but perhaps she was filling Stonefist in more than me. If so, I should thank her. If Razi got the impression I was involved in a conspiracy to subvert him, he'd probably be even madder at me than if Moss hadn't intervened at all.

Moss turned toward me. "Officer Phair. You remember how the cleaning lady said she saw a man in the New Age Alchemical building with long gray hair and mutton chops?"

I pointed to the church. "This is the guy?"

Moss nodded. "We matched his photo from the DMV database. Now, this is a priest we're talking about, but we should nonetheless assume he's armed and dangerous. I need the two of you to help me secure the suspect without anyone getting hurt. If this church is built like most, the living quarters will be in the back. We'll start on the first floor, secure the exits, and move our way to the second and third floors if necessary. Any questions?"

Whatever misgivings Stonefist might've had about being called to the Delta district disappeared upon hearing we'd be chasing a person of interest. He placed a hand on his holster and undid the clip. "On your command, Detective."

Moss looked at me. The warmth and camaraderie she'd showcased while giving me a ride home the night before was gone, and in its place was a cold determination. She radiated an energy that suggested anyone who got in her way would have a *real* bad time, and suddenly I understood how someone as small and pretty as she was had made it not only through training academy but through the customary stint on patrol.

I nodded. "Ready when you are."

"Good. Follow me."

With Moss leading the way, we headed up the stairs and into the church. The interior was more or less what the exterior promised: row upon row of wooden pews worn smooth from age sitting on a sea of off-white marble tile, all under a high ceiling criss-crossed with rib vaults. An elderly trollish woman sat in one of the pews on the right side of the central aisle, head bowed as she muttered her prayers, but the rest of the nave was empty, including the pulpit at the front, situated under a sprawling mosaic depicting a white-robed creator who dwarfed a sea of humanoid creatures beneath him. Moss, Stonefist, and I hurried past the pulpit to one of the doors on its side, guns drawn and held against our sides.

Moss pressed herself against the wall and whispered as she pointed into the corridor beyond. "I'll check the first door. Phair, take the second. Stonefist, the third. We'll rotate once each is clear. Watch the staircases." She pointed them out, one at each end.

We nodded. Once again, Moss led the way. She stopped at the first closed door on her left. As she pushed her way in, gun held before her, Razi and I kept moving. I stopped at the second door, swallowing my apprehension as I tested the handle. It gave, so I threw the door open and lurched inside.

I found myself in a bedroom, roughly the same size as the one Cliff and I shared. A bed was tucked against the far wall, and half of the remaining space belonged to a desk underneath a window facing a ragged garden. A young man sat at the desk, his head bowed and a marble idol of the same guy from the mosaic clutched in his hands.

He turned at the sound of the door. "Can I help—?" He froze at the sight of my pistol.

"Roncalli," I said. "Where is he?"

Before the guy could respond, I heard Razi's frantic bellow from down the hall. *"Get on the ground! Now! Get down!"*

I turned and darted into the hallway, joining Moss as she ran toward the same door I was. We both darted into the room Stonefist had barged into—not a bedroom, more of a study crossed with a chantry. On one side of the room, a richly furnished desk sat underneath alcoves set into all three nearby walls, each holding a statue with the religion's Creator in different pious poses. On the other side was an elaborate shrine, filled with votive candles, incense, and minerals, of all things.

More importantly, it was where my training officer knelt upon the back of an old man with long gray hair and thick mutton chops, screaming at him while he jabbed his revolver between his shoulder blades.

I pulled my handcuffs and slapped them on the old man's wrists while Moss pulled Razi off the old guy. "Thank you, Officer Stonefist. You can holster your sidearm now."

Moss patted Razi on the arm as she dragged him to the side of the room. The non-verbal display seemed to appease him, as he nodded to her with a smirk on his lips. Nonetheless, Moss shot me a glance as she moved to my side, a bug-eyed look that expressed her shock at Stonefist's tactics as well as any remark could've.

Throughout the process, the old man on the floor begged and pleaded for mercy. "Please, let me go. I'm a man of God!"

Moss ignored him as she grabbed his right arm, motioning me to do the same for his left. "Come on. Let's get him in a chair and see what he has to say for himself."

CHAPTER TWENTY

Roncalli was understandably rattled as we pulled the chair from behind his desk and pushed him into it. His eyes were wide with fear, and he kept blathering, switching between complaining about his wellbeing and making appeals to his Lord and Savior, all while giving casting looks at Razi. To her credit, Moss figured out pretty quickly that she wasn't going to get much out of the man while Stonefist lurked, his hand hovering over his holster. Once the priest had been dumped in the chair and his curate who'd I'd stumbled upon down the hall shooed off, she asked Razi if he had any latex gloves in the car. When he confirmed he did, she asked that he grab a few so we could search the room without contaminating the scene and to call for forensics while he was at it. I could see from the look in Razi's eye that he wanted to make me do the work instead, but unlike the night before when I'd asked Detective Dean if there was anything I could do to help, Moss made a direct request of him unprompted. With a grumble and a readjustment of his weapons belt, he nodded and headed out.

Moss sat on the desk, turning her attention to the old guy

while I guarded the door. "My apologies for that, sir. Officer Stonefist can get a little overzealous at times. My name is Ginger Moss. I'm a detective with the NWPD. You're Giovanni Roncalli?"

The old man's eyes flitted to the door, but his nostrils no longer flared, and the vein in his neck had stopped throbbing. "You may refer to me as Brother Roncalli. Now what in the world is this all about? You realize this is a place of worship, don't you? We abhor violence of all kinds within these walls, and combat is strictly forbidden."

"Is it, now?" said Moss. "My apologies if I hadn't pegged you as a pacifist. Do the tenants of your religion also prevent you from sending threatening letters?"

Roncalli cocked his head. "Excuse me?"

Ginger inspected her fingernails, switching topics abruptly. "Do you mind telling me where you were last night, Brother Roncalli?"

"For the most part, I spent the evening here in the chantry, then upstairs in my quarters while I slept. Why?"

"And for the rest of the evening?"

"What do you mean?"

"You said, *for the most part*," said Moss. "Which means there was another part. Why don't you tell us where you were earlier?"

Roncalli rolled his eyes. "I see. So this is about my trip to New Age Alchemical."

Moss smiled. "Tell us about your relationship with Gus Tovar, Mr. Roncalli."

The priest lifted a finger, forcing his other hand up with it as they were handcuffed together. "I assure you, I was there at the invitation of Mr. Tovar. If he's claiming I trespassed, that's hogwash. You can't change your mind after the fact and decide to press charges."

Moss was a pro. She didn't show any emotion, nor any surprise at Roncalli's claims. "What time did you arrive at New Age?"

Roncalli shrugged. "I'm not sure. Around seven?"

"Mr. Tovar was there when you showed up?"

"Of course he was," said Roncalli. "As far as I can tell, that man never stops working."

Moss lifted an eyebrow, as if to say *he's stopped now.* "What were you there to talk to him about?"

The pastor sighed. "I've corresponded with Mr. Tovar several times. When I first heard he was pursuing the development of a chemical process to turn lead to gold, I figured he had as good a chance of succeeding as any man who's tried in the past, which is to say next to none, but then word came of that Lumaris woman and her trek to find the Philosopher's Stone, and suddenly it seemed necessary for me to have a chat with them both. But Tovar wouldn't listen to reason. I tried to convince him alchemy is beyond a science. It's a force not fit for mankind to understand, and it's for that reason the Creator has hidden its secrets from us from the days of time immemorial."

I knew I was there to guard the exit, but I couldn't help myself. "Hold on. Turning lead to gold? Are you saying Gus Tovar wasn't a chemist, but an *alchemist?*"

Thankfully, Roncalli didn't seem to notice my slip of present to past tense. "Of course. It's in his company's name. New Age *Alchemical.*"

I blinked. "I thought that was just a fancy alternative spelling."

Moss wrestled back control of the conversation. "Let's back

it up, Mr. Roncalli. You're saying the purpose of Gus Tovar's work at New Age was to discover a method of turning *lead to gold?*"

"Correct," said Roncalli. "Now, I can't say with any certainty if he's made significant progress in that endeavor, but based on my conversations with Miss Lumaris, I think he could be closer than he's let on. It's not a knowledge we are fit to hold! Has he not heard of the tales of King Zumis of Mauricia? How his kingdom collapsed and was swallowed by the earth due to his thirst for gold? I'm not a literalist, mind you, but the texts were written for a reason. They speak to the fundamental truths of humanoid kind, even if in historically inaccurate metaphors."

Moss lifted a hand to get the man to slow down. "That's the second time you mentioned this Miss Lumaris. Who is she?"

Roncalli sighed, looking exasperated. "She's the founder and head of an archeological consortium named Lumaris Digs. I think she used to be a college professor, but she started her own company when she was able to secure funding to search for the fabled Philosopher's Stone."

"And what is that?" I asked.

Roncalli's eyes widened. *"You don't know what the Philosopher's Stone is?"*

His look made me think I hadn't paid enough attention to my high school history teacher, but Moss made me feel better. "I've never heard of it either. We're police officers, not historians."

"Theologians," corrected Roncalli. "But regardless, I'm shocked you're not familiar with it. It's a famous alchemical artifact, heavier than the heaviest metal but a dusty reddish in color, like fresh picked saffron. The ancient texts say the Lord and Creator infused it with a spark of the divine force, that not only can the stone transmute lead to gold but also heal the infirm, turn green the leaves of a plant long dead, extend the lifespan of the man who holds it in his hands for decades or even centuries, and perhaps even be used to create life itself. Still, most of those who seek it do so out of greed, and it's the Stone's ability to turn lead into the most precious of metals that has primarily shaped its legend."

Moss held up a few fingers. "Let's try to keep this story grounded in reality rather than myth. So this Lumaris woman struck out to find this fabled stone?"

"That's right." Roncalli leaned forward in his chair, and his voice lowered. "And according to her, *she found it.*"

Moss lifted an eyebrow. "Really?"

Roncalli's posture returned to normal. "Well, that's what she's claimed. I never saw it, and I'm not sure I take her word for it. Many people have claimed to have found the Stone over the years for publicity stunts, showing fakes at fairs or trying to sell them to gullible old tycoons hoping to prolong their inevitable deaths. But whether or not she actually found it, her history at New Welwic University shows she's no charlatan, so I figured I should talk to her to warn her of the Stone's dangers."

I blinked, trying to process everything. "I'm not sure I follow. What does any of this have to do with Mr. Tovar?"

"Well, I thought that was obvious," said Roncalli. "Tovar stole the Stone from Flora Lumaris—or at least, that's what she claims. Again, it's possible she's untrustworthy."

Ginger sighed and rubbed a couple fingers against her forehead. "I thought you said he was working on a chemical—sorry, *alchemical* method for turning lead to gold. Why would he need this stone?"

"I don't know," said Roncalli. "Perhaps Tovar is the charlatan and his supposed research into the transmutation of lead is nothing more than balderdash and poppycock, so he decided to tease the secret of transformation from the Creator's own Stone. Or his entire operation is a front. I don't know, but regardless, I told him the same thing I told Lumaris. That the secrets our Creator hid from our eyes were done so purposefully, and that if he continued upon his path, a foul end would befall him, and rightfully so."

Moss snorted. "Funny you should say that given how Tovar met his end."

The old man blinked. "What?"

Moss hopped off the desk and crammed her hands into her jacket pockets. "Gus Tovar was shot to death last night. We found him not long after you claim to have been in his laboratory."

Roncalli gaped and swallowed air. At the same time, heavy footsteps echoed up the hall. Razi emerged through the door, holding the box of latex gloves from the car. He pulled a couple and shoved the box into my hands. "CSU's on their way."

"Good," said Moss. "You two perform an initial sweep while we wait."

Roncalli finally found his voice again. "Wait... Tovar is *dead?*"

Stonefist started sifting through the piles of junk on the shrine while I moved to the desk, pulling on the gloves as I did so. Meanwhile, Moss took another step toward Roncalli. "Indeed. So did you shoot him because he refused to give you the Philosopher's Stone, or was it simply out of principle?"

"I did no such thing!" screeched the priest. "I swear to you, I had no idea the man had been murdered. I wouldn't... I *couldn't...* I'm not capable of such an act!"

I threw open the desk drawers, fingering through fountain pens and prayer beads as I looked for anything incriminating. As I opened the larger drawer on the bottom right, however, something caught my eye. A metallic gleam poking out from underneath a pile of papers.

My eyes widened as I pushed the papers to the side. "Uh... Detective Moss? I think Brother Roncalli's pacifist vows might not be quite as concrete as he made them out to be." I held up the revolver I'd found hidden in his drawer, a Jones & Westman Model 3.

Roncalli did his best impersonation of a fish as he shifted his gaze from me to the gun and back to Moss, his cheeks puffed and his eyes wide. "I... I've never used it. I don't even own ammunition. It's to scare thieves away, that's all. This is a rough neighborhood. The auto-shop next door has been broken into twice in the past year, and drunks from the bar sometimes start fights in the alley out back!"

I cracked the cylinder to the side and checked the chambers. Indeed, the thing wasn't loaded, and to me the gun didn't smell as if it had been fired recently, but that would be for the forensics team to determine, not me.

For what it was worth, Moss seemed to think the presence of the gun was reason enough to take action. "Stonefist! Phair! Get this man back to the precinct. I think it's time we move this interrogation somewhere more formal."

CHAPTER TWENTY-ONE

D etective Moss called the 5th Street precinct home, so that's where we took Roncalli. The building was bigger than the Williams Street version, two stories taller and more of a cube than a rectangle. As I understood it, the city's various police precincts had been acquired piecemeal over the centuries, converted from apartment complexes and jails and bakeries, or on rare occasion built from scratch when the building that had previously occupied the plot of land collapsed from dry rot or structural faults. It wasn't surprising. New Welwic was so old every building was built on the bones of another, sometimes five or six others. Anyone willing to dig a hole deep enough could find whole abandoned civilizations beneath the dirt. No joke, either. When the subway was built forty years ago, the city turned up so many artifacts the museums refused to take them all.

Still, it meant each precinct was different than the others, and it seemed to me the 5th was nicer than the one I called home. Thanks to its oblong construction Williams Street had more natural light, but the 5th Street precinct had a more classic appeal. Past the welcome desk, the main floor was entirely open, with only the occasional stone column blocking the view from one end to another. Officers and detectives alike worked from their desks, some bunched into clusters for partners and teams. The morgue was built into the basement, as were the holding cells, evidence rooms, and records vaults, and assorted offices, laboratories, and conference rooms occupied the floors above. I wouldn't bet money on the 5th not being a remodel, but it was as close as I'd seen any precinct come to looking like it was built for the job.

I sat on a bench outside one of the interrogation rooms on the main floor, where we'd delivered Roncalli for Moss to continue her questioning. Though I imagined some sound-proofing had been stuffed into the walls, if I strained my ears, I could just make out the flow of conversation inside—or at least I could when everyone around me stayed quiet.

Razi shifted on the bench and grunted. "I know you had something to do with this, by the way."

I tore my focus from the paneled wood door across from me. "What?"

"You thought I wouldn't suspect anything?" said Razi. "I already told you I've got you figured out. There's no way we were the closest unit to that church. Dispatch requested us for a reason. I don't know why. Maybe you've got one of your girl-friends working the radios and you sweet-talked her into sending the good calls our way. Whatever it is, I'm onto you."

Razi was close to the truth, but I wasn't about to admit it, not when he hadn't forced me to beat up a homeless person or give a ticket to a toddler in at least two hours. "I didn't sweet talk anyone. And are you honestly upset we got called to assist? You just admitted it was a good call."

"I got to bust an old man for murder," said Razi. "Of course it was fun, but that's not the point. You're not supposed to be having a good time. *You're* supposed to be doing whatever the hell I tell you, slogging your way through whatever septic tank of crap I point you at."

My jaw tightened. "So you admit you're torturing me."

Razi's eyes widened in mock surprise. "I'm not trying to hide it, girl. The point of this exercise isn't to get anything productive done, in case you hadn't figured that out. It's for you to learn your place, and that place is on the lowest rung of the police ladder. You're a rookie beat cop, not a detective's assistant. Get that through your skull."

I cocked my head. "Who said I was trying to be a detective's assistant? I did as Moss asked, nothing more."

Razi smirked. "You didn't have to *say* anything. Your actions are proving it for you." He grunted as he stood, shifting his belt under his paunch. "I'm going to get a coffee. Might grab some forms for you to fill out on the way back. Better loosen your writing wrist."

Stonefist sauntered off, and I checked my wristwatch. Half past six, so I still had three and a half hours of Razi's torment in front of me. I could do it.

I turned my attention back to the interrogation room, focusing on the voices within. Thankfully, the noise from the main floor, or the pit as Moss referred to it, didn't totally carry down the hallway.

After a moment I caught Roncalli's voice. "Well, I'm really not sure why. I suppose Miss Lumaris could've had her own plans for the Stone, but I was under the impression she already had a buyer. The same man who funded her expedition."

I heard something that resembled Moss's voice, but it wasn't loud enough to carry through the plaster.

Roncalli responded. "I don't remember. Doherty, perhaps? He's a businessman. I think he runs a lead enterprise."

Once again, Moss said something my ears weren't fine-tuned enough to catch. Maybe if I was a pure-blood elf instead of having the odd ancestor here and there...

Once again I heard Roncalli. "I don't know, Detective. I never saw the Stone myself. I promise! I didn't even notice the man's safe, so how would I know if it was open when I left?"

There was more muffled speech, followed by the screech of a chair sliding unsuccessfully across the floor. The door clacked as it opened, and Moss slid out. I stood in response, perhaps out of respect for the Detective's rank, or perhaps to make it look like I hadn't been sitting there snooping.

There was a reason Moss was a detective, though. Her eyebrows crept up as she closed the door. "Phair. You're still here." She flashed me a smile. "Listening in?"

I felt my cheeks warm. "Uh..."

Moss snorted. "Relax. I'm not going to bust your chops, I just figured you'd be gone by now. Where's your training officer?"

Some of the tension left my shoulders as I realized Moss wasn't going to add her weight to the pile of suffering Stonefist had been building all day. "Went to grab coffee for himself and paperwork for me, which I'm sure could wait until we get back to Williams Street, but it's not as if I'm going to say anything."

"Yeah, don't. That'll make things worse." Moss looked up the hall as if to make sure we were alone. "I know we talked about him last night, but seeing him at the church? Holy harvest. I feel for you, girl. How are you holding up?"

I didn't want to burden Moss with the truth, so I told her a version of it. "I'll get through it. I didn't join the force with the expectation that every day would be sunshine and roses." Although I *had* joined the force with the expectation I'd spend the lion's share of my time improving people's lives and easing their pain, one way or another.

Moss nodded. "Good for you. Head up, eyes on the prize. Tell him whatever you need to get through the day, but don't let him change who you are inside. We need as many good people in the department as we can get." She stared down the hall for a few more moments before turning back to me. "So... What do you think?"

I lifted an eyebrow. "About what?"

"About the case." Moss nodded toward the interrogation room. "You were listening. What's your take on Roncalli?"

I hesitated. "Detective, I'm a rookie patrol officer. I'm not sure you should be soliciting my opinions on this."

Moss sucked on her teeth. "Are you smart, Phair?"

That one threw me for a loop. "Excuse me?"

Moss looked at me blankly, suggesting she hadn't meant it as an insult. "Pretty simple question. Do you consider yourself an intelligent woman?"

I gave her the benefit of the doubt and assumed she wasn't playing me for a fool. "Yes. I do."

"How are you at reading people?"

"Depends. Men who I'm romantically involved with, not great. Otherwise, pretty good."

Moss laughed. "Fair enough. What I'm getting at is that detective work isn't a hard science. There's no degree program. I got this position by proving to my captain and to Detective Dean that I knew what I was doing. Mostly, the job's about paying attention and picking up on inconsistencies. I'm not trying to trap you into saying something dumb or out of line. I'm asking for your opinion because as far as I can tell, you've got your head on straight and your heart is in the right place. That and you probably know as much about alchemy as I do."

I snickered at that last bit, but Moss's kind words were exactly what I'd needed after so many hours of Razi's negativity. "Thanks, Moss. I appreciate that. But to answer your question, well... it seems to me Roncalli's story is exceedingly elaborate for someone who's trying to cover their ass for murder. I mean, he didn't even give an alibi. He put himself at the crime scene more or less at the time of Tovar's murder. So either he's telling some version of the truth, or he's *really* bad at spinning a yarn."

Moss smirked. "Yeah, I don't think he killed anyone either, although I'm surprised we found a gun in his office. Ballistics will tell us soon enough if his pistol was the one used to shoot Tovar, though. I'm just trying to make sense of this whole alchemy business. Turning lead to gold seems like a load of tripe to me, but I've learned something doesn't have to be true for it to provide a motive. If someone thought Tovar was in possession of the secret to unlimited wealth, that would absolutely be worth killing for."

Personally, I thought the real question was whether Tovar had been murdered over the mystical stone Roncalli mentioned or something else he'd discovered on his own, but my train of thought was derailed by the sound of approaching footsteps. I turned, expecting to see Razi returning with a sheaf of papers in hand, but instead it was Detective Dean. He was missing the sport coat he'd worn the night before, but his pressed slacks and tailored shirt were snazzy enough without it. His cheeks and jaw were smoothly shaven, his hair parted to the side with a touch of mousse to keep it in place.

He cocked his head at me, a measure of surprise crossing his chiseled features. "Officer Phair. What are you doing here?"

Moss saved me from having to explain myself. "Phair and her training officer responded to my call for backup at Saint Onassi of Reins. Helped me apprehend Brother Giovanni Roncalli, who's in interrogation right now. I was bouncing ideas off her."

"Oh." Dean's jaw remained taut, as if he wanted to say something but decided to keep it to himself. "Well, we appreciate your help, Officer. You're free to leave. Moss and I can handle things from here."

It wasn't an order, but Dean made himself perfectly clear nonetheless. I responded with a quick salute before heading toward the break room in search of Stonefist.

CHAPTER TWENTY-TWO

I sat in the Williams Street ladies changing room. My locker hung open in front of me, but I hadn't mustered up the energy to change out of my uniform into street clothes. A lingering fatigue lay over me like a lead blanket, though the sensation was more mental than physical. Outside of patrolling Miller's Creek Park and assisting Moss at Saint Onassi's, most of my time on shift had been spent either in a chair or a bucket seat, but Razi's aura had been omnipresent throughout. After we'd left the 5th Street precinct, we'd put a few dozen miles on the odometer before retiring to Williams Street for another round of Razi's patented over-the-shoulder wheezing and grunting as I filled out forms. Some of his vehemence from the afternoon had faded, whether from fatigue, thanks to our detour at the church, or because he thought his point had been made, but even though his heart was no longer in it, his demeanor remained as toxic as ever.

I sighed, thankful for the changing room's privacy. Apart from Captain McGuire, only a handful of women called Williams Street home, and while a part of me thought it might be fun to share the space with a few close friends with whom to gossip, for now I was happy I had the room to myself. That way, no one could witness the effects of Razi's campaign against me.

Outwardly, I thought I'd done well. I hadn't yelled at him or challenged him, other than questioning him briefly regarding his motives at the park. I hadn't scowled or rolled my eyes, at least not in his line of sight. I hadn't even let my smart mouth get the best of me, which was a big win in my book. But despite my stoic exterior, gosh darn it if Razi hadn't wormed his way into the soft parts beneath.

I knew that was what he wanted. To get in my head. To make me suffer so I'd stop fighting. To make me wilt so he could scoop me up and mold me to his liking like wet clay. I understood his game plan as well as he claimed to understand mine, and I knew that letting him get my goat was akin to letting him win, but how could I not let his behavior affect me? I'd made the decision to join the NWPD for one reason—to see what would happen when I dedicated myself to others instead of myself for the first time. The motivation evolved over time, of course. As I went through training academy, I found I liked the excitement and physicality that police work offered. When Cliff and I started dating, that gave me another reason to stick to the path I'd chosen, and now as I found myself exposed to Tovar's murder I found that I liked the mysterious allure of solving a case, too, but it was the chance to make a difference in people's lives that put me on the bench where I currently sat.

And Razi's damn attitude had me wondering if my very reason for being here was a lie.

In Razi's world, obedience and self-preservation trumped altruism and nobility. Policing was about getting people to behave by any means necessary, and to Razi, the cudgel was a more effective tool than the pulpit or the helping hand.

Of course, Razi's worldview was just that—*his*. His veteran status didn't somehow make his opinions on policing right, but the fact that he'd managed to go so far in his career while retaining said opinions made me wonder how widespread they might be. What was it Moss said to me in the hallway? *We need as many good people in the department as we can get.* That implied Stonefist's actions, while enough to raise a brow, weren't enough to get him reprimanded. Rather, Moss's statement made it seem like he might be more the rule than the exception, and if so, what the hell was I doing in a uniform at all?

I shook my head and tried to brush the feelings off. I couldn't let myself get discouraged. Other than Razi, everyone I'd met in the department, from the techs to the photographers to Dean and his team, all seemed perfectly professional. Chances were Razi was an outlier, and the fact that I thought otherwise was an artifact of the foul mood he'd put me in.

I stood and changed out of my uniform, locking up my sidearm before heading out and onto Williams Street. The night air was cool but not yet crisp, hanging in that nebulous zone at the beginning of fall where the season had technically changed but the winds hadn't gotten the memo yet. I'd spent enough time loitering in the changing room that it was almost eleven, but there were still a few folks out and about as I headed toward home. The shops near the precinct were all closed, but some of the restaurants closer to the park had lights on inside, and the chatter of conversation drifted from groups of patrons sitting under covered tables at the roadside, shielded from the road by metal banisters and thin stretches of rope.

I walked through one group's cloud of cigarette smoke,

coughing as I hopped onto the crosswalk and into Miller's Creek Park. There, the smell of fresh earth replaced the unpleasant smoke, and the rustle of leaves hid the roar of car engines and the screech of poorly maintained brakes. Gravel crunched under my feet as I walked, and in the distance, I heard the burbling of the long dead miller's creek. The occasional lamppost stood along the path, each creating a cone of yellow that stopped short of where the next started and faded to darkness past the edge of the gravel. No one else shared the path, leaving me alone with thoughts of a soft mattress and a warm body at my side once home.

As I rounded a bend that fed into the final straightaway into the plaza, I heard a sharp crack. Not the crack of a dead branch giving its regards to its tree before tumbling to the ground, nor the crack of a dry twig being stepped on. It wasn't loud enough to be gunfire, either. It was a more brittle sound, the sound of snapping mortar, or as morbid as the thought might be, the sound of a bone breaking.

I paused and looked behind me. No one followed in the cones of light, nor was there anyone in front of me. To the sides, however, I couldn't see more than ten feet into the darkness before the trees swallowed every last speck of the lampposts' effort.

Actually, that wasn't quite true. As I squinted into the darkness, I caught a hint of a glow. Something opaque and swirling, deep purple in color and nearly as dark as the surrounding trees. Was it smoke from a firework? The sound I'd heard had been more of a snap than a bang, and who in the world would be setting off fireworks in the park in the dark of night? Or rather, a *single* firework?

The purplish haze deep hovered there, deep within the

forest, neither lifting nor dissolving. As I stood there peering at it, a shiver ran through me. Goosebumps prickled my skin, and I had the sudden sensation of being watched. My hand drifted to my waist, but of course my pistol was tucked safely away in my locker at the Williams Street station.

Out of the gloom, two points of light appeared. I heard a faint crunch, and my voice caught in my throat. I took a step backward, but before I could run, the points of light bounded toward me. A squirrel, black of fur, hopped into the lamppost's cone of light, darted across the path, and disappeared back into the darkened forest.

My heart hammered in my chest, but as I turned toward the purple haze, I found I couldn't make anything out from the backdrop of solid black.

I shook my head as I turned toward the plaza. I couldn't believe I'd been scared out of my socks by a squirrel, but I nonetheless found myself walking faster than normal as I headed toward my apartment.

CHAPTER TWENTY-THREE

Cliff was gone when I woke up, which wasn't a surprise based on the amount of light streaming through the bedroom windows. A clock on the wall told me it was ten until ten, so with a groan, I rolled out of bed, dug a pair of jeans and a comfortable long-sleeved top from my dresser, and wriggled into them.

A yawn nearly crippled me as I headed into the kitchen. Our Sherman puffed as I pulled on the handle. Cool air hit me in the face as I bent down to look inside, but I needn't have bothered. The thing was as bare as a centenarian's skull. A few drops of milk lingered in the bottom of an otherwise empty bottle, and a single apple rested on its side in the vegetable crisper, its skin as wrinkled as newborn pup's. At least it wasn't moldy.

I closed the fridge and sighed. I might've changed apartments, but not my shopping habits. In the weeks I'd spent living with Cliff, we hadn't really discussed our domestic responsibilities. Cliff hadn't pressured me to do the shopping, which I appreciated after Mick's constant badgering, but at the same time, just because we hadn't discussed it didn't mean I could shirk the task indefinitely. Cliff might be more relaxed when it came to having food on hand than Mick was, but I hadn't held up my end of the social contract we'd entered into. Not once since moving in had I cleaned the apartment, and only once had I brought home a load of groceries. I worked, same as Cliff did, but as a woman, wasn't it my responsibility to do more of the domestic stuff? That's what society would have me believe, but in a perfect world, two partners would spilt the most noxious of any chores on their to-do list, wouldn't they?

A voice in the back of my head reminded me that splitting tasks meant half of the whole was still my responsibility. I groaned and resolved to pack the fridge with edibles before my shift started, but only after I filled my stomach with something other than an apple that predated the foundation of New Welwic.

I'd never been a fan of purses, so I slipped some cash and my apartment key into my pockets and headed out. Cliff's and my apartment was on the third floor, so I padded down the stairs and hopped out, crossing 8th as I headed back into Miller's Creek Park. There was a diner on Williams not far from where I'd passed the smokers the night before that was only open for breakfast and lunch, and while the food wouldn't satisfy an epicurean, they knew how to scramble an egg and fry bacon with the best of them. The air was crisp and cool as I walked, and for the first time it felt like fall had arrived. It wouldn't be long before the trees in the park turned brilliant shades of orange and red, and I almost wished I'd grabbed a jacket to throw over my shirt. *Almost.* I always ran more hot than cold.

As I walked along the gravel, several people passed me going the other direction, muttering curses. It was upon the third scowling face that I caught the trend, and it only took me a moment longer to realize the cause behind it. At the plaza in the center of the park, a pair of police officers in navy uniforms blocked the path. One was ridiculously tall, approaching seven feet but narrow in the shoulders, and the other was a good half-foot shorter than I was, with a short black beard that swallowed all light that approached it.

The guy with the midnight void enveloping his face held up a hand. "Sorry, ma'am. Park's closed. Official police business. You'll have to go around."

I peered over his shoulder. Several more officers milled about the fountain in the center of the plaza, but the real action was on the path heading toward Williams. Yellow police tape had been strung between trunks, blocking the trail entirely, and beyond it, I could see more officers tromping through the trees.

"What's going on?" I said.

"Nothing that concerns you, ma'am," said Officer Blackbeard. "Now turn around, please."

"You can let me through," I said. "I'm a police officer, too."

Tall and Lean snorted. "Sure you are."

I felt my cheeks warm. "I am, Slim Jim. I work at Williams Street. The name's Phair. You can ask Sergeant Zaxby." A larger than normal figure burst through the trees and approached the tape, a massive ogre in a tailored chocolate-colored suit. I recognized him immediately. "Wait... is that Justice?"

Slim Jim's brow had furrowed at the mention of Sergeant Zaxby, but Blackbeard's eyebrows rose to meet his. "You know Detective Justice?"

"Sure," I said. "I mean, not *well*, but we've talked. Seriously, what's going on here? Was somebody murdered?"

The two cops stared at each other, and by their looks I knew somebody had.

Slim Jim frowned after reading his partner's face. "We shouldn't say anything. You're not on duty."

Blackbeard nodded. "Yeah. Trust us, the less you know about this, the better you'll sleep at night."

"The hell I will," I said. "I live on the edge of the park. I walked through here on my way home after second shift ended last night. If someone got murdered, I want to know."

"After second shift?" Slim and Blackbeard shared another look. "So what? Like ten o'clock?"

A creeping dread spread through me, like a droplet of blank ink through a glass of milk. "Later. Around eleven. What aren't you telling me?"

The two guys continued to stare at each other. "I think we should take her to Justice."

My heart rose into my throat. *"What aren't you telling me?"*

Blackbeard eyed me. "What did you say your name was?"

"Phair. Penelope Phair."

Blackbeard lowered his voice. "This doesn't leave the brotherhood, got it? Someone found a woman in the woods this morning, a ways off the main path. She was mangled pretty good, and the worst part? The first officers on the scene found a tarot card on her."

CHAPTER TWENTY-FOUR

My vision darkened, and for a moment all I could hear was the *thump thump thump* of blood in my own ears. My heart raced, and I couldn't breathe. The Tarot Card Killer. He'd been here. In the park. As I walked home. He'd murdered a woman not far from the path. The strange purple haze I'd noticed. The snap, as if of bones. It could've been him. Mangling a woman. Tearing her body limb from limb, mutilating her, desecrating her remains. And I'd been right there. If I'd stepped off the path to investigate, if I hadn't hurried home, if I'd been drawn toward that strange glow...

It could've been me.

"Hey, Phair? Phair! You okay?"

I registered Blackbeard's voice as my knees buckled. I heard Slim shout, felt the grip of his massive hands as he caught me around my back.

"Crap on a cracker," said Blackbeard. "Get her seated. She looks like she's going to faint."

Slim escorted me into the plaza. I stumbled onto the paved circle, my feet feeling like bricks stuck on the end of wet noodles. With Slim's help, I flopped onto a nearby bench. As he made sure I wasn't going to fall off, Blackbeard took off toward at the caution tape by the trees, and I thought I caught Justice's name.

"How are you feeling? Can I get you anything?"

Slim's face swam into focus in front of me. It wasn't a pretty one, too oblong and sunken for my tastes. His eyes were different colors, one brown and one green, but I used it to my advantage. I stared at the green one and focused on my breathing. Pushing air in and out, in and out. I was okay, I told myself. I could've died, but I hadn't. What I was feeling was a natural response. Fight or flight. I'd survived, and there was no reason to let terror govern me now.

"Can you hear me? Hello?"

I nodded, tearing away from Slim's green eye. "Yeah, I can hear you. I'm fine."

The guy straightened. "Good. I don't need you blacking out on me."

I knew the panic had started to recede because I felt a familiar combative response I so often did when men dismissed me. "Don't worry. Wouldn't want to take you away from your tough job of guarding the fountain."

Slim frowned as Blackbeard returned. In his wake followed the massive Ogden Justice. He nodded to the two officers and spoke in his deep, radio voice. "Thanks. I can take it from here."

Justice crossed his arms as the two officers walked away. He didn't sit down, just regarded me with curiosity. "Officer Phair, was it? You seem to keep popping up for some reason."

"*For some reason?*" Another bout of the same annoyance I'd felt with Slim surfaced. "I live here. This is the path I take to work and to snag breakfast."

"Is that what you were up to now? *Getting breakfast?*"

I frowned. "Did Blackbeard not tell you why I'm here?"

"You mean Officer Tannenbaum?" Justice glanced at them. "He said I should talk to you. Didn't mention why."

I took a deep breath. "I got off work at about eleven last night. Walked home, through here."

Ogden's eyes widened. "*Holy crap.* And you just found out...?"

He didn't have to finish the thought. "Yeah."

Justice bellowed at the cops who'd escorted me to the bench. "Tannenbaum! Wyatt! Get this woman a water, or a coffee! Something, damnit! Move!" Justice sat down next to me, and his face softened. "Sorry. I assumed you were nosing around. It's my fault. We're trying to keep a lid on things, and... well, I made the wrong assumption."

I nodded. "It's okay. No apology needed."

"So how much do you know?"

"Almost nothing," I said. "Like I said, I was on my way to breakfast when I ran into those two. It's only because I wouldn't stop badgering them that they told me about the dead woman and the, ah..."

"Tarot card," said Justice. "It's okay. You can say it. It won't summon the bogeyman himself. So you walked through here from the Williams Street entrance last night at eleven?"

"I got *off work* at eleven. I probably walked through at eleven fifteen." I glanced into the forest past the edge of the plaza. "Detective, what happened out there?"

Justice shook his head. "Couple of teens found a woman near the creek at about seven-thirty. First responders arrived at quarter till, and Detective Dean and I arrived at half-past eight. As to the woman?" Justice grimaced. "Trust me, you'd rather I didn't go into detail. I've seen some ugly things in my time in homicide, and that one ranks up there. Suffice it to say she had a tarot card sewn in between the layers of her dress. The rest is up in the air. But frankly, what I can tell you about that poor woman is a lot less important that what you might be able to tell me. I haven't gotten a time of death from the coroner, but you might be the closest thing to a witness we have, Phair."

Left unsaid was the fact that neither of the first two tarot card murders had any witnesses either, leaving me as perhaps the first person with any first-hand knowledge of the serial killer's slayings, as minimal as it might be.

I swallowed hard. "I was walking along the path, maybe a couple hundred feet from where it spits into the plaza. I heard a snap, not like a tree branch, but something more brittle. Maybe a... bone?"

Justice grimaced and nodded.

"It seemed to come from my right, so to the west I guess. I stopped and looked into the woods, but they were dark. Nonetheless, I thought I saw a faint, swirling glow, purple in color. More of a smoky haze than anything else."

Ogden's eyebrows furrowed. "What do you think it was?"

"I don't know. My first thought was a firework, but the sound didn't fit, and I didn't see sparks. It wasn't quite like anything I'd ever seen. I almost thought I was imagining it."

Justice dug a notepad out of his jacket. He flipped it open and took a few notes. "What did you do then?"

"I froze," I said. "Something about it rubbed me the wrong

way. I got goosebumps on my arm. For a second I considered booking it out of there as fast as I could, but then I heard another, smaller crunch. A squirrel darted across the path at my feet. I tracked it to the other side of the forest where it disappeared into the darkness. When I turned back, the purple light was gone."

Blackbeard returned with a waxed paper cup filled with steaming coffee. I didn't particularly want it, but Justice insisted the man get it, so I took it and gave him my thanks.

Meanwhile, Justice frowned and tapped his notepad with the tip of his pencil. "This squirrel. What did it look like?"

I blinked. "I don't know. It was smallish. A black squirrel, not one of the more common gray ones. Why? Is the squirrel important?"

Justice shook his head. "I don't know, but we found a dead black squirrel not far from the scene. I'm no expert in squirrel necropsy, but the thing looked fresh. No flies, eyes weren't clouded. It couldn't have been dead for more than a day."

"You think the killer...?"

Justice shrugged. "I don't know what to think. We've got a ton of work to do, and very little about this murder makes sense at the moment." He flipped his notepad closed and returned it to his pocket. "The one thing I can say for certain is that Dean is going to want to have a detailed conversation with you."

"I don't know that I have much else to tell, but I can repeat to him what I saw. Is he at the crime scene?" Justice had said I didn't want to see the deceased, and I believed him.

"Nope." Ogden stood. "Another matter drew him away. He should be at the precinct. Fifth Street. You should head there ASAP—although you can get that breakfast you mentioned first if you'd like. I know better than to stand between a woman and her food."

The quip made me want to smile, but the panic and fear that descended on me upon learning what happened the night before hadn't quite lifted. Instead, I stared into my coffee. "You're smarter than most then, Detective, but I think I'll pass. As it turns out, I don't have much of an appetite anymore."

CHAPTER TWENTY-FIVE

At the request of Detective Justice, Officer Blackbeard gave me a ride in his squad car to the 5th Street precinct. He didn't say much as he drove, which I appreciated. As rattled as I was about the Tarot Card Killer, I didn't want any of the officers to pity me or treat me with kids gloves just because I'd had the misfortune of being in the vicinity of a violent murder. I was a cop, same as the rest of them, and I wanted to be treated like one. Although Blackbeard initially thumbed his nose at me, he'd changed his tune as soon as it registered that I was an officer of the law. Even though I wasn't wearing a uniform, he'd accepted me as soon as he'd received Justice's tacit approval.

If only Razi could be so easily won over.

Blackbeard pulled into the parking garage that butted against the building and pulled into one of the open spots next to the side entrance, the ones reserved for short term visitors. A shiny blue Howardson Dervish parked in the spot nearest the entrance, complete with whitewall tires, chromed bumpers, and a gleaming hood ornament displaying a fierce shield maiden,

Howardson's signature mascot. The license plate on the trunk read "MRLEAD."

I thanked Blackbeard and hopped out of the squad car, eyeing the decked-out Dervish as I crossed into the station. Though I'd gotten to explore the first floor when I'd accompanied Moss and Roncalli the day before, I wasn't an expert on which specific corners each detective called home, so I stopped by the front desk and hailed the officer seated there.

"Excuse me," I said. "I'm looking for Detective Alton Dean."

The guy eyed my woven shirt and jeans. "And you are?"

"Officer Penelope Phair. I'm off duty."

He nodded toward the elevators. "Third floor. By the north-facing windows."

I took the stairs instead, figuring the exercise would do me good. Once I got to the third floor, I realized I had no idea which direction was north, so I skirted the dividers that separated the floor into cubicles, peering over the tops looking for placards any time I found myself across from any windows. As I made it halfway around the perimeter, I caught sight of Moss's name between two of the dividing walls. Figuring Dean's desk wouldn't be far off, I dove into the maze looking for signs of Dean.

I didn't find him, but I did find his desk. Like the man himself, it was neat and tidy, with most of the paperwork contained in a pair of wire organizers or constrained to the edges, tightly stacked and marked with strips of colored paper that stuck from between the pages. Dean's nameplate sat in the middle of the desk, and there was a framed detective's certification affixed to the partition. Of personal effects, there were only two: an old hourglass, fashioned of blown glass, hand-carved wood, and tied together with fine strands of rope, and a statuette of the same eagle that was embossed on the official police seal, one holding a pair of balance scales in its claws. Notably absent were photos of family members or girlfriends.

One thing stood out from the rest, that being the items dumped in the center of the desk. A manilla folder marked coroner's report had been slapped there haphazardly, Gus Tovar's name printed on the tab. I pushed it to the side and found another report underneath it, this one from forensics. I didn't look at either, but I couldn't help but glance at the item preventing the first folder from laying flat: a metal slug, deformed from impact, but instead of lead it appeared to be made of solid gold.

I heard footsteps, and I shuffled the reports and bullet back into place on Dean's desk. I looked over the movable partitions only to find a man I'd never met walking through the maze.

"Excuse me," I said. "I'm looking for Detective Dean."

The guy pointed in the direction he'd come from. "I think he's in interrogation six with that Doherty guy."

"Doherty?" I said.

The guy shrugged. "I don't know. Some businessman."

I thanked him and followed the general direction of his finger into a corridor. None of the rooms were marked, but as I approached a pair of doors on my left, I heard voices. One was big and bombastic, the other more even and relaxed. Dean's.

I paused in the hallway. There wasn't a bench to sit upon as there had been outside interrogation one on the main floor. The voices came from behind the door with an inlaid panel of frosted glass, but I suspected I knew what was behind the adjoining door, one that was as plain as a bowl of cooked rice.

The prudent choice would've been to return to Dean's desk

and wait there until the man was done with his questions, but there was another option. Not the smart choice, but the more intriguing one. I looked up and down the hall, and finding it empty, I tested the handle to the unmarked door.

It gave, and I stepped into a simply furnished observation room. A table and a couple chairs were pushed against a one-way mirror looking into the interrogation room. Beside the table was a hulking contraption with a bunch of knobs and dials and a pair of spools attached to the top, each of them containing a length of magnetic tape. I hadn't seen one of the machines before, but I was fairly sure it was an audio recorder, though this one didn't seem to be turned on.

Detective Dean's voice drifted through vents set in the wall between the rooms. "So, Mr. Doherty. Tell me about Flora Lumaris."

Dean sat in a bare metal chair. Across from him, behind a stainless steel table that had seen its fair share of abuse, sat a man of advanced middle years. He had a tuft of white in his otherwise jet-black hair that looked as if it had been dyed into place, but other than that, his age didn't really show. He was broad-shouldered and clean shaven, with a few wrinkles in his brow and at the corners of his eyes, and he wore a suit that cost him a pretty penny, though not as much as the thick gold ring he wore on his right hand. If the man had been looking for a legal alternative to brass knuckles, he might've found one.

Doherty responded, his voice big and brassy. "For the record, Miss Lumaris contacted me, and did so before I ever met Mr. Tovar. At the time she was working at New Welwic University. At first I feared she wanted to express an environmental concern about my facilities, but instead she offered a business opportunity."

"When was this?" asked Dean.

"Two years ago, give or take. Upon meeting, she outlined her plan to find the Philosopher's Stone, a substance that can supposedly turn lead to gold. I was skeptical, of course. As a man who's built his empire on extracting and processing lead ores, I've heard every myth there's ever been about the transmutation of lead, but Miss Lumaris isn't a historian or even a religious kook. As it turned out, her background was in geology, and she knew as well as I did that lead is often found in the same minerals that silver and gold are. I won't go into the details of her proposal, but the crux of her claim was that the myth of the Philosopher's Stone is based in science. That there's a mineral catalyst, if you will, that when subjected to the right conditions of temperature and pressure can turn lead into the gold and silver that's found in those same ores. This, she claimed, was the true secret of the Philosopher's Stone and what she wanted to help me uncover."

"Help *you* uncover?" said Dean.

Doherty smiled. "What she really wanted was my money to fund her expedition, as well as rights to the industrial processes derived from the Philosopher's Stone, but I didn't earn my millions without learning how to negotiate. I thought her pitch was intriguing, and after a few rounds of proposals and counter proposals, we came to an agreement and off she went."

Dean nodded. "So when did Tovar enter the picture?"

"I approached him around three months later," said Doherty. "I kept thinking about Lumaris's argument, that a mineral could catalyze the transformation of lead. It seemed to me that if it was true, a chemical could be produced to achieve the same result. So I approached Gus, who had a background in inorganic chemistry and post-transition metals, and after some negotiating, I hired him to spearhead a research project to see if the transformation of lead to gold via chemical rather than mineral means was possible."

Dean leaned back in his chair. "So you were funding an archeological expedition *and* a fledgling chemical enterprise? That must've been expensive."

Doherty smiled. "Business has treated me well, Detective. I've made a lot of safe bets in my life, but I've also taken risks. Not all of them paid off, but the ones that did made me rich. Yet every crown I've earned would be peanuts next to what I could generate with the ability to turn my lead enterprise into a gold and silver empire. I figured the risk was worth the cost."

"Except it wasn't," said Dean. "Because Gus Tovar is dead."

Doherty snorted. "Trust me, I'm more upset about this than you are. First Lumaris has her sample of the catalyst material stolen, now Tovar gets murdered. I might as well have flushed a hundred thousand crowns down the toilet. If I didn't know any better, I'd guess someone was trying to ruin me."

"Or keep whatever secret Lumaris and Tovar were close to uncovering hidden," offered Dean.

Doherty smiled. "From my perspective, Detective, that sounds like the same thing."

I could only see the back of Dean's head, but I imagine he didn't smile back. "Mr. Doherty, could you tell me what you were doing between the hours of seven and nine PM two nights ago?"

"I was at work. I think I didn't leave until about seven-thirty. My driver took me home. I'd guess I got there about eight, maybe quarter after."

"And your driver? He could confirm that?"

"Of course." Doherty's brows furrowed. "But you couldn't

possibly think *I* had anything to do with Tovar's murder or the theft of the Philosopher's Stone, could you? *I'm* the one who's lost his entire investment as a result of these crimes."

"Possibly," said Dean, his voice cool and indifferent. "Then again, you're also the one with the most to gain by taking full control of such a valuable trade secret, and it does strike me as odd that you're unwilling to go into the details of your contractual agreements with Ms. Lumaris and Mr. Tovar. I'm not much of a businessmen myself, Mr. Doherty, but even I know that a hundred percent of a deal is more than some fraction of that."

Doherty's face darkened. "Indeed. Well, Detective, my apologies, but I think I've given all the assistance I can with your investigation. Certainly all that I *intend to* without my lawyer present."

"No need to call him right away." Dean pushed back from his chair. "You're free to go, Mr. Doherty. Thank you for time."

The lead tycoon didn't need to be told twice. He stood, gave Dean a disproving glance, and stomped out of the room.

Dean followed him out, closing the door behind him. I turned toward the exit, but before I could move, I saw the handle to the observation room turn. The door opened, and in stepped Detective Dean.

He glared at me as he closed the door. "I thought I heard someone enter the room. What the hell are you doing here?"

CHAPTER TWENTY-SIX

My heart leapt into my throat, and I broke into a cold sweat. I hadn't planned what to say in the event I got caught snooping, so I panicked and said the first thing that came to mind. "I don't think he did it."

Dean blinked. "Excuse me?"

"Mr. Doherty. The lead guy. I saw his car in the parking garage. It's definitely not the one that fled the crime scene."

Dean's eyes turned to ice. "You seem to be confused about why I'm unhappy. *You're not supposed to be here.* This room is for detectives and commanding officers and on rare occasion witnesses to listen in on suspect testimony, not snooping rookie beat cops who don't have anything better to do. Now listen to me, and listen good. I don't know what your game is, but you're way out of your league. Detective Moss may have taken a shine to you, but I sure as hell haven't. Now if you don't get out of here in two seconds—"

"Detective Justice told me to come!" I blurted out.

Dean cocked his head. "So now you've made friends with Ogden, too? You must have quite the silver tongue."

My cheeks burned, not from anger but from embarrassment. I could barely stand to look Dean in the face. "No. Look, I'm terribly sorry. Justice told me to talk to you. I was heading to breakfast this morning through Miller's Creek Park when I found out about the murder, except I'd walked through the park last night, probably around the same time as that woman's death, and when Justice found out he insisted I tell you my story face to face, it's just that—"

"Whoa, whoa, whoa." Dean's face lost its frosty chill. "You were walking through Miller's Creek Park last night? At what time? Ten-thirty? Eleven?"

"Around eleven-fifteen. Like I said, Justice told me you'd want to interview me yourself, but when I got to your desk, you weren't there. This guy said you were in the interrogation room, and... I don't know. I just walked in here, and once I started listening I couldn't tear myself away. I know that was inappropriate of me, and if you need to censure me, I'll understand, but—"

Dean closed on me and took me by the shoulders, his hands strong and firm. It was only once I felt his touch that I also noticed a wet sensation tickling the corner of my eyes. I wasn't much of a crier, but the embarrassment of being caught by Dean combined with the lingering terror of learning what happened in the park were testing my limits.

"Hey. Slow down. It's going to be okay." He let go of me to pull the chairs out from the desk. He eased me into one before taking a seat himself. "Please. Take a deep breath, think carefully, and tell me *everything* that happened last night."

I actually took several deep breaths, but when I started talking, I found it hard to stop. I told him everything, more than I'd told Justice. I gave Dean every detail I could about my timing and path through the park, the smoky haze I'd seen, the sounds I'd heard, the squirrel that crossed the path. Dean poked and prodded, gently asking questions to get every last scrap he could out of me. Eventually, after encouraging me to dig deep and put myself in the moment, to draw every clue out of my mind that was humanely possible, he sighed, leaned back in his chair, and stared into the empty interrogation room. He stayed there for over a minute, quiet and pensive. He cut quite the striking figure against the one-way mirror.

Dean's demeanor had changed the instant I'd mentioned the park, but I didn't know if he was still angry with me. I spoke softly, hoping for forgiveness. "I'm sorry that I can't offer more. When I saw that purple aura, it gave me a weird feeling. I still don't know what it was, and something told me to get the hell out of there as fast as I could."

Dean waved a hand. "Don't be sorry. You're the closest thing we've had to a witness in any of these murders. And don't minimize what you saw. It may not mean anything yet, but you saw *something*. Eventually I'll make a connection..." He turned to me, his face warmer than it had been at any of the times I'd been around him. "That's something for me to chew on later. In the meantime, how are you?"

I blinked. "What do you mean?"

Dean gave me a sympathetic look. "I'm a detective, Officer. I kind of know how to read people. There's no shame in feeling scared, lost, guilty even. Those are all normal feelings when you've had a brush with death. You had the fortune, or misfortune perhaps, of responding to a homicide your first day on the job. You seemed to handle that well, but this is a different animal. When it's your life on the line, it weighs on you differently. It preys on you."

Something about the way he said it made me think Dean had been in a similar situation once upon a time—or someone he cared about had. Maybe someone close to him.

I nodded. "Yeah. It's a weird sensation. I don't like it."

Dean gestured at my clothes. "Based on your attire, I'm guessing you're off duty."

I nodded. "My shift starts at two."

"The hell it does," said Dean. "You're at Williams Street, right?"

"I am, but—"

"I'm calling Captain McGuire," said Dean. "I'm going to make sure she gives you the day off. Given what you've been through, there's no way you should be on duty today."

"That's really not necessary."

"It is," countered Dean. "You're in shock, whether you realize it or not. You need time to decompress. Take the day off. Rest. Eat. Sleep. Spend time with your loved ones, if you have any. The job will still be here for you tomorrow. Trust me, we're not that close to eliminating crime in New Welwic."

I couldn't help but smile a little. "I appreciate your concern, but—"

"This isn't a recommendation, it's an order." Dean stood and gestured toward the door. His tone brooked no argument.

I nodded as I stood. "Yes, sir. I'll do my best. Thank you."

I took a couple steps, but Dean's voice stopped me before I reached the handle. "One more thing, Officer Phair."

I turned. "Yes?"

Dean's face had gone cold again. "Your presence in the park? The tarot card murder? It doesn't excuse your behavior here. Stay out of the Gus Tovar case. Am I understood?"

A bit of color returned to my cheeks as I bobbed my head. "Yes, sir. Loud and clear."

Dean nodded, and I left.

CHAPTER TWENTY-SEVEN

I stood in front of my stove, pushing grains of rice around a pot with a wooden spoon. I glanced at the cookbook I'd checked out from the library, trying to figure out where I'd went wrong. I'd never made a risotto before, but I was pretty sure it was supposed to be a rice dish, not a soup. I'd added the stock and wine, but had I mixed up the measurements? The recipe said to use three cups in total, but had I used quarts instead? How much was in a quart anyway?

I sighed. After leaving the precinct, I'd forced myself to get something to eat, even though my appetite hadn't returned. It proved to be a smart choice as the act of putting food in my belly helped clear my head, although that might've been more due to the scoop of chocolate ice cream I treated myself to than anything else. With food still on the brain after leaving the restaurant, I stopped by the nearest branch of the New Welwic public library and snagged a few cookbooks, because I sure as hell didn't have any at home. I'd mulled over Dean's advice to spend quality time with the people I loved, and while I wasn't entirely sure I loved Cliff, he was the closest thing I had at the moment, not counting Nana of course, and given the sorry state of our refrigerator, I figured I could kill two birds with one stone, cooking Cliff a nice meal that we could share when he got off duty.

My plan started out successfully enough. I'd only gotten lost twice navigating the grocery store, and none of my paper bags exploded on the way home, comically pelting the sidewalk with oranges and flour and a dozen eggs. I'd even tucked everything within the fridge in a manner that seemed both practical and efficient, but the seas turned more turbulent after that.

For one thing, I wasn't totally sure I'd bought the right ingredients for the dish I'd picked out. The recipe called for short grain rice, but all grains of rice were short, weren't they? I'd never heard of foot-long rice, that was for sure. To make matters worse, once I checked the cookbook when I got home I realized I'd forgotten to buy mushrooms. Still, I had carrots, so I figured I could chop those up and throw them in at the last minute and it would be fine.

Nonetheless, it was the rice soup that concerned me the most. There really did seem to be about four times too much liquid, but then again, it was only half-past four. Dinner didn't need to be ready for another hour. Perhaps if I cranked up the heat, the excess liquid would boil off. But would that affect the rice? How much did rice grow? Was it like noodles, which kept swelling as long as you left them in the pot? Maybe I could fix it by scooping some of the liquid out, but how would I avoid losing the rice? I didn't think Cliff owned a colander.

As I stirred the stock, wine, and rice, a smell tickled my nose. Not a good one, either. Something burnt and smoky. I knew I was a bad cook, but even *I* couldn't set fire to soup. So what was it? Were grains of rice sticking to the bottom of the pot?

That's when I remembered the bacon.

I threw open the oven, and a cloud of thick smoke poured out. I recoiled, coughing and choking as the black mass boiled into the kitchen. I snagged a dish rag from a nearby counter and whipped it through the air, trying to clear the smoke to no avail, so I backed into the dining area, hacking and wheezing as I threw open the nearest window. Whatever wind currents there might've been outside had no interest in entering my apartment, so I ran into the bedroom and opened the window there in hopes of coaxing them in. The smoke had started to dissipate when I returned to the kitchen, but only enough to reveal the root cause of the problem was still in full effect. The bacon I'd set on a pan in hopes of freeing stovetop space for my risotto had carbonized, and what little fat remained hissed and popped angrily.

I bunched up the dish rag and dove into the smoke, reaching into the oven for the hot pan. I pulled it free and slammed shut the door, though now I'd only succeeded in moving the bacon into a spot where the smoke could travel freely in any direction. I stood for a moment in indecision, and the bacon took advantage. With a loud pop, a fat droplet of boiling hot grease sprang free from the pan and landed on my forearm. I howled and threw the pan halfway across the kitchen.

My aim wasn't terrible. The pan clattered as it hit the counter and slid into the sink, but the charred bacon husks and black-flecked fat within didn't find such a natural home. They went flying, splattering across the back wall and the cabinets above.

I clutched my arm and hissed. "Argh... Shit, shit, shit."

It was only then that I heard the thump of the front door. *"What in the world...?"*

I turned to see Cliff entering the apartment. His nose wrinkled at the smell, and his eyes were wide with shock—though at the scene before him or the act of me cooking, I might never know.

I sighed. "Great. This is all I need."

Cliff tore his eyes from the disaster and focused on me. He rushed over as he saw me holding my arm. "What's going on? Are you okay, Nell?"

I grimaced. "I'll be fine. Burned my arm. The damn bacon grease got me."

Cliff's gaze drifted to the stove. "Got a good portion of the kitchen, too."

For the second time today, I felt like I was on the verge of tears. "Oh, gods damnit! I was trying, Cliff. I really was!"

Cliff put his hands on my shoulders. "Hey, relax. It's okay. You're hurt, not injured right? The rest doesn't matter. It's just burnt bacon." His nose wrinkled, and he lifted a finger. "Give me a sec."

Cliff rushed to the closet and pulled out an electric fan I didn't even know he owned. The thing whined as he plugged it in, but I immediately felt a tug on my clothes as it pulled air through the bedroom and out the dining room window.

Cliff hurried back to me, his eyes soft and compassionate. "Sorry, Nell. I walked in, there was smoke everywhere. You caught me off guard. But honestly, forget the bacon. The important thing is you're okay."

I shook my head, feeling like a failure. "I was trying to do something nice for you. Cook you a real meal for once, and of course it goes to hell. This day is a disaster!"

Cliff squeezed my shoulders. "We can salvage something. It'll be fine. What are you doing here anyway? I could've sworn you had second shift. Am I so sleep deprived that I'm already forgetting things?"

"No, Cliff. I got sent home."

His eyebrows rose. *"Sent home?* What did you do?"

A burst of anger roiled through me. "I didn't do anything, Cliff. I got sent home because of what happened in the park last night."

"The park?" Cliff glanced at the windows again. "Oh. *That.* Well, yeah, but I didn't get sent home because of it."

My jaw fell. He couldn't be that dense, could he? "Cliff, I walked through the park. At eleven-fifteen. I was there. I was there when... When..." I couldn't bring myself to say it. Thinking about how close I'd come to falling into a serial murderer's snare took me back to the spot I'd found myself this morning, confronted with the truth, scared, panicked, in shock and in disbelief. My throat constricted and my heart began to race.

Cliff's face went slack. "My god. Nell, I didn't think about that. I'm so sorry. You must be a mess."

Cliff folded me into a warm embrace. He wrapped an arm around my back and interlaced the fingers of his other hand into my hair. As he pulled me in, he kissed me on the forehead. His arms were strong, and they pressed me tight against his well-muscled chest. For my part, I held on tight to him, too. I buried my face in his shoulder, breathing his scent, needing his strength. It was only once I felt safe in his arms that the wall behind which I'd been piling my emotions all day finally broke. Tears trickled into the cotton of Cliff's shirt, and with them flowed my fear and relief and guilt and sorrow that I'd thus far refused to let out.

Cliff rubbed my back and stroked my hair. "Hey, now. It's going to be okay. I'm here for you, Nell."

As I stood there, feeling the strength of Cliff's compassion, I realized Detective Dean was right. I needed to share in the strength of others, to spend time with them, to vent and laugh and love, to let them remind me I was still alive, still human. And it wasn't a desire, it was a need. I *needed* Cliff. Needed his love. Needed his caress. Needed his body, pressed hard against mine, and I needed it now.

I pulled my head free from Cliff's hand and kissed him, hard. I drank the taste of his lips, probing for his tongue with mine as I ran my hands up his back into the short hair at the nape of his neck. Cliff moaned and leaned into my kiss, his lips gentle, his hands drifting to my waist and onto the curve of my bottom. He pulled me against him, and I felt something stir beneath the fabric of his pants.

I pulled back, sucking air as I tore at the buttons on Cliff's shirt. Cliff seemed confused but receptive. "Uh... Okay. *Yeah.*"

Cliff snaked his hands under my shirt, caressing the bare flesh of my midsection as I grabbed him by the belt. I yanked on it, trying to unbuckle it as I pulled us through the open door of the bedroom. I stumbled and tripped, but Cliff caught me. We both slammed into the footboard, but neither of us cared. I threw open Cliff's shirt as he unbuttoned my jeans, each of us kissing and biting at each other's lips hungrily. My pants bunched around my thighs as I worked on Cliff's, neither of us willing to tear our mouths from each other long enough to focus on the clothes. Eventually, I slipped my jeans past my knees and kicked them off while tugging Cliff's trousers to the ground. His manhood sprung to attention, hard as a rock. I pushed him to the bed and jumped on top of him, a shudder running through me as I slid him between my legs.

Cliff moaned, and I did too as I slammed into him. I drove myself into Cliff hard and fast, planting one hand on his bare chest and the other on his shoulder. Cliff reached around and grabbed me hard by the cheeks, ramming me into him with even greater force. His mouth opened in ecstasy. He stiffened and a groan escaped his lips. He pulled me hard against him, but I kept gyrating. A rush built inside me, I rocked against him harder, and as I felt the rhythmic pulse of Cliff inside me, I screamed. A shudder ran through me, euphoria running rampant, everywhere except for the point where my thighs met my butt where a vicious cramp had started to take hold.

I flopped onto the bed next to Cliff, panting as I massaged the knot that had formed at the base of my glutes. Cliff lay there, too, breathing hard and not saying a thing.

To his credit, he broke the silence first. "Wow."

"Yeah."

We lay there for another thirty seconds, sucking air before Cliff tried again. "I guess we're good on that rain check you promised me."

I brushed my wild hair out of my face. "Yeah."

Cliff turned onto his side, wrapping an arm around my bare waist. "So... what now?"

I snorted as I stared into his warm brown eyes. "What do you mean, what now? Now I need to cook a new batch of bacon."

Cliff laughed. "That's not what I meant. What I meant was... are you okay?"

I pressed a hand against my ribcage, feeling my heart beat

hard inside. The romp had been cathartic, but the feelings that triggered it were still there, muted as they might be. "I think so. For now, anyway."

Cliff trailed his hands along the tops of my thighs, as if he hadn't been fully satisfied, regardless of what the state of affairs between his legs suggested. "Are you going to be okay going forward? I mean, when you get back to work?"

That was the million crown question. "I don't know, Cliff. I guess I'll have to wait and find out."

CHAPTER TWENTY-EIGHT

T he problem with being forced off duty was that I had to make the shift up the next day on what should've been my day off. To make matters worse, the precinct didn't have need of any officers for second shift, so I got stuck with the first one while Cliff got to sleep in for once. I drained a cup of coffee at home and another two at the precinct before I started to feel human.

Then again, making my shift up had auxiliary benefits I hadn't planned, first and foremost among that I didn't have to deal with Razi. Instead, I got paired with an old, doughy officer by the name of Weems whose pants probably had to be special ordered to fit his gut. Weems didn't talk much. He did most of his communicating through grunts and wheezes, and he wasn't a career training officer like Stonefist was. He didn't seem to care that I was a rookie, that I was female, or anything about me at all. He just bobbed his head and sat at his desk and shrugged when I asked him what we should be doing. Eventually, either thanks to a dark glare on behalf of the acting sergeant or by divine interference, he told me to get my things and meet him at

his squad car, number thirty-five. When I got there, I found
Weems in the passenger seat. He told me to drive, which was
both exciting and terrifying given my progress at the academy,
but he didn't have me go far. He pointed me a few blocks north-
east of the precinct, eventually telling me to park in a vacant lot
outside a pawn shop. Once I'd killed the engine, Weems settled
into his seat and closed his eyes, and it was only when I asked
him what we were doing that he told me to keep a lookout for
anyone suspicious going in and out of the shop. According to
him, the owner had complained of items going missing, and it
was up to us to keep an eye on it, but within two minutes of
Weems' explanation, his eyes fluttered closed again and a quiet
wheeze fluttered his lips with each of his breaths. If what he'd
told me about the shoplifting was true, he didn't seem too keen
on putting a stop to it.

I leaned back in my seat, the coffee I'd swilled doing a better
job at keeping me awake than Weems. I watched people head in
and out of the store without any real idea of what I was looking
for. The radio crackled a few times with calls for other units,
never waking Weems from his slumber. I'd started to wonder if
I'd do anything of value at all today when again the radio
crackled at half-past ten.

"Unit thirty-five, I have a message for Officer Phair. Please
respond."

I picked up the handset. "Officer Phair speaking. What
seems to be the problem?"

The radio crackled. "Detective Ginger Moss at the Fifth
Street precinct has requested you call her at your earliest convenience, Officer."

"Copy that." I set the handset down and glanced at Weems.

His chest rose and fell slowly, and his eyes hadn't so much as flickered at the sound of my voice.

I sighed and shook my head as I exited the vehicle. There was a payphone not far from the entrance to the pawn shop, so I hopped inside and picked up the receiver. When the operator responded, I gave her my badge number and asked for Moss at the 5th.

The phone rang a few times before a familiar voice answered. "Detective Moss speaking."

"Hi, Detective. It's Officer Phair."

Moss's voice wasn't what I'd call coarse, but it nonetheless softened upon hearing my reply. "Phair. Hey. Thanks for the call. Hopefully I'm not interrupting."

I snorted. "Are you kidding? I'm currently staking out a pawn shop while my partner for the day saws logs in the passenger seat of our car. I don't think I've ever seen anyone fall asleep so easily at ten-thirty in the morning."

Moss snorted. "It's a learned skill. Only the old-timers seem to have it down pat. I'm still working on it myself."

"So what can I help you with?"

Moss was quiet for a second before answering. "To be honest, I was off yesterday, and I just found out from Justice that you were in the park when the Tarot Card Killer struck. I wanted to check in and see how you were doing, woman to woman."

I shrugged, even though there wasn't anyone there to see me. "To tell the truth? Yesterday was rough. I held it together pretty well until I got back to my apartment, but Dean was right to make sure I got sent home. I had about ten different emotions coursing through me, and I sort of exploded all over my boyfriend when he got home." I thought about Cliff's and my frantic romp. "Uh... metaphorically speaking, of course."

"I get it," said Moss, her voice crackling over the phone. "I've been in a few situations where I feared for my life. I've always been good at keeping my head on straight while the fur is flying, but afterwards? You need to decompress, one way or another, and while the health benefits in this job aren't terrible, the department doesn't do a great job when it comes to moni- toring mental health. There's still an old boys' club attitude around here that any injury that can't be sewn together can be treated with a bottle of your favorite hooch, but I don't share that opinion. I guess what I'm trying to say is, if you ever need a sympathetic ear, I'm only a phone call away, even if it's after hours—or especially if it's after hours, given how full my plate's been lately."

"Thanks," I said. "I appreciate that. But at least for now, I feel okay. Maybe it's that I'm too tired to feel anything. I didn't think switching between shifts would be quite this jarring."

Ginger snorted again. "I'm not sure it's the shifts. Sounds like you have the same genetic condition I do where you can handle anything in the moment and deal with the baggage later, which is good for you. It's a vital survival trait for police work."

I thought about the terror I'd felt when Razi and I were called to New Age Alchemical to investigate Ilovar's shooting. As scared as I'd been in the car, I'd pushed my fear to the side and gotten the job done as soon as we arrived on the scene. "Seems like it."

"Anyway," said Moss. "I won't keep you—unless you want me to."

"What do you mean?"

"Well, doesn't sound like you're doing a whole lot at that

stakeout of yours, and I could use a hand again. I need to interview a Mrs. Elva Doherty for the Tovar case. Thought you might be willing to provide backup."

My mind ran to the scene I'd witnessed in interrogation six the previous day. "Is she related to a lead tycoon, by any chance?"

"She's the ex-wife of Cab Doherty, a metals magnate, yes. You've heard of the guy?"

I guess Dean hadn't filled her in on my spying session. I wasn't sure I wanted to tell her about it, either. "Look, Detective, I appreciate the offer, but after I spoke to Dean yesterday about the murder at Miller's Creek Park, he told me not to interfere in the Tovar investigation. I don't want to get in trouble."

I could almost hear Moss blinking in confusion. "You wouldn't be interfering. Like I said, I should have someone with me, just in case. Dean and Justice are both busy. If it's not you, I'll have to call someone else."

I glanced at the squad car, where Weems continued to drool over his shirt collar. I might've sighed.

"I won't tell Dean if you don't."

I'd told Moss the truth. I didn't want to get into trouble—but I also didn't want to waste my time staring across an empty lot hoping for a theft to occur before my waiting eyes. "Do you have an address?"

CHAPTER TWENTY-NINE

You know how every city has a neighborhood where the homes are surrounded by manicured topiaries, where people wear furs in the middle of summer, and where the dogs being walked have jeweled collars and wear sweaters of the finest wool? Well, the people who live in that neighborhood are the butlers and cleaning staff for the folks who live in Brentford, the oldest, swankiest, snootiest district in all of New Welwic.

The Brentford home I pulled up in front of was modest by the local standard. Only three stories tall, with marble columns on the main, a facade of rust red bricks on the stories above, and two dozen windows facing the street. Thick green creepers grew along trellises to the second story, and a pair of carved granite lions stood guard on either side of the portico. I parked the car on the circle drive in front, paved with more of the red bricks that made up the building itself. Moss still hadn't arrived, so Weems took the opportunity to settle into his seat and close his eyes once more. Apparently, he needed his eighteen hours a day of beauty rest. He was ugly enough to warrant it. Then again, perhaps I was being too harsh. Maybe he had narcolepsy.

I'd been in the drive about five minutes when I heard the deep rumble of Moss's Howardson Hornet. I got out of my squad car and waited for her on the steps as she pulled up behind me and killed the engine.

Her car door clunked as she stepped onto the bricks. Once again, she wore the stylish leather jacket I'd gotten so used to seeing her in, but she'd matched it with a pair of faded jeans and a simple gray tee. She gave me a nod. "Phair. Good to see you." She glanced into the car at my partner du jour, whose mouth hung open and whose eyes were closed. "I didn't ask over the phone, but what happened to Stonefist?"

"He has the day off, as far as I know," I said. "This is my makeup shift."

"Right." Moss pointed at the car. "This is?"

"Weems. Either he was up all night, or Mr. Sandman holds a grudge against him."

"How long have you been here?"

"Five minutes, give or take."

Moss shook her head. "I know I said that was a learned skill, but I'm impressed nonetheless. We'll leave him. You and I can handle anything we run up against."

"I don't know," I said, eyeing the house. "Don't people this rich have armed guards and attack dogs?"

Moss laughed. "All these folks might be criminals, but they don't need thugs to protect them. That's what the judicial system is for."

I blinked. "Wait... *what?* I was joking."

Moss waved me up the steps. "So am I—sort of. I mean, not *every* super rich person got their wealth by cheating and defrauding the little folk underneath them, but a non-negligible portion of them did. Dean, Justice, and I don't spend a ton of time investigating folks in Brentford—they don't get their hands dirty with murder often—but the fraud and white-collar guys basically live here. Not that any of the folks they indict ever see the inside of a cell, but still…"

Moss might've noticed the disappointed look on my face as we reached the front door, because she gave me a sheepish smile. "Sorry. I'm not normally so cynical. I guess seeing people living in solid gold houses awakens the curmudgeon in me." She rang the doorbell.

I tried to put the jaded take behind me and focus on what lay before. "So what's my role here?"

"Honestly?" said Moss. "Not much. I'll ask Mrs. Doherty the questions. Just keep your eyes open, and if for some reason the socialite takes a swing at me, you can hop on her and get a few good swings in before you break out the cuffs."

I heard footsteps, and the door opened. The guy who stood behind it had a head of neatly combed gray hair and wore a black suit. He looked at me the same way he might a door to door vacuum salesman. "May I help you?"

Moss flipped her badge. "Detective Moss, NWPD. This is Officer Phair. Is Mrs. Doherty in?"

The butler's right eyebrow lifted. "I'll have to check if she's busy…"

Moss slipped inside before the butler could lock her out. "That's a yes. We need to speak with her regarding an active investigation."

The butler swallowed air and frowned at Moss. I took advantage and sidled through the half-open door as well, which solicited another evil glance from the butler.

The man sighed. "Very well. Wait here. I'll go find her."

Jeeves shuffled off, and Moss snorted. "Didn't even offer us a drink. What a cad."

I used the opportunity to look around. The place was like my great-grandmother's house on steroids. The foyer was higher, the floor shinier, the furniture older and with a darker layer of varnish, but it all had that same old-world feel. A chandelier hung over us, with a hundred different crystal shards reflecting the light of the bulbs in as many different directions.

"You said this was Doherty's *ex*-wife, right?" I said.

Moss nodded. "Either she made out like a bandit in the settlement, or the guy's *really* loaded."

It didn't take long for me to hear footsteps again, but these were lighter and had a sharper clack than the butler's did. A woman appeared from around a marble pillar, gliding toward us in a chiffon dress that wasn't quite long enough to hide a pair of strappy heels. She clutched a half full wineglass in her right hand, and she held her left at her breast, her wrist back and her fingers pinched.

The woman was no spring chicken, but she was attractive nonetheless, with a full bosom, slender arms, and a face almost free of wrinkles. The piqued look she gave us as she stopped didn't do her any favors, though. "I understand you're with the police?"

"That's right." Moss flipped her badge and gave the introductions again. "You're Elma Doherty?"

"I am."

The woman didn't offer anything else, nor did she invite us further into the home. I could tell the interview was going to be as fun as having teeth pulled.

To her credit, Moss didn't let any of the anti-wealth sentiment she'd expressed to me on the stoop creep into her voice. "Sorry to bother you, Mrs. Doherty, but we're investigating the murder of one of your husband's business associates. We were hoping you might be able to answer some questions for us."

"Murder?" Elma's free hand flicked toward her face, and I thought she might start chewing on the nail of her pinky. "Are you suggesting my ex-husband *killed someone?"*

"Cab Doherty isn't a primary suspect in the investigation at this time, no."

"Oh." Elma's face fell, as did her voice. "And here I thought he might finally get what's coming to him. Shame."

Moss gave me a bug-eyed look, one I returned pound for pound.

Moss cleared her throat. "We understand you're divorced. Do you mind telling us about the breakup?"

Elma looked about the foyer with disinterest as she took a sip of her wine. "Will my doing so hurt Cab's legal defense?"

Moss shared another look of disbelief with me. "Well, the investigation is still ongoing. So... there's hope."

Elma perked. "Very well then. Cab and I divorced two years ago. He was an insufferable drip who cared more about his business than about me or anyone else. He worked late and rarely confided in me. I wish I could say he ignored me because he was with another woman, but I don't think he's ever expressed interest in flesh and blood. The only thing he cares about is stacked bills. Anything else?"

"You got this house in the divorce?" Moss gestured to the foyer.

"Well, I didn't buy it myself," said Elma.

"Did you receive any other assets?"

"You're talking about cash? I got enough, at least for the moment."

"No stock in Cab's companies? No bonds?"

Elma cocked her head. "None. Why? Are Cab's assets important to his investigation?"

If Elma hadn't yet figured out that we weren't here to get dirt on Cab, then I wasn't about to break it to her.

Neither was Moss. She smiled. "We're sorting through the facts. To be clear, you don't have any continuing financial arrangements with Mr. Doherty? He doesn't pay alimony?"

Elma looked down her nose at Moss. "I may not have sharpened my business acumen much under Cab's influence, but I learned to take my cash upfront, Detective."

"Probably a smart move," said Moss. "If you don't mind me asking one more thing before we leave: do you know anything about your husband's efforts to turn lead to gold?"

Elma blinked. "Excuse me?"

"You said you divorced two years ago. According to Mr. Doherty, he hired a woman by the name of Flora Lumaris at that time to find an artifact for him that might turn lead to gold. Did he talk to you about any of that?"

"He did not." Elma's face hardened. "What did you say this woman's name was? Lumaris? Is she attractive?"

That caught Moss off guard. "Well, she's an elf. She's reasonably good-looking I suppose. But that's not—"

Elma snarled and screamed. "*I knew it!* So he *was* cheating on me after all. That scoundrel! That snake! Welby? *Welby!* Get me the phone, this instant!"

Elma Doherty's wine sloshed from her glass as she stormed off in search of the butler. As she disappeared, Moss turned to me and spoke quietly. *"Oh. My. God."*

"Yeah," I said. "Even without knowing Mr. Doherty, I can guess why he divorced her. Did you get what you needed?"

"All that I'm going to get, I think." Moss nodded toward the door. "Let's get the hell out of here before she comes back. And if for some reason I later realize we need to talk to her again, I'm sending Justice."

A stiff breeze blew as I stepped onto the portico alongside Moss, whisking the stink of Elma Doherty's vacuous hate off me.

Moss shook her head. "That woman's a piece of work. And I thought I *already* held rich folk in low regard..."

"Divorce can change people, and not always for the better," I offered. "I saw that with my parents. The hate can run deep. It's not always easy to let go."

"All that may be true," said Moss, "but don't run to her defense. That woman was a walking sack of wet cats before her divorce. Tell me I'm wrong."

I snorted. "I won't argue that. Is she a suspect in the investigation now?"

Moss looked at me sideways. "How do you figure that?"

"Well, you decided she warranted an interview, even if only a short one. If you're looking for evidence rather than me just guessing why you're here though, she admitted that she hates Mr. Doherty's guts and that she has no lingering financial stake in his companies. If she wanted to screw him over, she might be willing to sabotage the research projects he was funding. Wouldn't be any skin off her back."

Moss stopped at the base of the steps and chewed her lip. "Believe it or not, spite alone usually isn't a strong enough motive for someone to commit murder. There are lots of people out there who hate somebody else's guts, but you have to have a screw loose to hate someone enough to murder them. Usually when people kill out of anger it's not premeditated. It's a spur of the moment sort of thing, like during bar fights or when a guy walks in on his wife nailing the neighbor. Almost every premeditated murder involves a motive beyond simply hurting the victim. Nonetheless, let's just say I'll be adding Elma's name to my big board rather than crossing her name off."

The wind gusted, bringing with it a clean scent of oncoming rain. In the thick of downtown New Welwic, it probably would've just pushed the gasoline exhaust and hot garbage stink my way. I guess exorbitant wealth could even buy fresh air.

Moss shivered in the breeze and stuffed her hands in her pockets. "You read a lot of mystery novels growing up, Phair?"

"Not especially," I said. "Why?"

"You have an analytically-inclined mind. Most of the patrol officers I come across are of the Stonefist and Weems variety, which is to say they're a few sprinkles sort of a sundae. You mind if I bounce some ideas off you?"

I couldn't lie. I liked spending time around Moss, and not just because her snazzy leather jacket and good looks gave her a stereotypical aura of cool. Moss treated me like her equal even though I wasn't, and the calls I'd made at her side were easily the most mentally stimulating work I'd had since starting. Then again, Dean had been clear in his instructions.

"Wouldn't this be something better suited to Justice or Dean?" I said.

"Sure," said Moss. "But they're not here. You are. I don't know about you, but I'm the kind of person who needs to throw ideas at the wall until one sticks. If I wait until I corner Alton to talk things over, I'll have lost my train of thought. Better to go over the evidence while its fresh."

I hesitated.

Moss, like the detective she was, noticed. "What's wrong? Is this about Dean telling you not to poke your nose into the investigation? Did you piss him off?"

I grimaced. "I think so."

Moss frowned and shook her head. "I bet this is about the Tarot Card Killer. He's been an ass these past few weeks. It's all he thinks about, and it's wearing on him. Spilling over into other areas of his life. After all, it's not your fault you happened to be walking through the park when that psycho broke thirty of that poor woman's bones."

"He did *what?*"

Moss's eyes widened. "You didn't know? Sorry. Look, the point is, don't worry about Dean. He's under a lot of stress. Just help me spitball ideas, okay? You don't even have to provide feedback if you don't want. You can smile and nod or shake your head. I just need to think out loud."

I'd never been very good at resisting advances I secretly wanted, as every boyfriend I'd been romantically involved with could attest to. "Okay. Shoot."

Moss stared into the bushes as she reached inside her brain. "First on the list of suspects in Gus Tovar's murder is Cab Doherty. He hired Tovar to develop a chemical process which could turn lead to gold, which would be a huge financial boon for him given his sprawling lead processing enterprise, but he doesn't have a strong motive for offing Tovar. For one thing, we haven't found evidence that Tovar unlocked the secret Doherty was after, and even if he had, Doherty's motive for killing the guy would be to avoid paying him a cut of his earnings. Someone has to be pretty miserly to use murder to increase his earnings by twenty or thirty percent."

"And on theoretical money, to boot," I said. "We're talking about money Doherty *could* earn, not that he has earned."

Moss nodded. "Then there's his ex-wife. I hadn't seriously considered her a suspect, and I still don't, but she has motive. Hate, which as I mentioned, isn't a strong impetus for someone to kill. Not to mention I can't picture her as the murdering type. She's too vapid to pull something like that off."

"She might've hired someone," I offered.

"Doubt it," said Moss. "That requires finesse to keep it under wraps, and you have to know the right people. Unless her butler used to run guns for the mob, I doubt she'd even know where to start. That leaves us with that elven woman."

"Who?" I said.

"Flora Lumaris," said Moss. "The owner of the archeological firm, or geological enterprise. Whatever you want to call it. She claims she found a sample of the so-called Philosopher's Stone, though if we're to believe her it's a mineral like any other, albeit it an extremely rare one."

I shrugged. "Sorry. I don't know anything about her other than the bits and pieces I heard from you and Roncalli."

"Justice interviewed her yesterday," said Moss, rubbing her chin. "She thinks Tovar stole her mineral, but she doesn't have proof. Whoever took it, it was a professional job, not amateur hour. They didn't leave many clues."

"Speaking of Roncalli," I said. "Isn't he still a suspect? I mean, he put himself at the crime scene, and we found his gun that he claimed he didn't own."

Moss sighed. "Sadly, he's off the list. We got ballistics back on his revolver, and it's not a match. The thing has never been fired, so far as we can tell. On top of that, we found a witness who put him on a street corner about ten blocks from New Age Alchemical at the time of Tovar's death. He's out."

I wracked my brain. "What about other people in Tovar's life? His family and friends. Maybe he wasn't murdered over his work. Could be someone wanted him dead for another reason."

Moss tipped her head back and forth. "Could be, but I'm not buying it. We did a little digging on the guy. No wife, no kids, no social life we could uncover. Pretty much a workaholic. And you have to remember the safe in his laboratory was open, implying something was stolen. Personally, I think it's the Stone. He stole it from Lumaris and someone stole it from him in turn. It's the only thing that makes sense. Either Lumaris stole it back, or..." Moss's brow furrowed, and she grew silent.

"Or what?" I asked.

"Well, Lumaris made it sound as if the theft of the Stone was a professional heist, right? What if Gus hired the thieves to steal the Stone from Lumaris but couldn't pay them? Or alternatively, what if the thieves were smarter than the types who pull your average smash and grab? Maybe they did a little digging after the fact and realized how valuable the Stone was, so they returned to Tovar and demanded he cut them in on the take. He refused, so they shot him and stole back the Stone. They could be trying to extort Doherty as we speak."

"Has he reported that?"

"No, but if he thinks the thieves might destroy the Stone or go to a competitor, he might be unwilling to involve us." Moss snapped her fingers a few times. "I like this. This makes sense. We'll have to touch base with Doherty. Grill him again and see if he cracks. If he doesn't, we might have to talk to his driver to see if he's had any clandestine meetings he hasn't told us about. In the meantime, we'll have to return to Lumaris. See if we can pry loose more details about the guys who robbed her. Maybe we'll recheck Gus's finances, too. See if we can figure out if he paid the thieves directly or if he used New Age Alchemical funds instead."

Moss smiled. "See? What did I tell you, Phair? You're the grease I needed to get the wheels in my head spinning."

I smirked. "You're calling me greasy?"

"In the best kind of way. Thanks for the help. Guess I'd better let you get back to it." Moss clapped me on the arm as she headed to her Hornet.

As she started her engine, I stared at the squad car. Weems still slumped in the passenger seat, sawing away at invisible logs. I wasn't sure what *it* Moss was referring to, but I was pretty sure the rest of my day would be downhill from here.

CHAPTER THIRTY-ONE

I woke up the next morning while it was still pitch black out, the incessant ringing of my alarm clock refusing to let me melt back into my pillow. With a groan and eyes barely cracked, I dragged myself into the kitchen where I found the toaster humming and Cliff already stirring eggs in a pan. I gave him a kiss as I poured us some coffee from the pot we'd made the night before and sat down at the table. We'd both pulled first shift for the next three days, so for once we'd be able to share some meals.

Time wasn't on our side for breakfast though. We plowed through our eggs and toast and scurried off into the night, walking through the park and onto Williams Street. As far as I knew, our relationship remained a secret, so I waited by the nearest intersection for a minute as we approached the precinct, not wanting to be seen walking through the front doors at my beau's side.

I couldn't wait long, though. By the time I got inside, changed, and walked to the briefing room, the clock was only a minute shy of six. Cliff was already there, looking bright eyed and bushy-tailed in his navy blues, as was Razi, looking decidedly more gruff from his seat in the back. Razi gave me the evil eye, and his scowl suggested I'd done something to grieve him without knowing it, but I ignored him and Cliff alike as I took a free chair toward the front. The shift sergeant was there, a military type by the name of Anderson with a crew cut and a muscular neck. He waited behind the lectern, staring at the clock as the hour's final seconds ticked away.

Just like Zaxby, he cleared his throat as the minute hand reached the hour. "Morning, officers. Not too much to go over today, thankfully. We had a fire overnight at an office building on the corner of Mount Warren and Third. Firefighters arrived at the scene at about four. They've contained the blaze, but they've only started to canvass the wreckage. To the best of our knowledge, nobody was inside at the time, not even any cleaning staff. We don't anticipate casualties, but it's possible someone who wasn't on the official registry was inside doing god knows what. We'll know soon enough, I guess. Arson detectives will be on the scene shortly. We'll need a few of you to help direct traffic outside, and it's possible arson will call in for help throughout the day.

"We also received word from the narcotics division at HQ about a new tactic dope dealers in midtown are using to shift product. Apparently, the dealers have recruited some of the homeless to act as intermediaries. The transients set up shop at street corners, under bridges, the usual, begging for change. Buyers come up, drop off their payment, and walk off. They come back a few minutes later, at which point the beggars have shifted the product into their change cups. The buyer picks up the product as if they were dropping off more change, and nobody's the wiser. The point is, if you never had a reason to shoo the homeless off public property, now you do. Be especially wary of transients who have containers in which to hide the goods. If you see anyone with a guitar case, a satchel, anything of that nature, be sure to investigate."

The sergeant shuffled some papers, scanning the pages as he did so. "Let's see here. That's the important stuff. Now to assignments. Frum and Briggs, you're on traffic at the fire. Peebles and Wixom, I need you to respond to a call from a grocer on Seventh about some possible storefront vandalism. The rest of you are on peacekeeping duty at Rucker Park. For those of you who don't know, there's a rally scheduled to start at nine on the south lawn by a group known as Everyone Counts, except they spell it like the number one instead of the word. Cute, right? Their permit lasts from nine to twelve, but chances are some of them will be there early and they won't disperse until after lunch. Usually, these things draw counter protestors, and there are always those who like to instigate violence for no other reason than to sow chaos. Be sure to stop by the armory for shields, helmets, and vests, and stay safe out there. Roll out!"

I stood as everyone shuffled toward the exit. Cliff gave me a smile as he passed, but I didn't return it—not because I didn't want to, but because Razi was bearing down on me like a freight train, and the scowl *he* wore could block out the sun.

"Well, well," said Stonefist. "Glad to see you're finally back."

Finally? I'd been off duty a single day, but I didn't bring that up with Razi. I figured the first words I spoke to him shouldn't incite an argument. "Good to be back, Officer Stonefist. For the record, it wasn't my choice to be taken off duty." Which was true, even if I'd later realized the value of Dean's decision to have me sent home, as well as appreciated the events that transpired during it.

Razi snorted. "Sure it wasn't."

I'd already committed to a non-combative morning, but I couldn't help myself. I lifted an eyebrow. "Are you aware of what happened?"

"I heard," said Razi. "You happened to be in the park the same evening that tarot card crackpot offed some lady. So what? You didn't stumble into him. He didn't hold you at gunpoint. As I heard it, there's no reason to believe you were anywhere near the guy when the murder occurred, and yet for some reason you get a day off because of it? Please."

I gritted my teeth, feeling the anger Razi was so good at generating roil in the pit of my stomach. "First of all, it wasn't a day off. I made up my shift yesterday morning while you were free to sleep in, and second of all, the Captain made the right call ordering me to stay home. I was emotionally compromised. It was a draining day."

Razi rolled his eyes. *"Emotionally compromised...* Remember when we met I said I didn't care if you were black, white, blue, gray, male, or female so long as you got the job done? I'm rethinking that now."

The anger had warmed from a simmer to a boil. "What are you saying? That if I was a man, it wouldn't bother me to be turned into filet by a serial murderer?"

Razi sneered at me, thumbs in his belt loop. "I'm saying it's all a load of bull, and you know it. This wasn't about you being in the park. It's about you cozying up to the detectives spearheading the investigation."

I blinked, unable to believe what I was hearing. "Are you

honestly suggesting I *faked* placing myself near a murder to get closer to Detective Dean and his crew?"

"What I'm *suggesting*," said Razi, "is that you either don't have a clue what your role as a patrol officer is, or you're refusing to accept it. Luckily for you, I have a feeling today is finally going to provide you with a helpful lesson. Now come on. We have items to check out from the armory."

CHAPTER THIRTY-TWO

Rucker Park was one of the city's oldest and largest, with dozens of acres of wooded paths, botanical gardens, and greenways. There were playgrounds for children, volleyball courts, tennis courts, and scrummage fields, but for the time being, I found myself on the wide expanse of lawns at the park's southern edge. The grass was a vibrant green and smelled as if it had been freshly cut. Birds trilled in the trees at the edge of the lawn, and the occasional sound of children's laughter drifted over from the nearest playground to the north. If I were stretched out on a blanket with a book in hand and Cliff at my side, the morning might seem idyllic, but instead I stood there, shield in hand and a baton in the other, watching as a crowd of protestors gathered near the street.

I wasn't very tuned-in politically, so I hadn't heard about the Everyone Counts movement, but I caught the gist of it from the makeup of those gathered. I saw ogres and trolls, dwarves and elves, half-giants, faeries, and even the occasional pixie flitting in the air above the crowd, through given their reputation for mischief, they might've been looking for marks whose wallets they could swipe. Many of the protestors held homemade signs and banners, some promoting the movement's eponymous slogan, others preaching various egalitarian creeds: equality, justice, and fairness for all.

I wasn't blind or dumb. I knew some of New Welwic's racist past: neighborhoods that had been red-lined to exclude immigrants and half-breeds, the lack of a police presence in slums, mayors and commissioners and even police captains who were invariably human or who only had trace amounts of elven blood running through their veins, all of them men. But I didn't think the prejudice against non-humans was a particularly big issue anymore. New Welwic had been around for so many centuries, with human and non-humans mixing for the length of it, that I'd be surprised if anyone whose parents hadn't moved to the city within the last twenty years wasn't of mixed ancestry. The gods only knew the full extent of what races went into making me, even if I did pass as human in everything except the slightly too warm hue of my skin.

Then again, whether or not the folks who'd assembled were mixed breeds perhaps didn't matter because for all intents and purposes they *looked* like full-blooded dark elves and dwarves and trolls, and maybe it was appearances that made all the difference.

Pushing aside the validity of the movement or the necessity of the protest, those assembled didn't seem like they had any intention of starting a fight. As far as I could tell, none of them were armed with anything more than the sticks which they'd attached their signs to, and as I stood there, watching their numbers swell on the grass as they chanted and waved their banners at passing cars, the worst offense they seemed guilty of was spilling off the assigned protest area into the parking lot and the neighboring greens.

For his part, Razi stood nearby, grunting and swearing about how the armored vest he wore made him sweat and itch. He didn't do anything dumb, like rushing the crowd with his pistol out or yelling insults at the protestors to incite them. It was a refreshing change from the intimidation tactics I'd seen him unleash on everyone from bartenders to candy salesmen, but then again, half the precinct's first shift officers were standing beside us, so perhaps his attitude change was more about keeping up appearances than anything else.

As the first hour of the protest shifted into the second, I too felt the weight of the armor and the heat of the sun beating on my neck. I shifted, my feet starting to ache, and I wished I really did have a blanket so I could lay down on the grass and rest my legs.

Razi noticed me squirming. "We're not even halfway through this peacekeeping party, Phair. Don't tell me you're ready to throw in the towel."

I snorted. "As if you haven't spent the past hour grunting and scratching your privates."

Razi smiled. "Maybe I have, but could be we're in luck. We might not be standing around much longer. Take a look."

Razi pointed, and I followed his finger. A few cars had pulled into the parking lot, and from them a group of regular human Joes emerged. They hung on their half open doors, pointing and yelling at the protestors. I wasn't close enough to hear more than a general din, but for their part, the protestors weren't having any of it. They yelled back and shook their signs and jabbed accusatory fingers in the direction of the newcomers, but each group kept a good dozen paces away from the other.

"Great," I said. "Agitators. Just what we need."

Razi smirked. "What? You're not excited at the prospect of actually doing your job?"

"You're jazzed about quelling a possible riot?"

Razi's smile spread. "It's all about keeping the peace. Protect and serve, Phair."

As if on cue, I saw something fly out of the corner of my eye. I didn't catch what it was. It might've been a rock or an apple, but from the reaction of the protestors, whatever it was landed among them. A hole formed in their midst, and the tenor of their chanting turned more hostile. The sign shaking and shouting intensified, but it was one young troll breed who took action. He rushed forward and swung a stick that may or may not have previously held a sign at one of the agitator's cars. I couldn't hear the snap and crunch of the taillight breaking, but I saw a shimmer as sunlight reflected off the shower of glass slivers that flew into the air.

Razi shoved me in the shoulder as the rest of the beat cops around me surged forward. "That's our cue. Come on, rookie."

We ran across the open expanse of field in front of us, and in that short moment, the situation at the intersection of the park and the parking lot descended into chaos. Several more fist-sized items took flight, and I heard someone cry out in pain. A window on the parked cars exploded as a rock flew through it. A punch thrown by one of the automobile gang knocked a protestor to the ground, and people started to run in all directions, even before they saw us coming.

We'd run through minimalist drills on crowd control at the academy, so I knew the basic principles. Our goal was to separate the rival factions to keep the violence from escalating and to subdue individuals who refused to stand down. It seemed simple enough in theory, but as soon as I found myself inside the perimeter of the crowd, theory went out the window.

There were people everywhere. Angry people, yelling, pushing, shoving. Fearful people, screaming, crying, running. Some people fought, others fled, and it wasn't immediately clear which was which because as many people ran into the melee as from it. Who was on which side was only clear based on their racial makeup, but it became immediately obvious to me that we were about two minutes too late to separate any one faction from the other.

As I tried to gather my wits, someone screamed in my ear. Someone else slammed into me, knocking me two feet back. Some of the other officers also took shoves and jostles, and they responded quicker and more forcefully than I did. Shields became battering rams, pushing people back, slamming them to the grass and concrete. Batons swished through the air, some making that *whisk whisk* sound as they chopped air, others landing with meaty thuds and producing pained cries.

Somewhere behind me I heard Razi's bellow, telling people to back up or get wrecked, but despite the maelstrom around me, I felt disconnected from the action, as if I was a higher being observing from a celestial plane. My feet stuck rooted to the trampled grass, my shield and baton arms frozen in ice, yet all around me chaos reigned. People shouted in anger and fear. My fellow officers lashed out indiscriminately, and still I stood there. I didn't fear for my safety. Anger didn't boil inside me. I just took it all in, and all I could think about was my role—*our role*—as police officers. We were here to keep the peace—Sergeant Anderson's words as well as Stonefist's. Was that what we were doing? We hadn't started the fight, but we sure as hell weren't stopping it, either.

An overweight ogre teen barreled past me, tearing me from my reverie. He ricocheted off another officer and stumbled to the ground. The officer in question apparently took it personally, as he ditched his shield and jumped on the teen's back, wrestling him to the ground as he tried to regain his footing. The officer wrapped his arm around the husky teen's neck and grabbed the baton with his free arm. The poor kid gurgled and hacked as he collapsed to the grass, but the officer didn't lay off him.

Something in me snapped, and I sprang into action. I slammed the officer with my shield and knocked him off the kid. The officer rolled into the dirt and sprung up, baton gripped tight and ready for action. His nostrils flared as he stared past me. "Who the hell did that?"

"I did," I said over the din. "You were choking that kid."

The kid, still coughing and gurgling, stood and took off as quickly as he could. The officer glanced at him as he darted off, his face beet red. "You let him get away! *What the hell is wrong with you?*"

I couldn't believe *I* was the one getting screamed at. "He couldn't breathe. He could've died."

The officer's face contorted in rage, but before he could yell at me more, I felt myself yanked back. I spun, my baton still in hand, half-expecting to be confronted by a group of the teen's ogre friends, but it was Razi who stood there, his face as red and angry as the officer's. "What in the name of the gods do you think you're doing, Phair?"

I still had my dander up, and being grabbed by the arm and spun around brought back images of Mick and his abuse. "What does it look like I'm doing? I was trying to make sure that guy didn't get seriously hurt!"

"By knocking him to the ground?" shouted Razi.

"What?" It took me a second to understand. "Not *the officer*. That kid he was strangling."

I'd seen Razi's anger and frustration firsthand. I'd even seem him surprised, but for the first time, he looked at me absolutely dumbfounded. "How do you still not get it?"

The crowd around us had started to disperse, with only a few officers still breaking up fights or pushing back protestors. A few of the dumber folks on both sides still yelled and pointed fingers, but most had fled. "Get what, Stonefist?"

"Protect and serve, Phair. I told you that a minute or two ago."

"Exactly," I said, feeling my cheeks burning. "That's what I was doing. I was protecting that poor kid."

"We protect each other, you idiot!" screamed Razi. "Gods! We're not here to coddle a bunch of lawless rioters and thugs! We're here to protect normal law-fearing folk from them, and above all else, we're here to protect each other! We have each other's backs. We protect ourselves from criminals as readily as from lawsuits and prosecution. The brotherhood comes first. *Always!* How have you not figured that out yet?"

I knew Razi's outlook on policing. He'd made it clear from our first shift, and yet I couldn't quite convince myself he'd seen what happened. "What about protecting each other from making a terrible mistake, huh? Where does that factor in?"

Razi's brow furrowed. "What the hell are you talking about?"

"That officer was about to make a horrible mistake. He could've killed someone, innocent or not. What then? Even if you don't give a shit about anyone else's wellbeing, I prevented one of our own from shooting himself in the foot."

Razi shook his head angrily. "He wasn't making the mistake. *You* are by not toeing the line. We serve the folks whose taxes fund the department. We protect them and everyone else who obeys the law, but we protect each other *first*. We do that by always sticking up for each other, no matter what, no matter the circumstance, and when the shit hits the fan, we stand by each other. We make our brothers and sisters in blue look good at their worst moments, because we know they'll do it for us in turn. *That's* what this brotherhood is all about, and if you don't get that through your thick skull real soon, you're going to find a boot in your ass and the door locked up tight behind you. I'm a patient man, Phair. I've taught all kinds and turned them into functional officers, but I can't help the blind, so open your eyes."

Razi stormed off, heading toward a group of patrol officers who were still working to disperse the remains of the crowd, but I stood still, my feet once again having grown roots. My teeth ground together in rage, but there was more than anger toward Razi bubbling. I was embarrassed and sad, because my eyes *were* open.

All the way.

CHAPTER THIRTY-THREE

I sat in the precinct break room, letting the heat from a cup of coffee leech into my hands. I stared into the depths of the liquid, at the ripples that undulated from the center of the cup with each of my heavy sighs. As dark as the brew was, it wasn't as black as my thoughts. Past the thin surface of the drink lay a swirling tornado: folks running, rocks flying, my fellow officers unloading upon terrified civilians with batons, and at the center of it all, I stood.

Me. I was a part of it. As much the problem as the solution.

I heard footsteps, but I didn't look up. A pair of glossy shoes entered my field of vision, and I heard a familiar voice. "There you are."

It wasn't Razi's. I looked up to find Cliff crossing to the coffee pot. "Save a spot for me on the couch. Boy, my feet could use a rest. I feel like I haven't sat down all day."

Cliff pulled a paper cup off the stack. The pot gurgled as he filled it, and the carafe clacked as he slid it back into the machine. Cliff held the cup close and inhaled the coffee's scent, sighing in pleasure despite it holding all the olfactory joy of an old tire.

Cliff took a sip. "Ahh. That hits the spot." He sat next to me. "I don't know about you, but my TO and I just finished booking four different people. One assault against an officer, two on inciting violence, and another for lewd conduct while resisting arrest. That one was kind of funny, though it involved exposed male genitalia, so perhaps it's not a fit topic of conversation. Good thing you were on the other end of the lawn. Suffice it to say I hope that's the most action we see for the rest of the shift. I'm not sure we could fit many more in the cells, anyway. We need some to make bail first."

I continued to stare into my coffee, as chatty as a corpse.

Cliff shifted forward. "Hello? Did you hear me?" His voice softened, and it grew quieter. "You doing okay, Nell? Did you take a punch out there or something?"

I didn't feel like talking, but if not with Cliff, then whom? I looked up from my brew and locked eyes with him. "Cliff... we're not helping anyone."

In the two-plus months I'd known him, I'd unearthed most of Cliff's admirable qualities: his rugged good-looks, his physical strength, his gentle nature, and his inherent sense of right and wrong. A razor sharp wit wasn't among them, though, and the befuddled look he responded with proved it. "Huh?"

I sighed. "We've talked about why we each joined the force, Cliff. You said you'd always wanted to be an officer, but that wasn't the case for me. My Nana was a captain, and she's a huge influence in my life, perhaps the biggest I have, but... I made the choice to serve because I was adrift at sea. I was floating without purpose, without a heading, and after seeing the people my

Nana helped throughout her life, myself included, I thought that's what I'd been missing. Even though I didn't know what to do with my life, I thought I might feel better about it if I spent it helping others instead of wallowing in self pity. Making a difference. Picking people up when they'd been pushed down. Maybe that's still what I need, but I have no idea because *I'm not doing that*."

Cliff squinted. "Is this about the rally?"

"Yes. No. Sort of," I said. "It's mostly about Razi. He keeps getting under my skin. Telling me we're here to protect each other more than people out there who really need it. Telling me things about the department that sound cruel and indifferent but that I can't convince myself are without merit, not based on what I've seen with my own two eyes. The rally's part of the larger whole."

Cliff shifted in his seat. "I'll admit, things got out of hand pretty quickly, but I think we reacted in the way we were supposed to. We didn't intervene until violence broke out among the protestors. I guess you could argue we should've been down there sooner, right among them the whole time, but there was no reason to believe anything was going to happen until someone threw a rock."

Cliff seemed to be missing that my crisis of confidence wasn't due to the rally. The rally was just the straw that broke the griffon's back. Even pushing aside my interactions with Razi that he hadn't been a party to, though, I couldn't believe Cliff hadn't seen the chaos with the same glasses I had.

I set my coffee aside. "Cliff, how can you possibly think we reacted the right way? I agree, we should've acted as soon as those counter protestors arrived, but once we got into the crowd, everything devolved into madness. There were people screaming and crying. I saw officers beating people for the simple crime of standing nearby. For the love of all gods, one of them jumped on a kid and started choking him. He could've died!"

Cliff's eyebrows rose. "I didn't see that, so I can't comment. And yeah, things got crazy, but I don't know how else we're supposed to react when everyone loses their minds. We needed to get control of the situation. Sometimes that means using force."

My brow furrowed. "I wouldn't say *everyone* lost their minds. I'd say a bunch of racist dirtbags showed up and started chucking rocks into peaceful protestors, and *then* they all freaked out when we rushed them in body armor."

Cliff shrugged. "I don't know what you saw, but from where I stood, it looked like both sides were itching for a fight."

I frowned, and my jaw tightened. *"Both sides?* Don't give me that crap. The rally was perfectly peaceful until the other side showed up."

Cliff stood. "What do you want me to say, Nell? I guess I didn't see it the way you did. The sergeant predicted violence might break out, it did, and we used necessary force to stop it. That's part of police work. You can't solve all problems peacefully. Some people won't listen to reason, and large groups of people almost never do. You ever heard of the term groupthink? People act irrationally when they're part of a mob."

"But that's what I'm saying, Cliff. The protestors weren't a mob at first. They were just a crowd until outside agitators turned them into one, and for the record, we started out as a crowd, too. It wasn't until we ran into those people that *we* turned into a mob. We just happened to be better armed than they were."

Cliff sighed and gave me a sympathetic look. "I don't know what to tell you, Nell. I've got to get back to work. I'll see you later."

I watched Cliff exit the break room, and while anger simmered under my surface at the simple fact that he hadn't agreed with me, more than anything I was disappointed. I *knew* Cliff, at least I thought I did. I figured if anyone would agree that our department's response had been overly violent and reckless it would be him, yet he hadn't seen a thing wrong with what we'd done.

His words echoed in my head. *We used necessary force to stop it. That's part of police work.* In a sense he was right. I wasn't naive. I knew some situations could only be solved with force, but it was the question of what was necessary and what wasn't that bothered me. And sadly, as I looked back on the past few days, I couldn't think of a single use of force by myself or Stonefist that *had* been necessary. Not one.

I shook my head. I knew somewhere beyond the break room door Razi was waiting for me, eager to rub my concern in my face, and I couldn't leave. I didn't want to face whatever I had to do next, because it wasn't what I'd signed up for. Maybe Nana's experience had been a fluke. I'd always assumed things had changed in the decades since she'd served, but I thought they'd changed for the better.

I couldn't ignore my problems. I'd learned that lesson many times over. I had to confront them and solve them, one way or another. But the best way I could think of to solve my current problem—quitting—would only create a host of others.

It also wouldn't be the right thing to do. The moral, responsible thing.

Over the murmur of my thoughts, I heard the station's PA. "Call for Officer Phair. Please report to the nearest phone."

With a sigh, I pushed myself to my feet and headed out.

CHAPTER THIRTY-FOUR

I picked up the phone at the front desk and waited while the operator connected me. I half expected to hear Detective Moss's voice again, but it was a cooler, masculine voice that answered. "Detective Dean speaking. Is this Officer Phair?"

I composed myself quickly. "Yes, sir. What can I do for you?"

"Do you have a pad and a pencil available?"

I dug them out of my pocket. "Yes, sir."

"I'm going to give you an address. Fifty-seven forty Beaumont Avenue. There's a parking lot next to it. I need you to meet me there."

"Yes, sir." I jotted the address down. "I'll be right there."

Dean hung up before saying another word. I returned the phone to its receiver, confused but intrigued. An abandoned parking lot might be a great place for a clandestine meeting, but not in the middle of the day. Nonetheless, I couldn't think of any other reason Dean would want to meet with me outside his precinct.

I shook my head, curiosity momentarily pushing aside the feelings of doubt about my job. I ventured into the maze of desks on the main floor, looking for the one Razi and I shared. Sure enough, I found my TO there, his chair tilted back and his feet propped up.

He flashed me a smile. "There you are. Thought you might've gotten lost. I know the ladies room is stuffed in a corner, but you should've been able to learn your way back by now."

I took a deep breath and unclenched my teeth. "Detective Alton Dean called. We need to meet him at a parking lot on Beaumont."

Razi snarled. "Damnit, Phair. What did I tell you? You need to stop sticking your nose into investigations that don't concern you. That's not your job, and with the way you're shaping up, it's never going to be."

I wasn't ever in a mood for Razi's bullshit, but with thoughts of giving up on policing entirely swirling through my head, I didn't pull any punches. "Dean called *me*, Stonefist. He gave specific instructions. Didn't tell me what was going on, just to be there. Made it seem urgent. If you don't want to go, fine. I'll take the car and you can wait here, but if you try to keep me from following a direct order, I'll report you to Dean and the captain both."

I thought Razi might stand up, push his gut into me, and bellow some hot air into my face about respect and protocol, but instead he just snorted. "No need to get all huffy. Let's go see what your boyfriend has in store for you today."

Razi and I headed to the lot. Once again, Razi took the wheel, and after giving him the address, he headed out. We didn't say a word to each other as we drove, and I barely even looked in his direction. After ten minutes of silence, Razi pulled off Beaumont into a parking lot that was a lot less abandoned than the one I'd fabricated in my head. Razi pulled into one of only two available spots, but despite the dense population of cars, of people there were only a few to be seen.

I stepped out of the patrol car and headed across the lot to where Dean, Moss, and Justice stood. Razi's heavy clomps followed me, but I ignored the man as I stopped outside the group of three. "Officer Phair reporting, detectives. What can I do for you?"

Moss shot me a smile, but it was Dean who responded in a matter-of-fact way. "Officer Phair, the night of Gus Tovar's murder you reported you heard the roar of an engine, rushed to the alley behind New Age Alchemical, and spotted a car speeding off."

"Yes, sir." I'd reported it to him directly the night of.

"Do you think you could identify that car again if you saw it?"

I gave the question a brief consideration. "Definitely."

Dean flashed me a rare smile. "Good. We think it's in this lot. Let's see if you agree."

Moss tipped her head at me, as if to say, "Go on." I turned and gazed into the lot. I was certain the car had been black, which narrowed it to about fifteen vehicles, although there were a couple more present that were a dark navy. I'd reported to Dean that I thought the vehicle might've been a Pearl Townsman, but I wasn't enough of a car guru to know for sure. I stepped away from the group, leaving Razi behind me as I scanned license plates for anything that started with the letters AF.

A half dozen cars from the detectives I stopped at one of the navy ones. The back plate read AFG845, but the back of the vehicle was more boxy than the one I remembered, and as I peered around the side, I didn't find any fender skirts over the wheels.

I straightened and kept going. Eventually, I found one of the black vehicles whose plate didn't start with AF, but instead read AET944. The vehicle was a Pearl Motors Voyager, not a Townsman, but the car had the rounded back end and fender skirts I remembered. I moved to the driver's side and inspected the panels. I didn't see any obvious scratches in the paint, but as I knelt and took a closer look, I caught sight of an uneven gleam along the back door. I lifted my hand to block the sun, and without the bright light, I could see it. A stretch of black that wasn't the same as the rest. Someone must've repaired the door, but instead of repainting the whole thing, they'd only touched up the scratch in question.

I stood and waved to the group. "Detectives! I think I've found it."

They walked over, Dean at the head of the pack. He nodded. "This it?"

Given the description I'd given him, I couldn't imagine Dean hadn't already figured that out, especially if he suspected the car was in the lot, but I played along. "Yeah. I must've gotten the plates wrong. E instead of F, but I'm pretty sure this is it."

Dean regarded me with hard eyes. "Pretty sure isn't going to cut it, Officer. Is this the car or not?"

Moss and Justice looked at me without saying anything, and Razi lingered behind them, looking unsure of himself. I took one more look at the car and took a deep breath. "I'm sure this is the vehicle. There's a scratch on the side that looks to have been repainted. It's the one."

Dean stood there for a moment without saying a thing. Eventually he turned and nodded to Moss and Justice. "Alright. The suspect is Joseph Knalnut, owner of Knalnut's Fine Jewelry down the street. Justice, you're with me. Moss, bring up the rear. Officers? Come along. You can guard the doors in the event anyone tries to leave unexpectedly. Got it? Let's move out."

CHAPTER THIRTY-FIVE

I fell into step next to Moss as we headed through the parking lot toward Beaumont. Dean and Justice had already put a dozen paces between us, but I nonetheless lowered my voice. "So, uh... I feel like I'm missing something, or perhaps a handful of somethings. You mind bringing me up to speed?"

Moss flashed me a smile. "A lot's happened since you and I talked to the former Mrs. Doherty. Justice and I brought Flora Lumaris into the precinct and had a long discussion with her about the theft of her so-called Philosopher's Stone. I don't remember how much I told you about that, but it was a robbery. They held Lumaris up at gunpoint in her office, and while the two men who robbed her wore masks, they weren't the smartest of criminals. They parked their getaway car outside her place of business, and though Lumaris was shaken up by the encounter, she was nonetheless smart enough to look out the window when the thugs took off. She didn't get a license plate, but she got a passing glance at the guy who climbed into the passenger's seat. He ripped his mask off as he was getting inside. It wasn't a great look, but we brought the precinct's best sketch artist in to work with her. Once we had that, we brought in Newbury, the detective in charge of the robbery case—who should've already done the work I've told you about—and shared with him the notes. Thankfully, he wasn't useless. He thought he recognized the perp in the sketch, a career stickup man who goes by the nickname Iron Eddy.

"It took some digging, but with Newbury's help, we tracked Iron Eddy down and threw him in a cell. After letting him stew for a while, we confronted him with the evidence. Anyone with half a brain could've figured out a single witness's passing glance wouldn't be enough to a convict a guy of armed robbery, but apparently Iron Eddy's brain reserves were running on empty. He rolled over easier than a show dog. Gave us everything he knew as soon as we mentioned the possibility of a reduced sentence."

We headed north, following Dean as we hit the street. "So he told you who hired him?"

"He tried," said Moss. "Didn't have a name, but he gave a physical description. Older guy, human, lots of rings on his hands, used a jeweled cane to help him walk. Said he drove a black Pearl Voyager with an angel hood ornament, which the company only introduced two years ago. That helped us narrow down the possibilities when Dean pulled the DMV records this morning. We were able to narrow them further using what you told us about the first two letters of the plates you saw on the getaway car, plus what Iron Eddy told us about the suspect's age and gender."

I blinked, confused. "But I got the letters on the plate wrong. I thought it started with AF, not AE."

Moss smiled. "I know. When we narrowed down the results,

we didn't get any that matched, but Dean's smart. When our search turned up a bucketful of bupkis, he figured we should try substituting the F for an E. It's a common error, same as mistaking an F for an R. Once we figured that out, a suspect popped right up. Joseph Knalnut, owner of several jewelry stores around town." Moss pointed at a shop half a block in front of us.

I shook my head. "I don't get it. If you figured all this out, why did you need me to ID the car?"

"Because most detective work is conjecture," said Moss. "Just because it made sense that you might've misidentified one of the letters in the plate doesn't mean that's what actually happened, and our captain isn't in the habit of issuing warrants to search for stolen goods based on theories and guesses. Dean told him what he knew, and he provided him with a warrant to search Knalnut's home and place of business for anything related to Gus Tovar's murder on two conditions. One, that Iron Eddy finger Knalnut from a group of photos of random old guys, and two, that you positively identify the car you saw at the scene of the crime without prompting. So... here we are."

Dean and Moss had already entered, but I paused at the front of the shop. "So, Lumaris was wrong? Tovar wasn't the one who stole her stone?"

Moss shrugged as she pulled on the door, causing the shop bell to jingle. "That's how it appears, but who knows? Seems like there's more of this mystery left to unravel."

Moss headed inside the shop and I followed as Razi closed on us from behind. The place was laid out like most jewelry shops are, with glass display cases around the perimeter and an island in the middle, but it was bigger than most, with thousands of rings, necklaces, bracelets, earrings, brooches, and even tiaras on display. Employees in suits stood behind the glass cases, their faces slack as I took my spot by the door. A pair of customers at the edges looked just as confused. Dean and Justice stood authoritatively by the island, but clearly I'd already missed something as an old man with a cane flipped up a section of the counter and stepped through to the main floor.

"I'm Joseph Knalnut." Several liver spots shone through the man's thin hair, and his fingers had a least a half pound of gold and silver weighing them down. More obvious than his age, however, were the mottled bruises that covered the skin left uncovered by his suit: one between the fingers on his right hand, another on the back of his left, and a third on his neck near the edge of his jaw. "What seems to be the problem, detectives?"

Dean reached into his jacket as he walked around the edge of the island, producing an envelope that he handed to the old man. "Mr. Knalnut, we have a warrant to search the premises in connection to the robbery of Flora Lumaris and the murder of Gus Tovar. Do you have a safe on site?"

Knalnut gobbled air as he opened the envelope and scanned the document that he unfolded from within. "What? What's the meaning of this?"

Razi joined me on the other side of the door. The two patrons in the store looked appalled and headed toward us, eager to leave. Dean had told us to guard the exit, but I figured customers were free to leave.

Dean paid them no mind, his focus firmly on the old man. "A safe, Mr. Knalnut."

The old jeweler sputtered. "Yes. Several. In the back, under the counters."

"Moss." Dean flicked his hand. Ginger headed around him, though the counter gap to the back as she recruited employees to help her. "According to police records, Mr. Knalnut, you have a firearm registered to your name. Do you have it on site?"

Knalnut fanned the letter, his hand shaking. "Detective, I don't see how any of this—"

Dean's voice chilled, sending a shiver down my spine. "Answer the question. Is your firearm on the premises?"

Knalnut sighed. "It's on the right side of the store, third cabinet from the left under the counter. But you have to understand, this is a jewelry store! Theft is a constant threat. We need to have protection on hand."

Dean ignored him. "Justice. Check it out. Moss. Anything?"

"Working on it." She'd ducked behind the counter, as had one of the employees. I heard a clank and a metallic groan. That was followed by a moment of silence before I heard another. After the second, Moss spoke again. "Dean? Might want to check this out."

She straightened. In her hands, she held a mineral of some sort: a dull, reddish-brown rock with exposed crystals on one side and a bumpy texture on the other. Moss grunted, clearly struggling with the weight as she deposited the thing on the countertop.

Dean pointed at it. "Mind telling me what that is, Mr. Knalnut?"

The old man blinked a few times. "A geode. Quite rare, and quite valuable."

"Well, I believe the latter," said Dean. "But it also matches the description of an item stolen at gunpoint a week ago. Ever heard of the Philosopher's Stone?"

"Detective, I assure you, that stone was not stolen! It was given to me as a present."

"By Gus Tovar?"

Knalnut hesitated. "Yes."

"Did you know he'd been murdered?" asked Dean.

Another hesitation. "I'd heard."

Justice cleared his throat from the side of the room. "Dean? Got the pistol." He held it up, a beefy revolver with a shiny barrel and pearl grips. "Looks like a forty-five. Same as killed Tovar."

Dean pulled a pair of handcuffs from underneath his jacket. "Joseph Knalnut? You're under arrest for solicitation of armed robbery and for the murder of Gus Tovar. You have a right to remain silent, as anything you say can and will be used against you in the court of law."

Knalnut put his bruised hands up in supplication, exposing his knobby wrists. "Please! No handcuffs! I'm a hemophiliac, and I bruise at the slightest touch. I promise you, I'll come peacefully."

Dean closed on him, cuffs in hand as he eyed the bruises, but after a moment he slid them back into his belt. "Very well. Moss? Justice? You might want to swap those pieces of evidence, but bring them both."

Justice and Moss looked at each other and nodded, but Dean wasted no time. He directed Knalnut towards the door, though the old man didn't move quickly. Between the cane and the bruising, I didn't think there was much of a chance of his escape, but I nonetheless was on high alert as I escorted him and Dean back to the parking lot.

CHAPTER THIRTY-SIX

I sat in our squad car, a half-eaten grilled cheese sandwich in hand. We were parked outside a diner by the name of FlapJoe's, which I assumed was a pancake pun that involved the owner's name. Two other squad cars were parked next to ours, but unlike number eighty-seven, the other two were empty, the officers inside enjoying a meal and suffering Razi's company. Being the rookie, I was stuck outside, eating takeout a waitress had brought to my window while I kept an ear glued to the radio, waiting for calls from dispatch.

On the one hand, I knew being relegated to the car while the others enjoyed a hot meal was a punishment or at the very least a form of mild hazing, but I didn't care. It meant I got to eat my lunch out of earshot of Razi's entitlement and bluster. It meant I could relax, confident in the knowledge that for ten minutes I wouldn't have to grit my teeth while Razi made an off-color comment or threw out ideas about which low-income neighborhoods to patrol in search of busted taillights and expired plates.

Besides, despite the joint's hokey name, the grilled cheese was actually damned good.

I popped the last bite of my buttery sandwich into my mouth and chewed, relishing in the crunch of the bread and the silkiness of the cheese. As I wiped my fingers on the included napkin—they could've given me two or three, for crying out loud —the radio crackled. "Dispatch to eighty-seven. Officer Phair, could you place a call to the Fifth Street precinct?"

I wiped the last of the crumbs off my fingers and grabbed the receiver. "Copy that."

I left the second, uneaten half of my sandwich on the center console and hopped out of the car. I figured there was a phone inside the diner, but heading inside risked attracting Stonefist's ire, so instead I made for a pay phone on the corner. After giving the operator my name and badge number, she connected me to dispatch at the fifth.

"Hello, Officer," she said as I gave her my name. "Detective Moss wanted to speak with you. One moment please."

The phone made several clicks, and I waited as the call went through. Soon enough, I heard Ginger's voice. "Moss here."

"Hey, Detective. It's Phair. You need something?"

"Phair. Hey. No, for once I don't need your help. Just wanted to give you an update. Ballistics came through on the revolver we found at Knalnut's yesterday, and it's a match for the gun that killed Tovar. Pulled his prints off the grips, too. Looks like we got our guy."

"Oh. Good."

"We also did a little digging into Knalnut's financial records, and we found the money trail from Knalnut to Tovar. Knalnut has been as tight-lipped as they come, but it's not too hard to see what happened. Knalnut must've paid Tovar to orchestrate the robbery, and I guess their relationship soured when Tovar didn't deliver the stone to him. Hence the old *shoot shoot bang bang.*"

"But why did Knalnut want the stone in the first place?" I asked.

"Oh," said Moss. "I figured that was obvious. He's a jeweler. Quite a successful one, I might add. Anything that disrupts the economics of silver and gold probably would kill his business, so I guess he decided to get a head start on the killing."

I stood in silence for a moment. "Can I ask you something, Detective?"

"Shoot."

"Why are you telling me all this?"

"You've earned it, didn't you?" said Moss. "You've been on this case from the get go. You helped us at every stage, from IDing the getaway car to providing backup at Roncalli's and Mrs. Doherty's. I figured letting you know how things turned out was the least I could do."

"But I'm not a detective," I said. "I'm a beat cop, and not even a good one at that."

"What?" Moss bristled. "What makes you say that?"

I sighed. I didn't want to get into it. "I'm not sure I'm cut out for the job. It's complicated."

I heard some background noise on the other end of the line while Moss gathered herself. "You know, Phair, for someone who's as smart as you are, you sure are thick, and I'm not talking about your back end."

"Excuse me?"

"I asked that you call me to fill you in on the Tovar case, yes, but more than anything I wanted to thank you. You were instrumental in solving the murder, which for the record is not something most patrol officers can claim on their resumes after ten years on the job, much less a week."

"I was in the right place at the right time."

"Maybe," said Moss. "Or perhaps you *put* yourself in the right place at the right time. You made smart, quick decisions that created leads for us to follow. You've got a good head on your shoulders, and from what I can tell, your heart's in the right place. Don't dismiss yourself."

I snorted. "I thought my heart was in the right place, too, but maybe that place isn't the NWPD."

The phone crackled. "Is this about your TO?"

"Some of it is, but it's bigger than that."

"Look," said Moss. "Don't let him get to you. I told you before and I'll say it again, we need more people like you in the department, not fewer. Smart people. Honest people. People with integrity. Don't let one jackass with a skewed view of justice sour you on the whole system."

Moss's words should've been uplifting, but somehow I felt as despondent as I had at the start of the exchange. "I'll try."

"Seriously," said Moss. "Don't do anything rash. Stick it through, and you could go a long way. And if you're ever feeling down, just remind yourself: you helped put a murderer behind bars."

I didn't know what to say, so I settled for a white lie. "I appreciate that, Detective. It means a lot."

I heard more background chatter on the line. "No problem," said Moss. "I've got to go. Hopefully we cross paths again in the future, Phair."

"Yeah. See you round."

The phone clicked, and I returned the receiver to its home. I stood there, searching inside myself for feelings of joy or a spark of hope, but I found nothing. Objectively, I knew Moss was right. I'd done a good job. I'd helped solve a case, and I should be proud of that, even if I wasn't proud of my actions in the department as a whole. So why wasn't I? Why couldn't I compartmentalize Razi's jaded attitude and the precinct's riot response and focus on the good? Why couldn't I accept that I'd fulfilled a role I'd envisioned for myself at the start of my journey and pat myself on the back for it?

Moss's voice rang in my head. She'd said to remind myself of my accomplishments, so I did. "You made a difference, Nell. You put a murderer behind bars."

I stood in the booth, waiting for the words to take hold, but they didn't. Somehow, I couldn't convince myself I was telling the truth.

CHAPTER THIRTY-SEVEN

I sat at the dining table in Cliff's and my apartment. A plate of tuna noodle casserole sat before me, which I picked at with a fork whose tines were slightly bent. Cliff sat across from me at the table, doing a similar song and dance with his portion. He'd been reading in the easy chair in the living room when I got home, as he'd pulled the night shift for the next couple days, but we hadn't said more than a couple words to each other as I prepared supper and plated it.

Cliff's fork clacked against the porcelain, and his glass clinked as it returned to the table. He cleared his throat. "Nell, are we ever going to talk about this?"

I sighed. "I know, alright? This dish is terrible. It's burnt on top and the noodles are goo on the bottom. It looks and tastes like cat food, except only the mangiest alley cat would ever stoop to eating it. I'm sorry, okay? It's garbage."

Cliff snorted. "It's not the best casserole I've ever eaten, but that's not what I was talking about."

I looked up from the oozing noodles and waited for him to elaborate.

Cliff cocked his head at me. "You've been giving me the cold shoulder for a day and a half. This is about our disagreement in the break room, isn't it?"

I met Cliff's eyes. "I would've called it more of a spat or a tiff, but yeah."

"Can we talk about it?"

I flicked my fork in his general direction. "Be my guest."

To his credit, Cliff wasn't insulted by my attitude. "I've been thinking about your point of view, and in retrospect, I admit there were elements of our response in which I think we failed. I didn't see the choking incident you mentioned, but I did see violent outbursts by other officers. They lashed out, and while I understand why, because of the environment and the chaos, that doesn't mean it was right. We all could've kept our cool better. I think we could've avoided a lot of the violence if we'd acted sooner, and I'm sure even more of it could've been avoided if we'd communicated with the protestors better."

"I think you mean communicated at all," I said.

"Fair enough," said Cliff. "I acknowledge the response wasn't ideal. I'm willing to go to the sergeant, tell him what I saw, and make recommendations about how we could've reacted better, though I can't guarantee he'll listen to me."

I nodded. "I appreciate that, Cliff."

He leaned forward in his chair. "Nell, I know you're upset about the protest, but policing is a complex problem. There are good people in the world and there are bad people, and unfortunately some of both become cops. I'm not naive enough to believe otherwise. That said, I believe there are more good than bad, and even though a lot of us made mistakes the other day, I think most of the officers got caught up in the moment. On the whole, we do make a difference in the world. A meaningful one."

I shook my head. "I don't know, Cliff. I don't think I'm being naive either. I know some violence has to be met with violence. The idea that all problems can be solved peacefully through discourse alone is a myth. You can't negotiate with people whose goal it is to eliminate you, whether they be murderers or government thugs or anything in between. You can't always be warm and fuzzy and expect everyone to follow the rules. I get it. Policing is complex, and you have to accept some bad with the good... I'm just not sure *I'm* able to do it."

Cliff's brow furrowed. "What are you saying?"

I set my fork down. I didn't want to eat anyway, certainly not the noodles I'd massacred. "I don't think I made the right choice choosing policing, Cliff. I wanted to help people, and I don't see myself doing that. I feel as lost as when I got fired from my waitressing job and ended up on the street four months ago."

"Hey. Come on." Cliff put his silverware down and came around the edge of the table, kneeling next to me. "It can't be that bad, can it? For what it's worth, I think you make a great police officer. And I'm sure you *are* helping people. You just have to accept that you can't help *all* of them."

I hesitated. "But what if that's how the system works? What if the system was designed for us to help some people and not others, and the ones who really need the help are the ones being excluded?"

"If the system is the problem, how do you plan on changing it from the outside?" said Cliff. "If the good, honest, kind officers like you throw up their hands and leave, who's left?"

I snorted. "You sound like Moss."

Cliff lifted an eyebrow. "Who's Moss?"

"One of the detectives in the murder case I've been wrapped up in. I've told you about her like five times, Cliff."

My boyfriend blinked. "Oh. Guess it must've slipped my mind."

I smiled. "Yeah. That happens a lot. Thankfully, you listen when it actually matters."

Cliff took his cue and smiled back. "So... we're okay?"

"Yeah. We're good." I leaned in and kissed his cheek. "Thanks for checking in."

"You bet." Cliff glanced at his watch. "And now, I'd better change. Got to get ready for my shift."

I wasn't wearing my watch, but I caught Cliff's. "Now? It's not even eight. Your shift doesn't start for two hours."

Cliff straightened. "Well, I've got paperwork I didn't finish yesterday. I thought I might get a head start on it."

I glanced at Cliff's plate, upon which a heaping helping of tuna noodle casserole still jiggled. "And your belly hasn't weighed in on this decision at all?"

Cliff grinned hesitantly. "Well, ah..."

"It's okay," I said. "I don't blame you. Go. Get dressed and stop by a diner. I'll clean this up and eat an apple or something."

Cliff retreated to the bedroom while I cleared the table. The casserole made an ear-splitting clang as I dumped it into the garbage pail, as if I'd dumped a brick in there instead of something intended to be chewed. As I washed dishes, Cliff came out, gave me a kiss, and headed out.

As I dried my hands, I realized I didn't feel quite as helpless as I had earlier in the day. Against all odds, the combination of Moss and Cliff's support might've buoyed my spirits. Maybe they were right. Maybe the fact that I found some of the department's policies and Razi's attitudes hard to swallow meant I

was a perfect fit for the job. That wouldn't make Razi's assignments any easier to stomach, but a better sense of the bigger
picture might be enough for me to weather the storm long
enough to get a glimpse of the horizon. After all, I'd invested
quite a bit in becoming a police officer. The skills I'd learned in
the academy wouldn't translate much of anywhere else, and I
still owed my Nana for the tuition, even though she'd probably
waive the debt if I asked. I owed it to myself to give the job a
fair shot, and that meant slogging through the muck to get to
dry land.

Of course if I believed that, then why was there still a
gnawing uncertainty in the pit of my stomach that I couldn't
seem to shake?

As I stood there scratching my chin, my stomach growled,
and I realized the pit might be due to hunger rather than
anything mental. I ate some yogurt and fruit straight from the
fridge before heading into the bathroom for a shower. The water
felt good on my skin, and I stayed under the shower head for
longer than I needed to, rubbing the suds into the base of my
scalp and relishing the warmth. When I finally emerged and
toweled off, I changed into a night gown and curled into a sofa
chair with a book. Staring down the prospect of my first scheduled day off since starting my job, I figured I might stay up and
read a while, but as my lids began to droop and my head tipped
forward more than a few times, I gave up and retreated to the
bedroom.

Perhaps my body had been playing tricks on me, however, as
once I retired to a horizontal position, sleep eluded me. I tossed
and turned, feeling as if I'd forgotten something important, but
after revisiting in my head the actions I'd taken throughout the
day, returning the forms from my desk to the proper outboxes,

locking my locker at the station, turning off the gas to the oven, eventually I entered the world of dreams.

There, I found myself standing inside Knalnut's Fine Jewelry, except it was also New Age Alchemical at the same time. Gus Tovar lay on the floor to the side of the central island, his shirt stained red with blood. The open safe from New Age was there, too. Tovar's outstretched arm pointed toward it, same as it had at the scene of the murder, except this time the reddish brown Philosopher's Stone sat dead center at the base of the armored box. Knalnut stood to the side of it, his arms in the air, his bruised fingers and knobby wrists on full display. His eyes were wide as he stared at Tovar, and he shook his head in dismay. "I didn't do it! I didn't kill him. I swear!"

Dean stood to my side, shaking a pair of handcuffs at the guy. "Tell it to the jury, old man. The evidence says otherwise."

Justice appeared out of nowhere, looming over me. In his hands he held Knalnut's revolver. "Indeed. We've got you dead to rights." He pointed the pistol at Tovar's pale form and said in a deadpan, *"Bang."*

Dean pushed Knalnut against the island. He wrenched his hands behind his back and slapped on the cuffs. The old man's wrists purpled before my very eyes as he continued to shake his head. "I'm telling you, it wasn't me!"

Suddenly, Moss was at my side, too. She smiled as she clapped me on the back. "See, Phair? Told you. You should be proud. You've helped put a murderer behind bars."

I stared at the corpse. At Tovar's slack face, at his cracked wristwatch. I followed his outstretched arm, this time not to the safe, but to the gleaming bits of metal scattered across the floor. The remains of a stainless steel watchband, the links and pins I'd seen strewn across the floor of New Age Alchemical. I stared at them, then at Knalnut's rapidly bruising wrists. My heart hammered in my chest. I couldn't breath, and I felt Moss pounding on my back.

"Phair? Phair, are you all right?"

I felt a rush. My eyes snapped open and I sat up straight in bed. My heart continued to beat hard against my ribs as I stared into the darkness, but over it I heard my own voice, soft in my ears. "Good gods. We arrested the wrong guy."

CHAPTER THIRTY-EIGHT

I took the subway to the corner of Beaumont and Ninth and walked to the parking lot outside Knalnut's Fine Jewelry from there. I wore a broad-rimmed hat and sunglasses to go along with a saffron-colored sundress, none of which I was particularly comfortable in, but at least the weather was right for it: sunny and right on the dividing line between warm and cool, with just a hint of a breeze.

I strolled into the lot, feeling nervous despite the fact that I wasn't doing anything wrong, much less illegal. Still, I wasn't used to snooping. All the training I'd gotten in police academy was geared toward winning conflicts not gathering information, which seemed like a pretty big oversight on the department's part. Regardless, I made my way to the spot where I'd last seen Knalnut's Pearl Voyager a few days ago. It was no longer there, replaced by a cherry red Howardson Bumblebee, but I didn't fret. If my theory was right, it made sense the car would've been moved despite Mr. Knalnut's imprisonment.

Indeed, after searching the lot, I found the Voyager again,

parked at the edge of the lot against the bricks of the nearest shop. After double-checking the plates, I headed down the street toward the jewelry shop. I paused outside the door and took a deep breath to still my nerves. Again, nothing I was about to do was against the law, but I wasn't in the habit of lying, and if for some reason the employees inside the store saw past my hat and glasses and identified me, there might be career repercussions if not legal ones. Still, it was a risk I had to take.

The shop bell jingled as I pulled on the door. It was midmorning, so I hadn't expected many patrons inside, but the place was empty except for a single employee, a youngish man with a baby face wearing a crisp brown suit. I didn't recognize him from Knalnut's arrest, but I hadn't paid much attention to the staff. Hopefully if he'd been around, he hadn't paid much attention to the silent patrol officers guarding the door, either.

The man smiled as he saw me enter. "Good morning, Miss."

I appreciated the youthful title, if nothing else. I hated being called ma'am or madam. "Good morning." I headed to the displays, trailing a hand across the glass as I scanned the contents.

"Anything I can help you find today?" asked the young man.

My heart beat harder in my chest than it should've. "I suppose so. I'm here to look at rings."

"On your right, toward the back of the store." The young man held out a hand. "Any sort of ring in particular?"

I couldn't blush on command, but I tried to sound coy. "Well, yes. You see my boyfriend has insinuated there might be something he's going to ask me in the not too distant future, and I figured I should get an idea for the sort of thing I like, if you catch my drift."

"Certainly, Miss." The young man smiled as he moved his way down the display. "We specialize in all manner of engagement rings. Diamond, of course, are the most popular, but more and more ladies are choosing more colorful gemstones of late. Rubies. Emeralds. Amethysts in particular are on the rise. That said, the gemstone is far from the only choice to be made when selecting a ring. Metal is equally important. Gold and white gold are the most common choices, but some opt for platinum, and of course we also work in silver. We can meet any budget at Knalnut's. Finally, design is perhaps the most critical element." He waved his hand at the display. "Do you see anything that tickles your fancy?"

I peered into the glass, which house a two-tiered display that stretched for several feet in either direction. There must've been a hundred rings in the case, and apart from the obvious differences in color, I could hardly tell them apart. All were shiny and petite and pricey-looking.

"Well, I'm really not sure," I said. "I've always been a fan of floral designs."

"Say no more." The young man bent over and opened the back of one of the displays. "We have a number of rings that are modeled after roses, the traditional cultivated variety, not the wild ones. Why don't you take a look at this one?"

He pulled a ring from the case and set it on the counter. It was a diamond ring, that I could tell, but if it was supposed to look like a flower, I wasn't seeing it. "Where are the petals?"

"The petals aren't depicted per se," said the salesman. "The collection was *inspired* by roses. You can see it in the flow of the shank and the curves of the shoulders."

Shanks and shoulders? Were we talking about beef or rings? "I don't think this is quite the piece for me. What about this one?" I pointed to a random ring I had no interest in, but it happened to be at the front of the case.

The young man smiled. "Certainly, Miss. Not very floral if I say so myself, but an excellent choice. That's from our regency line. Expertly crafted."

The salesman once again knelt at the back of the case. He returned the rose-inspired ring before reaching for the one in front. As he did so, his shirtsleeves pulled up along his arm, exposing his wrist. I didn't suspect him of anything, but I nonetheless eyed it closely. He wore a watch, but it didn't look brand new, and I didn't see any evidence of scratching on his skin.

The young man placed the ring on the counter as he straightened. "Twenty-four carat white gold. Diamond center, sides, and accents. Truly a brilliant piece, worthy of a woman as beautiful as yourself."

I knew the guy was supposed to flatter me, and I wasn't buying it. I sighed, perhaps in an overdramatic fashion. "Oh, I don't know. This isn't quite right, either. Maybe what I need is something custom."

The salesman perked, and golden crowns danced in his eyes. "Why, certainly. We do custom pieces quite often. I have a binder full of design elements I could show you—"

I waved him off. "Yes, I'm sure, but there must be someone else I could talk to. Someone with more experience. An owner, perhaps?"

The young man did a fairly good job hiding his disappointment in being underestimated. "Of course. Mr. Knalnut is in his office in the back. I'll return in a moment."

The mention of Mr. Knalnut perked my interest, but if my theory was right, it wouldn't be the same one I'd met. Indeed, within thirty seconds, a man appeared through a door at the back of the shop as the salesman slid through behind him. He was of middle age, probably in his forties or fifties, with a salt-and-pepper beard, short shorn hair, and a sharp hook nose, and he wore an expensive suit with velvet lapels and pocket covers.

He extended a hand as he approached the display. "Good morning, Miss. I'm Hywel Knalnut, proprietor here. Welcome. You are?"

I took his hand, eyeing his wrist as I shook it. A hint of a watch poked out, but his shirt cuffs covered his skin. "Mabel Sudsbury. Pleased to meet you."

Hywel pulled his hand back and smiled, an oily sort of grin that probably worked wonders on old ladies but few others. "I understand you might be in the market for a custom engagement ring. Something floral in design?"

"I might be," I said. "But while this fine young man went to fetch you, I happened to spy one more ring that caught my eye. This one, right here." I pointed to another of the supposed rose collection that was against the front of the display. "Perhaps you could show it to me?"

Knalnut didn't show even the slightest annoyance in perhaps losing a pricier sale. "Certainly, my dear." He knelt and reached into the case. As the salesperson's shirt sleeve had, so too did his pull back as he reached for the ring. His watch came into full view, a bright and shiny and dare I say new Jagger-Lecant made of gold. As he grabbed the ring, I caught a glimpse of his wrist. The mottled purple skin stood out against the bright white of his shirt, just as I thought it might.

Hemophilia was hereditary, after all.

Hywel Knalnut placed the ring on the counter. "This particular ring is modeled after the winter rose. We went to great lengths to make the cup that holds the stone match the elegance and freedom of the winter rose's petals, and due to the wide bridge, if you catch the sunlight just right, you can almost see frost dancing across the diamond's faces." He smiled again. "So, Miss Sudsbury? What do you think?"

I smiled back, a sense of satisfaction spreading through me. "Mr. Knalnut, I think I can safely say I've seen all I need to."

CHAPTER THIRTY-NINE

I pulled off my sunglasses as I stepped into the phone booth. I put a few coins into the slot and waited for the operator to respond. When she did, I asked her to connect me to Shay Daggers and gave her an address. After a few clicks, I heard a ring.

A deep, meaty voice answered the phone. "Daggers residence."

"Hi, Baul," I said. "It's Nell. Is Nana around?"

"I think she's in the solarium. One moment, Miss."

I heard a clunk as he put the phone down. For a minute, all I could hear was the latent crackle on the line, but eventually I heard the muffled swish of fabric on fabric, followed by my Nana's familiar voice. "Shay Daggers speaking."

"Hey, Nana," I said. "It's me."

"So Baul told me," she replied. "How are you, dear? I've been so curious to know how your first week as an officer has gone. Any exciting arrests?"

"Yes and no," I said. "Honestly, Nana, I haven't had the best of weeks."

My great-grandmother lost some of her jovial tone. "I'm sorry to hear that dear, but to be honest, it's not unexpected. You've been thrust into a very different world than the one you're used to, and as childish as it is, there will always be hazing of rookies. It'll get better over time."

I sighed, thinking back to my conversations with Moss and Cliff. "It's not that simple, I'm afraid. There's more than hazing that's bothering me."

"What do you mean?"

I shook my head. "It's complicated. To be honest, I've had some doubts about whether or not I picked the right job, but that's not why I'm calling. Nana, can I ask you a serious question?"

"Of course, dear. Always."

"What was police culture like when you were a cop?"

I heard my great-grandmother sigh. "Well, that's a multi-layered question. How detailed of an answer do you want?"

"I only put a couple coins in the phone, so you should probably give me the cheater version."

"Okay," said Nana. "For starters, it was a male-dominated profession. As I told you, I was one of only a few women in the department when I joined, at any level, and I was the first female captain at the Fifth Street precinct. Sexism was common, including among the good ones like your Papa Jake. Even beyond that, there was an aura of machismo that permeated everything, as if solving problems with your fists was somehow better than solving them with your brain. People as a whole were resistant to change, especially those in charge, and there was corruption here and there, but overall I think the department was filled with people who took pride in their jobs and believed that truth and justice would ultimately win over lawlessness and fear."

"What about the idea of the police as a brotherhood?" I asked. "Did you ever get the sense you were looking out for each other at the expense of the people you were supposed to protect?"

"Not really," said Nana. "Don't get me wrong, there were some who abused their positions, but as a whole, I think we did far more good than harm. Why?"

I hesitated. "Nana, were you ever in a position where you needed to do the right thing, but you weren't sure if doing so was the smart choice?"

"Ah. I see." Nana's voice sobered. "As a matter of fact there were several, and not all of them were when I was an established veteran, either. I'd been on the job less than a year when a scandal hit the department. Several elder statesmen in our precinct were revealed to have taken bribes from a smuggler gang. Even our captain was implicated, though he wasn't really at fault. Jake showed me how important it is to stand up for what's right, even when the repercussions end up damaging people you care about."

I stood in the booth, listening to the crackle of the phone and the rumble of cars on Beaumont.

Nana gave me a moment, but only one. "You know you don't have to tell me what's going on if you don't want to, Nelly, but I'm always here for you. I'll always lend you an ear, if you wish it."

I sighed. If there was anyone I could tell, it was Nana. "I responded to a shooting my first shift. A scientist was murdered, and for a number of reasons, I've become more involved in the investigation than maybe I should've. The point is the detective in charge told me to stay out of his case, except I can't because I realized the man they arrested didn't commit the crime. I haven't told my TO, but he says our job is to protect one another. To shield each other from scrutiny as well as prosecution. I know he would tell me that if I open my mouth and speak the truth I'll not only make my superiors look bad but torpedo my career in the process, but I can't make myself believe that. I can't believe some unwritten code is more important that justice. That loyalty trumps the truth. I just can't."

"Then don't."

I blinked. "Come again?"

"Nell, when you told me you were thinking about joining the force, I thought that was about the best news I'd heard in years. Do you know why? Because you're smart, ambitious, and tough, but above all, because you have a good heart, the same heart Jake did. You're passionate and you make mistakes when you're mad, but deep down inside, you know what's right and wrong. Your emotions might've led you astray, but your heart never has. So don't stay silent. Speak up for what's right, and always make the choice that feels right, in life and *especially* as a police officer. Because if right doesn't matter, what point is there to doing the job at all?"

I took a deep breath, and for the first time since Razi spewed his hate at me in the car, my lungs felt full. The empty pit that had been gnawing at me for the past week had finally been filled, and I knew with what: courage and a sense of right.

"Thanks, Nana. I appreciate you saying that. I know what I have to do."

CHAPTER FORTY

A fter pushing my way through the front doors of the Williams Street precinct, I paused at the reception desk. An officer by the name of Kennedy sat there, a guy in his late thirties who I'd shared a word or two with during Sergeant Zaxby's daily briefings.

He looked up and gave me a nod as I approached. "Morning, Phair." He started to shift his attention back to whatever he had on his desk, paused, and tilted his head back up. His brow furrowed as he looked at my yellow dress. "Are you on service today?"

"Nope. Day off, but I need to speak to the captain. Is she in?"

"As far as I know." He craned his head in the general direction of the captain's first floor office. "What's going on?"

I shook my head. "Nothing you need to worry yourself about. Thanks, Kennedy."

I worked my way through the narrow hallway to the ladies room, where I changed into my uniform. I didn't technically need to, but I figured it would make my argument easier to swallow. Once changed, I made my way into the maze of cubicles on the main floor and headed to the desk I shared with Stonefist. To be fair, the desk was shared by more than the two of us, as other officers who pulled different shifts used it too, but luckily for me, there wasn't anyone there at the moment. I sat down and pulled some paper from one of the drawers. With a pencil in hand, I started writing.

I thought I might hesitate, that when faced with the moment of truth I might question whether I'd made the right choice, but I didn't. I knew I had a duty to report the truth and to strive to see justice done. I'd known it all along, even before Nana affirmed my preexisting beliefs, but knowing someone of her character stood beside me, even in spirit, made it easier. I wrote down every detail I knew about the Tovar murder, everything I'd gleaned from conversations with Moss and Justice and Dean, what I'd seen with my own two eyes at New Age Alchemical, and what I'd witnessed from my visit to Knalnut's Fine Jewelry earlier in the day. I knew I might get in trouble for conducting an unofficial investigation, even if it was on my own time, but I'd probably get in much bigger trouble for filing the report at all.

So be it. I'd made my bed, and I was going to lie in it.

When I finished writing, I placed my report in a manilla folder and headed toward the far side of the precinct. The captain's office sat there, the blinds drawn and the door closed. When they were open, the Captain generally welcomed conversation, but I tempted fate and knocked on the door anyway.

"Come in," came a muffled voice.

I opened the door and stepped through. Captain McGuire was a woman in her early fifties, broad-shouldered like me but with a flat face that looked as if it had been hit with a frying pan during her formative years. I'd only spoken with her briefly during my interview process, but during that short encounter she'd exhibited all the warmth of a dead fish.

Fountain pen in hand and a stack of papers before her, she looked at me with disinterest. "What is it, Officer?"

"I need to speak to you about a murder investigation, ma'am. It's important."

"Close the door," she said, waving in its direction. "Is this about the Tarot Card Killer? I'm sorry you got caught up in that."

Though she said she was sorry, her face didn't show it. Perhaps she just wasn't very expressive. "No, ma'am. This is about the Tovar case."

She cocked her head. "Which one?"

She didn't invite me to sit, so I didn't. "The murder of Gus Tovar at New Age Alchemical. It's Alton Dean's case."

The Captain frowned as she leaned back in her chair. "Officer, Detective Dean works out of the Fifth Street precinct, not ours."

"I understand that, ma'am, but I've nonetheless found myself involved in the case from day one. Officer Stonefist and I were the ones who first responded at the scene."

"And you can't take whatever information you have on the case to Detective Dean, instead?"

"The chain of command dictates that I deliver my report to you, ma'am." I leaned forward and deposited the manila folder on the edge of her desk. "In that, you'll find my full testimony in regards to the Tovar case. Everything I've observed and my conclusions. The evidence suggests Detective Dean arrested the wrong man."

Captain McGuire gathered the folder and drew it next to her, but she didn't open it. "The *evidence suggests it?*"

McGuire leveled me with a dismissive glare, but I didn't let it roil me. "Yes, ma'am. It's quite conclusive."

McGuire drummed her fingers on the top of the folder. "Officer, are you aware you're not a detective?"

"Yes, ma'am."

"And you're aware that this case is not under investigation at this precinct?"

"I am."

McGuire sighed and opened the folder. She scanned the first page. "Officer, I don't know anything about this investigation, but if you think you have pertinent information regarding it, I suggest you take it to Detective Dean. Filing a report is a formal process that you may not have fully explored the repercussions of."

"Captain, Detective Dean specifically told me to stay out of his investigation, and I didn't. I take full responsibility for that. However, I fear that if I take the information to him, he'll dismiss it out of hand or file a complaint against me directly. I'd rather the information be filed as a report to ensure it becomes part of the official case file. It's the only way I can be sure the information won't be ignored."

McGuire pursed her lips. "Are you *sure* about this?"

I took a deep breath. "Yes, ma'am."

McGuire nodded. "Very well. I'll make sure this gets into the right hands."

I didn't thank the Captain, because she hadn't agreed to do me any favors. She'd simply agreed to do her duty, which was all I could ask for. With a nod, I turned around and headed out.

CHAPTER FORTY-ONE

I had less than half a day left to me when I returned to my apartment, but I made the most of it. I read some of the book that nearly put me to sleep the night before, Cliff and I treated ourselves to a nice meal—out, of course—and I finished the evening by the radio, listening to a serial about kings and queens and jealousy and betrayal while a cool wind blew through the windows.

The best part was that I didn't feel stressed or upset or conflicted about any of it. I was so quiet Cliff even asked me if I was doing okay, but the simple fact was that for the first time since my initial shift with Razi I felt good about my decision to join the force. Part of it was accepting the role I played. As a rookie patrol officer, I wasn't in control of the calls I responded to, the tasks assigned to me, or the officers I was partnered with. Maybe I'd get chances to effect change in people's lives and maybe I wouldn't, but I'd always be in control of my own moral compass. No amount of hazing could devalue my beliefs, and no number of Officer Stonefists could force me to choose indiffer-

ence and self-preservation over service to the people I'd vowed
to protect.

As I'd come to that conclusion, I'd realized Cliff was right. I
was a good police officer, and no one could take that qualifica-
tion from me. Unfortunately, they *could* take my position away
from me entirely, and despite the earlier misgivings I'd
expressed to Cliff and Detective Moss, I really didn't want that
to happen.

Butterflies fluttered in my stomach as I sat down to my shift
briefing the next day, but only because I didn't know what
repercussions there would be from filing the report against
Detective Dean. Given the speed of most bureaucracies, there
was a good chance he wouldn't find out about it for a week,
which would be fine with me given Joseph Knalnut's trial probably wouldn't begin for months, but there were more immediate
effects my report could've engendered. Chief among them was
the reaction it elicited from Razi. There was always a chance he
didn't know a thing about it—I certainly wasn't going to tell him
—but he was far more tuned in to the gossip network than I was,
and rumors spread as fast in a police station as they did in an all-
girls school.

In the briefing, Zaxby droned on about the incidents that
occurred during the previous couple shifts. I must've zoned out
during his speech, as I barely caught the patrol assignment he
gave me and Razi. I struggled to catch up as everyone else filed
out of the conference room, and Stonefist fell into step
beside me.

"You with us today, Phair? You look a little out of it."

I shook my head as we neared the stairs. "Doing fine, Stonefist. Ready to get to work."

"You sure?" he said, his voice thick with doubt. "Because I

still remember what a cock-up Rucker Park was two days ago. If you didn't learn anything from that experience, I'm not sure there's a TO in existence who could drag you to your first anniversary at the precinct."

I glanced at him sideways as I headed to the first floor. "Don't worry, Officer. I learned plenty."

Maybe he didn't catch my sarcasm. He just grunted and kept clopping down the steps. When we reached the ground floor, Razi headed toward the armory, but I froze.

My stomach fell out from underneath me as I stared toward the captain's office, where I caught sight of Detective Dean storming out her door in the direction of the parking lot. "Oh, crap."

Razi stopped when he noticed I wasn't following him. "Phair? I swear, we're going to have a major problem if you can't focus today."

I didn't get a chance to address his doubts as Captain McGuire poked her head out of her office and immediately spotted me. "Phair. A moment, please."

Razi cursed as I headed around the first floor maze and into the captain's den. McGuire waved to the door again as she sat.

I closed it before coming to attention before her desk. "Yes, ma'am?"

"Did you happen to see who was leaving my office just now?"

I nodded, the butterflies now flapping their wings ferociously. "I did."

McGuire shook her head. "You'll recall I suggested you not file the report."

I swallowed hard. "I take it the detective wasn't pleased."

"He was not," said McGuire. "And I can't blame him.

Detective Dean is a busy man. He has numerous cases assigned to him, including some that are of a much higher profile than this Tovar case you chose to report upon, other cases you of all people should be aware of, so you can imagine he didn't take kindly to an officer fresh out of the academy thinking she knows how to solve crimes better than he does."

Whatever feelings of serenity and acceptance I'd felt the night before fled from me like a hare that had caught scent of a dog. "Ma'am—"

McGuire held up a hand. "You ignored a direct order from a superior, Officer Phair. Dean told you to stay out of his case, and for reasons known only to you, you decided to ignore that order and launch a private investigation of your own. That's not how we operate in the NWPD, and it shocks me someone who just finished their training would think that's an acceptable form of conduct."

I hung my head. "I'm sorry, ma'am. I was trying to do the right thing."

"The right thing to do, Officer, is to follow orders that are given to you. If it were up to me, I'd assign you any number of unpleasant tasks to drill the value of a hierarchy into your head, but alas... it's out of my hands now."

That brought my head up. "Excuse me?"

McGuire stared at me as if I were a piece of furniture. "Despite his obvious displeasure, Dean nonetheless came to me to discuss the matter face to face, which is a tactic I encourage you to add to your repertoire. Though I was prepared to reprimand you myself, he argued for a less traditional punishment, and to be perfectly honest, I didn't feel attached enough to you after a week of service to fight on your behalf."

My brow furrowed. "What do you mean a less traditional punishment?"

McGuire picked up an envelope from the side of her desk and held it out. "You've been reassigned, effective immediately. Dean demanded it."

I took the envelope between shaking fingers. *"Reassigned?"*

The Captain nodded. *"Effective immediately.* Dismissed."

CHAPTER FORTY-TWO

Several emotions churned inside me as I left the captain's office—disappointment, confusion, uncertainty—but among the others, a single one stood tall: rage. It wasn't an all-encompassing rage, though. I still believed I'd done the right thing. I'd stood up for what I knew was right. I'd remained true to my principles. I wasn't mad at Captain McGuire, either. I knew I'd get reprimanded in some form or another. No, my anger had a singular focus: Alton Dean.

I knew he'd be upset with me for interfering in his investigation. I knew he'd complain to his superiors and mine alike. I figured he'd file an official complaint against me, but to go directly to my captain and exert his influence to change her decisions? To use his position to change the form of my punishment to suit his whims? That was a low blow, a petty move I never expected someone as seemingly intelligent as him to stoop to.

Somewhere in the background I heard Razi bellowing at me, but I ignored him. I wasn't his charge anymore, and I had more pressing matters to attend to. Instead, I took off at a sprint toward the parking lot. As I burst through the side doors, I was fully prepared to canvas the lot in search of Dean, but I didn't have to look far. Just a few spots to the right of the exit was parked Dean's emerald green Howardson Viper, and leaning against the wall, smoking a cigarette, was Alton Dean himself.

I hadn't seen him smoking before, and I didn't care for the habit one bit, so I used my irritation at being enveloped by his acrid smoke cloud to further fuel my anger. I stomped toward him, one of my hands clenched into a fist, the other nearly folding the Captain's envelope in half from the force of my grip. "Hey. Dean."

Dean looked up and gave me a courtesy nod. "Phair."

"Don't Phair me." It was a stupid thing to say given that police officers referred to each other by their last names, but I was mad and looking for any reason to start a fight. "You can't dismiss me that easily, no matter what some piece of paper says. You might've thought you could slink out and never see me again while I'm stuck chasing pickpockets in the most desolate corner of the Erming for the next decade, but I'm going to say my piece and you're going to listen, damnit."

Dean lifted an eyebrow as smoke curled from the tip of his cigarette. "Pardon?"

"You heard me," I said, jabbing the envelope in his direction. "You might be angry that I interfered in your investigation, and you have every right to be. I disobeyed an order. I get it. But for you to come after me for reporting information on your case that either hadn't been considered or had never been observed in the first place is both cowardly and despicable. Retaliation is bull-shit. I did the right thing. I saw an innocent man who was being charged with a crime he didn't commit, and I spoke up. I did it through official channels so it couldn't be swept under the rug, and you know what? I'd do it again, even if I got stuck mopping restrooms for the remainder of my stint in the force. I don't care who you are, or who my captain is, I'm always going to stand up for what's right and make my voice heard. *Every time.* And if speaking the truth and making sure justice is served gets me on an unwritten shit list, so be it. At least I'll be able to sleep at night knowing *my* moral compass is pointing the right direction, which is something you'll struggle with for the rest of your life, even if you don't recognize it now."

Dean studied me carefully throughout my tirade. As I finished he snorted, and the corner of his lip curled up in a hint of a smile.

I felt the rage overtake me, and I had to consciously force my arms to stay at my sides. "You think this is *funny?*"

Dean let out a slow cloud of smoke as he glanced at the envelope clenched between my fingers. "Doesn't look like you read your reassignment yet."

"No. I haven't. I've been a little busy running down the man who decided to singlehandedly scuttle my career."

Dean lifted an eyebrow. He flicked a few ashes from the tip of his cigarette to the ground. "You sure about that?"

Something about the way he said it made me question everything I thought I knew. I tore open the envelope and ripped the letter from within. I unfolded it and scanned the text within, trying to get to the meat.

As I hit the second paragraph, my eyes bugged out. "Wait... *what?* You want me to *work for you?*"

Dean averted his eyes as he took another drag from his cigarette. "I'm not too big a man to admit I'm wrong. You were right. Joseph Knalnut didn't kill Gus Tovar. His son Hywel did. The bruise on Hywel's wrist from the broken watchband recovered at the scene of the murder proves it, but there were other red flags I should've seen. Joseph is weak. Old. He would've had a hard time handling a big forty-five like the one we recovered from his jewelry store. More importantly, he walks with a cane. How was he going to steal the Philosopher's Stone and make his getaway before you arrived? That thing weighs as much as a bag of wet sand, and the simple act of carrying it probably would've given him more bruises."

Dean shook his head. "The problem is I didn't give the case my undivided attention. For weeks now, I've been stumbling through work with blinders on. All I can think about is the Tarot Card Killer. You could say I'm obsessed, and you wouldn't be wrong. The things he does to those poor women... It's as cruel as it is disturbing. Finding him has consumed every ounce of my attention, and it's resulted in me making uncharacteristic errors in judgement. I delegated too much of this case to Moss and Justice, but they're overworked, too. None of us put the thought into this case that it required. We all just wanted it to go away so we could focus on more important things. All of us except you. So when your report made its way to my desk, after getting over my initial anger at myself for missing what should've been obvious, I got to thinking. Maybe three isn't enough. Maybe our investigative team could use one more."

"But..." I glanced at the letter in my hands to make sure I hadn't misread it. "I don't understand. I'm a few weeks out of the academy. I've never had any detective training."

Dean waved his hand, and smoke trailed into the air. "So? You made connections the rest of us failed to. That counts for a lot in my book, and for what it's worth, Ginger seems to think you've got what it takes, too. She talked you up. Said your head was in the right place, and if I had any questions about your heart, your impassioned speech just cleared them up. Besides, police academy teaches you as much about conducting an investigation as patrol duty does, which is to say not one whit. It's a skill you teach yourself, and the abilities involved are more innate than not. I knew I wanted to be a detective the moment I set foot in the Fifth, and all I needed was an opportunity to show everyone else I could do it. This is yours."

My brow wrinkled as I tried to wrap my head around things. "To be clear, what exactly are you offering?"

"An opportunity," said Dean. "No more, no less. Your rank won't change. You'll still be an officer, but instead of being stuck with a toxic TO you'll report to me. You'll work with Moss and Justice, too, of course, but officially I'll be the one responsible for your development. You won't be on patrol. You'll work cases with the three of us, learning the ins and outs of investigation as you go. It's not a guaranteed path to detective. Just a chance for you to show us what you've got."

I stood there, feeling like someone had pulled a rug out from underneath me. I'd expected to be yelled at, to be chastised and mocked, not praised for a job well done. I should've been elated, not only at the prospect of not being stuck on slum patrol for the rest of my career but at the chance to become a detective, something I'd only recently realized I desperately wanted. And yet... not everything about Dean's offer sat well with me.

Dean sucked on his cigarette, and the burning embers approached the filter. He blew out another cloud of smoke. "You're awfully quiet for someone who's been offered a hand up out of the dirt."

I licked my lips. On the one hand, I knew I should keep my mouth shut, thank Dean for his offer, and ask him when I should start, but I wasn't wired that way. As I'd already explained to him, I intended to stand up for what was right, no matter the cost, and that meant doing so even when the potential repercussions outweighed the rewards.

I took a deep breath. "I'm flattered by your offer, Detective, but before I agree to this, I need you to answer something for me. Why should I join you?"

I thought Dean might give me a flippant answer that referenced his status or the fact that the alternative was to pound pavement all day long at Stonefist's side, but he regarded me with a slightly furrowed brow instead. "What do you mean? What's bothering you?"

I met Dean's cool ice blue eyes. "You're familiar with the NWPD motto, of course. Protect and serve? I bought into that hook, line, and sinker when I joined the force. Still do, but it seems some people in the department have different definitions of who we should be protecting and serving than I do. I always figured we were supposed to protect those who need the most help and serve people other than ourselves, not protect ourselves and serve those whose pockets already overflow. So where do you stand? Who do you protect and serve? And perhaps more importantly, what have you done in support of your ideals? You're a detective. You solve crimes, but how many people have you really helped along the way?"

Dean dropped his cigarette butt to the concrete and ground it out under his shoe. He nodded to his car. "Come with me. I want to show you something."

Part of me wanted to force the issue and make him give me an answer then and there, but damn it if Dean didn't suspect I had a curious streak. Maybe in some ways it was a test. Tease me and see if I took the bait, as any good detective would.

I got in the car.

CHAPTER FORTY-THREE

Dean's Viper purred as he drove. The car's heavy walls and thick glass kept out most of the road noise, and my seat barely jostled as he rolled over the potholes at the side of the road. I didn't know how much Dean earned, but apparently there were benefits to being a highly regarded detective beyond the respect of his peers.

The radio crackled as Dean drove, but he didn't say anything. I ached to know what he intended to show me, but I figured if he was going to tell me he would've done it at the lot. Asking probably wouldn't change his mind.

Instead, I tried pursuing answers to another mystery that hadn't fully resolved itself. "So, seeing as you're offering me a chance to be a part of your team, would it be against protocol for me to ask you some questions about the Tovar case now?"

Dean glanced over his outstretched arm that grasped the steering wheel. "You're not officially on-board yet, but given that you kept us from trying an innocent man in the court of law and probably having our asses handed to us by a sleazy defense lawyer, I'd say you've earned it. What do you want to know?"

"Well... everything. I can't make sense of it. Why did Hywel Knalnut kill Gus Tovar? Why was he willing to let his father take the fall, and what was their connection to Doherty and Flora Lumaris?"

Dean kept his focus on the road. "As far as we can figure it, this all started two years ago. Cab Doherty hired Lumaris and Tovar to investigate the myth of turning lead to gold, Lumaris from an archeological perspective and Tovar from the chemical. Basically, everything Doherty told us was true. However, the case really starts when Lumaris recovered what she claims is the Philosopher's Stone, which is the mineral you saw Moss pull from the safe at Knalnut's Fine Jewelry. Our theory is that Tovar hadn't made any progress discovering a chemical process by which to turn lead to gold, but he'd strung Doherty along with falsified research to maintain his funding. When he heard Lumaris had recovered the mythical Philosopher's Stone, he feared it would work, which would mean Doherty would no longer have need of his services. So, he decided he'd steal it to prevent its secrets from getting out.

"Problem was, Tovar didn't know the first thing about pulling off a robbery. He also didn't have the money to hire someone to do it for him, as he'd been living hand to mouth off Doherty's checks, spending every last cent trying to make it look as if New Age Alchemical was a legitimate business. The rent on that building wasn't cheap, after all. So he approached Joseph Knalnut, figuring if anyone would hate to have the gold and silver business upended it would be a wealthy jeweler. Knalnut didn't originally buy Tovar's story given that he seemed to be working on a method to convert lead to gold himself, but apparently, he showed Knalnut the falsified research and was able to convince him that he posed no threat to his business, only the Stone did. After some haggling, he convinced Knalnut to hire thugs to hit Lumaris. The thugs delivered the Stone to Tovar, ostensibly so he could figure out a way to destroy it, thus hiding whatever mystical secrets it might possess forever.

"Of course, according to Knalnut—who was willing to talk once we'd charged his son and offered him a plea deal—Tovar wasn't being completely honest. He didn't touch base with Knalnut for several days after obtaining the Stone, and Knalnut began to suspect that instead of destroying it like they'd agreed he was studying it for his own purposes. Joseph confronted the man and demanded he turn it over, but Tovar refused, and since it was Knalnut who'd hired the thieves to hold up Lumaris, it was Tovar who had the legal leverage. He threatened to blackmail Knalnut if he didn't play along."

"So the elder Knalnut roped his son into helping him protect the family business?"

"Not exactly," said Dean with a smile. "As it turns out, Hywel Knalnut doesn't like his old man much, despite the fact that they work together, or perhaps because of it. He'd been acutely aware of his dad's dealings with Tovar, and after their fight, he saw an opportunity. He confronted Tovar at gunpoint, stole the Stone, and murdered him, figuring the truth would come out and his father would take the blame, leaving him with full control over their assets and jewelry business. Not a bad idea, really, though if his plan was to frame his old man, he could've made it easier on us. I guess he figured leaving a signed confession at the scene of the crime was too obvious and was counting on the best minds of the NWPD to uncover the truth eventually."

I scratched my head as Dean turned onto Fifth. "I don't get it. How didn't the elder Knalnut suspect something was up?

The old guy had the Stone in his safe, after all, and he said he knew Tovar had been murdered."

"Hywel apparently thought of that, too," said Dean. "After Tovar's murder, he mailed the stone to their store along with a faked letter from Tovar saying he was sorry for his actions and that he'd reconsidered his stance on who should hold the Stone. Old Joe thought it was strange, given the way Tovar had acted, but then a day later he saw in the paper that Tovar had been murdered. Knalnut figured Tovar had been in deeper with bad actors than he'd claimed to be, and he'd mailed the Stone to him to keep it out of enemy hands. Knalnut didn't think there was anything connecting the now dead Tovar to him, so he decided to keep his mouth shut and relish in the fact that he'd gotten the Stone in the end. If you ask me though, the elder Knalnut has started to lose his edge, because during interrogation he didn't seem to think that being in possession of the Stone would incriminate him. As if he hadn't hired goons to steal the thing before Tovar had been murdered."

I mulled Dean's tale as he stopped at a red light. "So Gus was a scam artist all along?"

"I don't know about that," said Dean. "His credentials in chemistry were solid. Without a background in chemistry myself, I can't say with any certainly if he was a kook or not, but he certainly burned through a lot of Doherty's money without a thing to show for it."

The light turned green, and Dean eased on the gas. I turned to look at him, his strong jaw and dark skin perfectly framed by the driver's side window. "If he was a scammer, how do you explain the gold bullet that was recovered at the scene?"

Dean glanced at me. "You know about that?"

"I saw a gleam of something golden the night of the murder,

and when I came to find you at the precinct after the Tarot Card Killer struck in the park, I saw it bagged on your desk."

Dean nodded. "Ballistics confirmed it was fired out of the same forty-five as the slugs that killed Tovar. Found glass fragments on it, too. Based on the trajectory, it must've passed through some of the chemical bottles that were broken during the shooting."

I frowned. "I know Hywel is a jeweler, but why would anyone put a gold bullet in their revolver? And only one?"

"Not sure. Hywel still hasn't admitted to the murder, much less enlightened us about his bullet preferences."

My brow furrowed, and I felt like my brain had gone fuzzy. "So the gold bullet recovered at the scene passed through an unknown number of chemicals before embedding itself in the wall. I hesitate to ask, Detective, but do we have any way of knowing how *long* that bullet has been gold?"

Dean gave me a sympathetic glance. "Officially? It was gold when it was loaded into the chamber, and it's always been gold. Maybe Hywel had a bit of a poetic streak in him to go along with his murderous one. But unofficially?" He shrugged.

Dean pulled the Viper into the Fifth Street precinct parking garage and snagged a spot near the side doors. I noticed them but I didn't really see them, as my focus had shifted back a week, transporting me to the scene of Tovar's death at New Age Alchemical. My voice felt small in my own ears. "So he wasn't a scam artist after all."

Dean put the car in park and killed the engine. "You want some advice? In this line of work, you never uncover all the answers. You never get the absolute truth, just something that resembles it. You have to be willing to let the occasional oddity go—not the ones that crack the case, mind you, but the little ones that niggle at you in perpetuity but don't change the course of events. If you worry too much about every single one of those, you'll go mad over time."

Dean got out of the car. I blinked and followed him out, trying to focus on the present. "So what did you want to show me?"

"Follow me. It's down the stairs."

Dean led me into the Fifth and down into the basement, where the walls were made of rough hewn stone and a chill seeped through them. We traversed the full length of one long hall before transitioning into another. Two more turns brought us to an alcove, inside of which stood a guard station that looked as if it hadn't been touched in a hundred years. Nobody stood at attention, but the iron gate beyond—which looked like it belonged in a castle more than a police station—was shut tight.

The lock on the gate, however, had been replaced within my lifetime. Dean pulled a keyring from his pocket, selected a key from a gaggle of others, and stuck it in the keyhole. The lock clacked, and the gate creaked as Dean pushed on it. He stepped through, and I followed him into a room filled with row upon row of filing cabinets.

Dean flicked his fingers as he walked along the side of the aisles. "This is the Fifth's record room. Don't ask me why it's in the basement or why it's a refurbished jail cell. As far as I know, it's always been here."

"Refurbished?" I said.

"Perhaps retrofitted is a better word. Regardless, this is what I wanted to show you." Dean stopped at one of the cabinets and opened the second drawer from the top. He pulled it out as far as it would go and patted the dozens upon dozens of manilla envelopes within.

I pulled one out far enough to get a glance at the tab on the side. "Your case files?"

"Every once since I made detective," he said. "What you have before you is a full reckoning of my history in the department, not counting the time I spent on patrol. Every case. Every criminal caught, every person charged. Every mistake I ever made, and every family who was able to find closure as they stared into the beaten faces of the criminals sent to prison at the end of their trials. You asked who I choose to protect and serve? What my motivations are? I think they're pretty similar to yours. I think truth and justice mean something. I think that even though we may not always get everything right, we should try our damnedest to get as close as we can, and when we make mistakes, it's our duty to learn from them. I don't think anyone's above the law, and I think it's our responsibility to make sure everyone is treated fairly, without prejudice or favor. Including each other. But you don't have to take my word for it. You can decide for yourself."

Dean pointed down the aisle to where we'd entered the records room. "There's a table and chairs on the far side. Not comfortable ones, mind you, but chairs nonetheless. I'll be at my desk when you've made your decision."

CHAPTER FORTY-FOUR

I'm not sure how long I sat at that table reading. I know I made a total of five trips to the filing cabinet, and by the end of the fifth, there was barely any room on the table for me to open new files.

The reading material wasn't exactly lyrical prose. It was dry and technical, filled with dates and names and lists of evidence, with almost no elaboration or insight into the parties involved beyond the motives of whoever was ultimately accused and tried. The files weren't really intended to be read from start to finish like a novel. While there were summaries and conclusions, there was a lot left to the imagination. The investigative journey Dean had taken through each case wasn't spelled out in black ink, rather left to be pieced together from witness statements, photographs, sketches, and patrol officer reports. Nonetheless, each folder painted a picture, one that became more bright and vibrant with each piece of evidence I sifted through and considered. As I read, it crossed my mind that Dean might've brought me into the records room to pique my curiosity, to make me get a glimpse of the sort of work a detective was thrust into on a daily basis, all so I'd get excited about the possibility of joining his team and accept his offer, and while that may have been a part of his motivation, I took Dean at his word.

I really think he wanted me to judge the worth of his career on its merits.

I didn't expect to find errors in Dean's past cases like I had with the Tovar murder, but true to Dean's word, the errors he'd made in previous cases were listed alongside everything else. Most of them weren't even what I'd call mistakes. More like faulty conclusions based on limited evidence, conclusions he later modified based on new clues that led him to correctly solving the cases. He wasn't perfect. He could be fooled and tricked, same as anyone else, but based on the dates of the cases, it was clear he learned from his past investigations. If he'd made the same mistake twice, I couldn't find it.

While it was reassuring to know even the best detectives make mistakes, it was all the things Dean had gotten right that drew my attention. It wasn't just the volume of cases he'd solved and the high conviction rate of his arrests that stood out. The speed at which he closed cases was also impressive. Most of the murders he investigated were closed within a week, and while I didn't know many crime statistics off the top of my head, that seemed pretty dang good. No wonder the Tarot Card Killer consumed Dean's every thought. The guy had been roaming New Welwic for almost two months, and as far as I knew, the department wasn't any closer to catching him than they had been when he first struck.

I'd moved on to my umpteenth file, a case where a woman in her mid thirties had been murdered and her husband had been charged with the crime. It was a sordid tale of infidelity and deception, but the hardest part to swallow was that the couple had children. The file included copies of their testimony regarding their parents' whereabouts on the night of the murder, but it was a hand-written note at the back of the folder that caught me by surprise.

It was from one of the children, Sadie McGovern, addressed to Dean. It wasn't long, maybe five sentences in total, thanking him for taking them in when their father was arrested, making sure they were warm, safe, and fed until their Nana could be found to take care of them.

Maybe it was the fact that she used the word Nana, same as I did for my great-grandmother, or maybe it was the fact that the letter was written in a child's shaky hand and full of misspellings, but something inside me broke. I felt tears rolling down my cheeks, and I had to wipe them away to keep the droplets from smudging the ink on the page.

As I sat there with the letter in hand, a loud metallic clang shot me from my seat. I raced to the mouth of the records room to find an officer stepping away from the now closed gate.

"Hey," I said, wiping my cheeks one more time for good measure. "What are you doing?"

He jumped at the sound of my voice, and he looked surprised when he turned. "Oh. Sorry. Didn't realize anyone was in there. Just locking the room up for the evening."

"*Evening?*" I glanced at my watch, and my eyes widened. "Holy harvest. It's after seven?"

The young officer unlocked the door and pulled it back open with a creak. "Yeah. You going to lock this up when you leave?"

"I don't have a key," I said. "But hang out a minute while I get the files put away and you can have at it."

I raced back inside and piled folders into my arms. I almost dumped a dozen files as I jogged between the table and the filing cabinet, but through sheer force of will, I got everything put away in three trips instead of five. I thanked the officer for waiting and took off in the direction of the stairs. I was huffing by the time I made it to the third floor, but I didn't slow as I headed across the mostly empty maze of cubicles in search of Dean's desk.

I needn't have hurried. I found Dean seated in his chair as I arrived, a desk lamp illuminating an open book on his desk.

"Hey," I said, my voice slightly labored. "You're still here."

Dean looked up from his book, and his chair squeaked as he turned to meet me. "I said I would be, didn't I?"

"Sorry I took so long," I said. "I lost track of time. So much so that you apparently ran out of paperwork and moved on to beach reads."

"I wouldn't call it that." Dean closed the book and showed me the cover. "Forensic Entomology: Examining the Utility of Arthropods in Criminal Investigation. It's interesting stuff, but I wouldn't recommend reading it after a meal."

I grimaced despite myself. "Oh. Sorry."

Dean put the book down and gave me a nod. "So. Have you made a decision?"

"Straight and to the point. Are you always so direct?"

"I try to be when it comes to work matters." He didn't elaborate, making me wonder if he was more nuanced in private. He also didn't ask me again, leaving me to fill the void.

I stuck out a hand. "I'd be honored to join your team, sir, if you'll still have me."

Dean grasped my peace offering and shook it. "I will—

assuming, of course, that you're willing to follow orders when I give them to you from now on."

"That won't be a problem, sir. After everything I've seen today, I believe in what you're doing. More importantly, I believe in you. If you tell me to run, I'll only ask where."

Dean smiled. "Don't go that far. I always encourage questions on my team. It's only by challenging the assumptions we hold that we learn and make progress."

I nodded. "Got it. I appreciate that, sir."

"Good," said Dean. "I'll see you tomorrow then. Nine o'clock sharp here at the Fifth. And one more thing, before you go."

"Yes?"

Dean cracked his book open. "You're a part of my team, now. Call me Dean, not sir."

"You got it... Dean."

He nodded. "Goodnight, Phair."

I wished him goodnight, too. He turned back to his book, and I headed for the stairs. I felt a lightness in my step as I walked. It wasn't joy, exactly, although I was excited about the prospect of returning in the morning to a job I didn't loathe. Getting to work investigations with Dean, Moss, and Justice was a massive step up for me personally and professionally, but at the same time, I knew my new assignment wouldn't right the various injustices I'd seen during my time with Razi. A shift in scenery wouldn't change the broader culture around me, even if it would put me in proximity to people who actually shared my ideals.

Still, there would be time for change later. If I could get a foot on the path to detective within a week and a half of starting my job, who knew how long it would take me to reach a position where I could enact real reforms. Nana might've been the first female captain of the Fifth, but maybe I'd be the first female commissioner of the NWPD. Why not?

The thought of her made me smile, and I vowed to give her a call to tell her the good news.

ABOUT THE AUTHOR

Hi. I'm Alex P. Berg, author of *Fair and Just*. Hopefully you enjoyed Penelope Phair's debut, because her life is only going to get more exciting and complicated from here. She'll need to step up her investigative game quickly as she, Dean, Moss and Justice try to solve the puzzling murder of an eccentric circus owner's wife in *The Burnt Remains*.

Can't wait for the next Penelope Phair adventure? Well, have you read my Daggers & Steele series? It features Nell's great-grandparents and homicide detectives extraordinaire Jake Daggers and Shay Steele, back when New Welwic was just going through the industrial revolution. The complete ten book series is available now, so what are you waiting for! Read it today! You can even buy the complete series in a single low-priced omnibus volume.

Word of mouth is **critical** to my success. If you enjoyed this novel, please consider leaving a positive review on Amazon. Even if it's only a line or two, it would be a *huge* help. Thanks!

Want to connect? Visit me at www.alexpberg.com or contact me on social media.

For a complete list of my books, please visit: www.alexpberg.com/books/.